Lost
in the
Stacks

An Anthology of Library Stories by Hawai'i Fiction Writers

Edited by:
Michael Little
Gail Baugniet
John Simonds
Rosemary Mild

Magic Island Literary Works • Honolulu, Hawai'i • 2025

Copyright © 2025 by **Hawai'i Fiction Writers**
Published in the USA by **Magic Island Literary Works**
     under the auspices of **Hawai'i Fiction Writers**
Printed in the USA by **IngramSpark of Lightning Source, Inc.**

Cover art by **Brett Botbyl.**
Cover design by **Larry Mild.**
Interior book design by **Larry Mild.**

Library of Congress Cataloging-in-Publication Data
Baugniet, Gail M: Editor, Author.
Little, Michael: Editor, Author.
Simonds, John: Editor, Author.
Mild, Rosemary: Editor, Author.
Botbyl, Brett: Illustrator, Author.
Garcia, Kelley: Author.
Jones, David W.: Author.
Jones, Shauna: Author.
Knox, Dawn: Author.
Mild, Larry: Author.
Newell, Bob: Author.
Page Jr, J.T.: Author.
Tigarden, Rose: Author.
Whytes, D.V.: Author.

ISBN 979-8-9863864-9-2

10 9 8 7 6 5 4 3 2 1

In Memoriam

In fond memory of Carol Catanzariti, registered nurse, labor attorney, Federal mediator, fellow writer, and friend. Carol's short stories and poems won awards and publication, inspiring other writers.

Acknowledgments

A special thank you to the Aina Haina Library and Epiphany Episcopal Church of Kaimuki for the use of their facilities for Hawai'i Fiction Writers' workshops and critique meetings.

Disclaimer

The publisher takes no responsibility for any author's story content. All narrators, characters (persons living or dead), incidents, and dialogues are entirely of the individual author's own references and responsibility.

Foreword
by Michael Little

This collection of library stories is dedicated to Librarian Holly Kwok and the staff at the Aina Haina Public Library in Honolulu, and to all those who make this neighborhood library a special place. The library has been the home of Hawai'i Fiction Writers workshops for a number of years. *Lost in the Stacks* draws its inspiration from all the libraries that have nurtured us over the years. Imagine that the book you are holding is, in some ways, like a library. Feel free to browse, to wander through its pages, to stop and sample a few short stories before selecting one to read. It's not a novel. It's the product of a number of local writers who all have much love for libraries. We hope that you will enjoy your visit. Thank you again to Holly and the friendly staff at Aina Haina, to the Friends of the Library, and to the folks who come to visit, including those who bring their children, who will grow up with fond library memories of their own.

Three Cheers for Libraries

"A library is a good place to go when you feel unhappy, for there, in a book, you may find encouragement and comfort. A library is a good place to go when you feel bewildered or undecided, for there, in a book, you may have your question answered. Books are good company, in sad times and happy times, for books are people —people who have managed to stay alive by hiding between the covers of a book."
　　—E.B. White, *Letters of Note*, Troy, MI, Public Library, 1971.

"If this nation is to be wise as well as strong, if we are to achieve our destiny, then we need more new ideas for more wise men reading more good books in more public libraries. These libraries should be open to all—except the censor. We must know all the facts and hear all the alternatives and listen to all the criticisms. Let us welcome controversial books and controversial authors. For the Bill of Rights is the guardian of our security as well as our liberty."
　　—John F. Kennedy, *Saturday Review*, 1960.

"Books permit us to voyage through time, to tap the wisdom of our ancestors. The library connects us with the insight and knowledge, painfully extracted from Nature, of the greatest minds that ever were, with the best teachers, drawn from the entire planet and from all our history, to instruct us without tiring, and to inspire us to make our own contribution to the collective knowledge of the human species. I think the health of our civilization, the depth of our awareness about the underpinnings of our culture and our concern for the future can all be tested by how well we support our libraries."
　　—Carl Sagan, *Cosmos*, 1980.

Table of Contents

Table of Contents (Continued)

Reading Room Romantic

by Larry and Rosemary Mild

Imagine being sent to the Library of Congress on your first assignment as a newbie lawyer. Yes, a senior partner in the Washington, D.C. law firm of Peabody & Ormandy ordered me to accompany a seasoned associate to that bastion of knowledge.

The Library of Congress is a complex of buildings in downtown D.C., each one named after a president of the United States.

Ben Gormain, the associate, had a legitimate research assignment in the law library, pertaining to historical mining rights. My task was to familiarize myself with the largest library in the world for future legal reference. We emerged from our air-conditioned office into mid-July's 90-degree heat. My lightweight summer suit, white shirt, and tie immediately began to feel sticky. But so what? I had passed the bar and I was a lawyer!

After settling ourselves in an Uber Toyota Camry, Ben briefed me. The original library was created in 1800 by President John Adams for Congressional use, but the British burned it to the ground in the War of 1812. Thomas Jefferson sold his personal collection of nearly 6,500 books to start the newly built Library of Congress that reopened in 1897. Ben, full of self-importance, informed me, "Visitors have to acquire limited-time group passes to enter the library, but I have long-term passes that will allow us unlimited access during the library's normal working hours."

The Uber driver let us out at the entrance on First Street. I looked up in awe at the Thomas Jefferson Building, flaunting its Italian Renaissance architectural identity—now called the Beaux Arts style: gray stone lavishly ornamented with arches and columns. But most astonishing, out front were the three fountains called the Court of Neptune—three larger-than-life bronze sculptures: the muscled, heroic god of the sea; sea nymphs on horseback; and a cluster of frogs, turtles, and a serpent.

Inside the Great Hall, Ben and I stepped onto a floor tiled in the signs of the zodiac. Twin marble staircases led to upper and lower floors. I thrilled to the very first display, the Gutenberg Bible Exhibit, surrounded by murals depicting the history of the written word.

At this juncture, Ben left me to pursue his own assignment while I wandered about, spellbound. Printers' hallmarks filled the triangular ceiling vaults above me. I found myself surrounded by magnificent art and feats of architecture everywhere I looked. On the second floor, I wandered into the Visitors' Gallery overlooking the fabled Reading Room—a massive circular shape. The three rings of tables were long and appropriately curved. I gazed up to see the stately mosaic of Minerva, Roman Goddess of Civilization and Wisdom, holding a long, unrolled scroll listing the sciences and arts and letters.

From my perch, I looked down into the Reading Room. Many of the tables were occupied by scholars with their noses in books, absorbing and recording knowledge with laptops and notepads. The quietude and serious air touched me with a sense of near-reverence. I had to go and sit among them—and be a part of it all. I hurried down the curved staircase and seated myself at a table in the middle row, basking in the spectacle surrounding me.

Soon, when my exhilaration came down to earth, I began to wonder, who were these dedicated people sitting around me? Mostly men and women much older than myself, many with glasses, a few males with beards, and none with disrespectful hats.

Two women sat on my left. I hadn't noticed them before, but

something fascinating was going on there. The younger woman had gorgeous fiery-red, shoulder-length hair, but I had yet to see her face. The older woman, with slate-gray hair pulled into a severe bun, turned pages of a large tome, searching for something. Red Hair wore what looked to be business attire, a simple aqua blouse under a beige suit jacket. She was fidgety, checking her watch, her body language telling me that she didn't want to be there.

I tried not to stare, but my male curiosity has an awfully strong pull. I don't know whether she felt that magnetism, but at last she turned toward me. I watched her slight frown transform itself into a delicious smile. Her oval face was beautifully sculpted, her fair skin blemish-free. Most fetching of all, a dimple appeared in her right cheek. I smiled back, a sort of goofy, embarrassed smile. Red Hair shifted in her chair as though she wanted to respond to me, but then thought better of it. Her matching red eyebrows rose to show the futility of speech in such a revered venue.

I understood the change in her body language, so I reached inside my suit jacket's breast pocket for my trusty little spiral pad and tore off a page. I lifted a pen from my shirt's pocket protector and scribbled a note asking her to dinner that evening. Foolishly, like a middle-school kid afraid of getting caught, I looked both ways before sliding the note across the open space between us. She read the note and chuckled, but then looked up at me and slowly shook her head—emphatically, No.

I don't know what I expected. After all, I was a stranger in a strange place. One could see her point of view; I had no one to vouch for me. But I was determined anyway, so I tore off another page from my pad. This time I decided to take it a little slower and introduce myself. I wrote my name, "James (Jaimey) Fuller, 25 and single." I also included my home phone number. I passed the note toward her, and this time she reached out for it. She read the note and chuckled, but then looked back at me and slowly shook her head—again, No.

Then she surprised me. She turned over the note, scribbled something, and passed it back to me. My heart danced—until I read what she wrote. "I'm Vivian, 26 and single." An older woman! How exciting! But there was neither a last name nor a phone number. No way to contact her. I wondered whether she was just being cautious or otherwise involved. Or was she merely shutting me down? I noticed her slender fingers with polished nails. No ring on her left hand, but I spotted a jeweled ring on the fourth finger of her right hand. Were they real gems or rhinestones? Was it a cocktail ring? An engagement ring? Remembering whether it's the right or left hand that holds those rings isn't my forté. I'm not a follower of Miss Manners.

But I wasn't going to give up yet. She had imparted some information—granted, not enough to move on, but enough to keep trying. Maybe, I thought, dinner is too much of a commitment for a first date. I tore out a fresh page from my pad and wrote, "How about a good old-fashioned cup of coffee? I'll throw in a pastry if you like." She grinned, showing perfect teeth as she read it. I waited for her response with baited breath. She turned the note over, took a little more time to write something, and handed it to me. Trying not to appear childishly overeager, I steadied my hand taking the note, and spent a moment adjusting my wire-rimmed glasses before reading: "Thank you, No. Perhaps another time and/ or place." Still no phone number or address. Slightly encouraging, but absolutely nothing to work with.

Feeling desperate, like time was running out, I had one more card to play. I tore off another page and wrote, "If we are to have any future at all, I will need your phone number or some way to contact you." I passed it to her and waited. Her smile evaporated, and she pressed her lovely lips together in a determined look, eventually shaking her head.

I knew it! Using the word "future" was stupid of me. I was devastated. Getting turned down happens sometimes, but this time was perhaps the cruelest ever dealt me. I spent the next ten minutes trying to analyze what I did or didn't do that was inappropriate or wrong.

In that same ten minutes, her gray-headed companion closed

the book she was studying, rose to her feet, and had a whispered exchange with Vivian, who nodded and stepped out into the aisle behind her. As Vivian walked out of my life forever, my sad eyes fixed on her backside silhouette—firm and shapely in the beige pants suit. Damn! I was letting my ideal woman get away and there was nothing I could do about it.

I left the room and bumped into a tour of the Jefferson Building, prompting me to tag along. It ended forty minutes later. Now my mind was awhirl with 400 languages, fifty-six printer's marks, Three Graces, Five Senses, works on Knowledge, Wisdom, Understanding, and Philosophy, not to mention all the murals and mosaics. After the tour, I figured I had done my assignment's due diligence, so I left the building and used my cell phone to order an Uber ride back to Peabody & Ormandy.

Half an hour later, I walked into my cubicle and flopped into my swivel chair. I laid my head down, nesting it in my folded arms with the intent to sulk for the rest of eternity. But I couldn't get comfortable; something on the desk was tickling my nose. I picked up my head to see what it was: a curled-up scrap of paper like one torn from my spiral pad. The note contained an unfamiliar phone number and nothing more. I turned it over to see the reverse side. Sure enough, it was the first of my notes to Vivian, but how did it get here?

On the desk phone, I dialed the number with a hundred explanations running through my head—some rational and some off the charts. I didn't know what to expect. With the receiver at my ear, I heard the phone ring, but I also heard a phone ringing a few cubicles to my left. Each of the succeeding rings seemed to be in perfect sync, but no one was picking up. I let it ring a few more times, and then I had a curious thought—from way out in left field. I was a lawyer, wasn't I? Time to pursue this thread of logic. I laid the receiver down on the desk, allowing the dialed number to remain ringing. The wayward phone elsewhere in the office continued to ring, as I thought it might.

I jumped up and stepped into the aisle. The ringing seemed

louder there. I walked the row of cubicles until I found the culprit phone. But no one was in this cubicle office. There wasn't even a name placard on the desk. I certainly wasn't going to go through the IN box. What if I got caught? Now I was really baffled. I stuck my head over the partition to the neighboring cubicle to query the woman there. She had her hand over her mouth trying to stifle a giggle.

"Whose cubicle is this?" I asked, beginning to feel belligerent.

"It's mine," said the melodic voice coming from directly behind me.

I turned quickly to face the owner and saw Vivian full on—red hair, red brows and emerald green eyes, the whole Vivian package. I wanted to hug her, but I said something idiotic instead.

"I asked you out nicely, and you're giving me the runaround? What the devil is that all about?"

"I was just having a little fun with you," she replied. "I wanted to see what you're made of. Come to the break room with me, and I'll explain everything."

"You tested me!" I blurted out when we got to the empty break room. "Did I at least pass, or was I guilty of something?"

"Oh, you got an A plus. You're acquitted on all counts, Jaimey."

"Acquitted of what? The crime of asking you to dinner?"

Vivian looked amused. "I get your point. But I don't date just anyone who asks. I need to know more about them. I'd seen you around the firm and recognized you at the Library of Congress."

My lawyer's instincts, newbie or not in my first job, forced me to ask, "Who was the woman you were with?"

"My mom," Vivian said. "She was doing some research for her book club and needed my help. I didn't want to rush her, but the timing was bad. I had an important email to send. Anyway, when I got back from the library, I made some inquiries about you. You seemed like a nice guy. I'm a second-year associate here, and you're a first-year associate. If you don't mind my superiority complex, I think dinner tonight would be excellent. You can pick me up at eight."

She handed me her business card. I turned it over, still suspicious. On the back she'd written her home address.

But dogged, perverse me couldn't let go. "What about your ring? Are you engaged?"

She laughed. Her cheeks colored, accenting her charming dimple. "Heavens no. The ring is on my right hand. See?" She held her hand up so I could get a good look. "It's just a bauble I enjoy wearing. If I were engaged it would be on my left hand. And it would be a diamond, I can assure you."

Wow. The lady lawyer was actually blushing. Now it was my turn to laugh.

§

A Cultural Palace

by Gail M Baugniet

Change may not always seem for the better, but it does lead to new life experiences and eventually to lasting memories. Almost four years out of my teens, and protesting a narrowing existence, I packed a few small-town belongings and headed a hundred miles south to the Windy City–Chitown. I had been hired to work for a collections lawyer on the ninth floor of the Chicago Loop's Temple Building on W. Washington Street. The busy street featured a newly built Civic Center dedicated two years earlier. Marshall Field's Department Store took up the next block heading east toward Michigan Avenue.

Across the avenue lay Grant Park, its spacious lawns sprawled along Lake Michigan's shoreline. As my luck would have it, anchoring the street on the corner of Michigan and Washington was the regally showcased Chicago Public Library. The building, with its Romanesque features and arched entryways, quickly became my second home in the culturally oriented city. I could not have imagined that a controversial farm animal—a pig, to be exact—would play into my latest life experience.

Although inconsequential to the decision-making process of my relocation, my chosen moving date proved a pivotal time for the country's political future. A match had already been struck to ignite a very long fuse shortly before this month of August in 1968.

* * * *

Following a sparse orientation, my work hours were filled with endless repetitive paperwork that required typing notices of past-due bills, in duplicate, and photocopying each notice for the collections manager's files. Time-consuming treks across Washington Street to file paperwork in civil court were infrequent, as few cases ever went to trial. Most debtors were anxious to avoid additional fees by settling their cases out of court.

While law office hustle and bustle was the order of each business day, window shopping and leisurely library visits offered me an inexpensive and peaceful respite from the strict deadlines of legal proceedings. Activities during the early weeks of my employment in the Loop were contained within that stretch of Washington Street. Strolls through the park, to Buckingham Fountain or along Michigan Avenue leading to the Chicago Art Institute, broke the comfortable pattern. But on a routine basis, the library on the corner offered a quiet escape from work and escalating political protests.

* * * *

I had visited the Chicago Public Library for the first time soon after settling into my studio apartment. Both were located a short walk from the Temple Building. After finishing work for the day, I had walked the couple of blocks to the library, climbing the steep flight of steps to the library's arched facade and entering through one of the Washington Street doors.

Rain had threatened again after a brief lull from a lunchtime shower. But I took the time to view bronze dolphins over the main entrance that greeted me before I ducked into the lobby. I unselfconsciously gawked at the vaulted entryway that rose three full stories. According to a small plaque posted on a side wall, the entry hall's grand staircase and walls were constructed of white Carrara marble. Running a hand over the smooth surface, I envisioned Michelangelo's statue of *David*, carved out of a damaged chunk of limestone from the same Italian quarry in the Tuscany region of central Italy.

Unfamiliar with the library layout, I approached a sprightly older librarian pushing an overloaded cart of books destined for return to the shelves and asked for directions to the mystery stacks. I had enjoyed a book by Arthur Hailey about a hotel in New Orleans and wanted to read his latest published novel, *Airport*, rumored to be loosely based on Chicago's O'Hare International Airport. I would first have to apply for a library card and didn't know how long the process would take.

Meanwhile, if copies of *Airport* were available, I could read a few chapters at a time while sitting in the library reading room after work. My dad had encouraged me to read mysteries by Dashiell Hammett. But I hadn't yet found the time, just as I had never been inclined to read books as a child. Only upon discovering Rex Stout's never-ending Nero Wolfe series, did I discover the pleasure of getting lost in a book's stimulating plot, most often a seemingly unsolvable murder mystery.

One of the library's benefits that I appreciated was an abundant supply of newspapers available for library patrons to read. I took advantage of this free service daily. During one visit, when I requested a current copy of the *Chicago Tribune*, the librarian mentioned that newspaper stands located outside of the library on Randolph Street had at one time allowed the public to read current editions of the paper for free as they came off the press. "Of course, that was before home delivery became practical." Handing the newspaper to me, the librarian added, "The headlines these days almost make you not want to read the news anymore."

With the Democratic National Convention scheduled for the last week of August, Chicago's police force was on high alert to maintain a calm atmosphere. The April assassination of Martin Luther King in Memphis, and then the Robert F. Kennedy assassination in Los Angeles in June, had made law enforcement across the country more vigilant. On August 12th, the *Chicago Trib* reported that E. Chicago Heights was under curfew due to civil unrest after several fires were set with railroad flares and a police sergeant was shot. On the 14th, the newspaper reported damage in that same area caused by Molotov cocktails and a hand grenade.

* * * *

Late one afternoon, I lounged on the library steps under a cloudless sky. On Friday, almost four inches of rain had fallen on the city, slowing traffic and discouraging protesters, while still maintaining temperatures over 90 degrees long after sunset. Today, though, comfortable temperatures with a steady wind off the lake and no rain in the forecast made for ideal protest weather. A taxi driver, stalled in traffic, turned up the volume on his radio during a broadcast of an editorial about Vietnam War protests airing on the WLS radio station. Peace activists were threatening to disrupt the upcoming convention at the Chicago Amphitheater. From his open window, the cabbie called out to no one in particular, "Whatdaya think of them peace activists?" In a self-assured voice, a young woman with a toddler in tow replied, "Many died for the beliefs those activists now protest. With everything that has been sacrificed, I'm not ready to accept their views." The cab driver nodded, apparently in agreement, then turned off the radio and edged his vehicle forward with the slowly advancing traffic.

Several other people in range of my hearing offered varying but less articulate opinions of the peace activists. If other discussions I had overheard were an indication, however, a majority of Chicago's population continued to assume that Mayor Richard J. Daley had the city's safety firmly in his grasp, regardless of what the protestors threatened. He had become mayor of the city in 1955 and every four years the majority of its citizens reelected him. After his first reelection, he reorganized the police department to better regulate the budget and oversee disciplinary situations involving officers. In 1960, he further bolstered his position by appointing Criminologist O.W. Wilson as superintendent of the Chicago Police Department.

Most citizens still trusted the mayor's ability to strong-arm the population. Others, who predicted that his iron control could not last forever, would experience little surprise when the pressure valve inevitably gave way. Now, only days before the start of the convention, unrest permeated the air. Whispered gossip in the library's reading room and between the stacks had led many locals to question how much longer before change became inevitable.

* * * *

By my third week in Chicago, my new library card had arrived in the mail. After another week of processing billing notices and avoiding groups of still relatively peaceful protestors, I patiently stood at the counter waiting for my selection of reading material to get checked out. Anticipating the 94-degree heat outside, I appreciated the comfort of the air-conditioned room.

The librarian furtively leaned across the counter toward me and whispered, "Be careful when you leave the library. Maybe don't go out the Washington Street exit." When I asked why, the librarian explained that some goofball protesters were holding a public rally in the Civic Center Plaza by that statue Picasso gave to the city. She rolled her eyes at the mention of the controversial creation before adding, "And things could turn ugly if the police get wind of the unlawful gathering, especially if the rumor of animal abuse is accurate. Best you exit out the Randolph Street doors."

Until recently, I had not been aware of an entrance to the library located off Randolph Street. Yesterday, I had finally taken the time to investigate and was pleasantly surprised to find an entirely separate section of the public library. I quickly learned of the building's fascinating history going back to 1897. After the Great Fire of 1871, which raged through Chicago's core leaving hundreds of thousands of people homeless and many thousands of buildings destroyed, the dedicated citizens quickly rebuilt. Soon British authors and statesmen donated thousands of books, many autographed by donors including Queen Victoria, poet Robert Browning, and naturalist Charles Darwin. Those books were first housed in an old three-story-high water tank salvaged from the destructive fire.

To my delight, I discovered that the Randolph Street portion of the library consisted of a four-story north wing. A curving staircase lined with Knoxville Pink Marble led to the Grand Army of the Republic (G.A.R.) Museum, which is dedicated to Civil War soldiers and displays artifacts of the Civil War. Tiffany windows and a sunlit stained-glass dome took my breath away as I stared in awe, a small-town girl incapable of assuming a blasé attitude.

Curious to know why the building housed two very distinct businesses, I posed the question to a friendly looking guide. He graciously explained that when the current location of the library was in the approval stage, a glitch arose on discovery that the property had already been approved for use by the G.A.R. He added that the satisfactory resolution was separate entrances for the two entities. While the building was now no longer in its prime, I could appreciate why so many local residents still considered this cultural treasure a palace for the people.

Nodding to the librarian who had suggested I leave by a different door because of possible unlawful activity nearby, I considered my options. Never one to avoid a bit of excitement, I chose to ignore the well-intended advice. Instead, I exited the library onto Washington Street and immediately headed back toward the plaza.

* * * *

I often ate my bag lunch sitting on the framework surrounding the sculpture everyone referred to simply as "the Picasso." The artwork had been gifted to the people of Chicago by Pablo Picasso, the world-famous artist, after he designed a miniature figure to be used as a model for the outsized structure. The unveiling of the 50-foot-tall, 160-ton structure took place in the Civic Center Plaza the previous year to lots of hoopla, and even more groaning, when the elongated face of the three-dimensional Cubist form registered in the minds of the unsuspecting public.

Ironically, no one ever thought to actually copyright the artist's work after it became part of the public domain on that August day in 1967. The limited common-law copyright protection had expired and no lawsuit or argument could change the ruling backed by the United States Constitution. Which likely explained how its likeness ended up on plates and cuff links, pajamas, and even the local telephone directory.

A boisterous but friendly crowd was gathered along the sidewalk as I approached the plaza. I was forced to step off the curb at Dearborn Street in search of a decent viewing spot. It was easy to assume the librarian had overreacted to any news I overheard about "goofball protestors" because this was clearly a peaceful rally, not a belligerent protest.

The upcoming Democratic National Convention gave hippies a reason to exist and rabble-rousers a platform on which to rabble-rouse in a relatively calm atmosphere. A suggestion of animal abuse at the Civic Center appeared to make little sense, unless someone had decided to spoof the plaza's famous towering structure known, among other less flattering names, as "a cow," though not specifically that of Mrs. O'Leary's legend.

As I strained to see what may have gotten the librarian so concerned about my safety, I spotted a raised platform next to the sculpture. Some protesters must have erected a stage for the purpose of voicing their current political concerns. I spotted a handwritten sign with the words "Youth International Party" scrawled in red letters. From articles I had read, this was the group of Yippies led by activists who had come to Chicago to protest the Vietnam War, along with other national issues, including the lack of racial integration. What better time and place to attract the most attention than around a political convention?

Tuning into bits of conversation, I learned that what the Yippies were advocating today was a third-party presidential candidate: a live pig! Deriding the official nominee of Democrats, Hubert H. Humphrey, and his opponent, the Republican nominee Richard M. Nixon, they were preparing to present their candidate for president of the United States, none other than Pigasus the Pig. As someone standing near me shouted out the name Jerry, a man stepped to the center of the platform. Enthusiastic chants and hand-clapping followed. But as the man attempted to introduce Pigasus to the crowd, he and his fellow protesters were flanked by a veteran team of police officers and quickly arrested.

The poor uncomprehending pig attempted to squirm out of

the ordeal, edging nervously toward the stage steps. The leash around its neck got caught on a post and toppled a protest sign. As several protesters corralled the animal, I noticed the pig's eyes wildly searching for an avenue of escape. Feeling its desperation, I could only hope law enforcement would deem the pig an innocent kidnap victim, not a politically protesting hog.

Deemed unacceptable by local law enforcement, and overseen by the city's esteemed mayor, the pig also was arrested and reportedly "squealed" on its perpetrators, which ultimately led to the arrest of several offenders. The crowd, which included me, quickly dispersed with no further altercations.

As much levity as the pig encounter offered to the good people of Chicago, the Pigasus protest highlighted the current political situation involving the ongoing war overseas and the racial inequality here in the United States. I couldn't help but equate both issues with this country's Civil War, thinking immediately of the G.A.R. Museum at the Chicago Public Library, which was dedicated to that war's soldiers.

Thwarted by police over the pig protest, during the weekend leading up to the convention peaceful protesters took to the streets and local parks. They blocked traffic and gave rambling speeches, mostly to protest the war in Vietnam and Vice President Humphrey, who was the leading Democratic presidential nominee. Police stood by in blue riot helmets, carrying billy clubs and black pistols. Soldiers stood ready with armored vehicles and bayoneted rifles. Along with other federal agencies, the Secret Service, FBI, and Criminal Investigation Division studied the hotel lobby crowds and searched for explosives. Thousands of protesters, Yippies, hippies, and tag-a-longs picketed the hotels of major political delegates.

Chicago cab drivers were on strike. The city's bus drivers were on strike. Electrical workers were on strike. Because I lived within comfortable walking distance of work, home, restaurants, and recreation areas, I was not deeply affected by the strikes. However, my boss recommended that I steer clear of the parks and convention center for the rest of August, due to escalating conflict between protestors and police. He said it didn't matter whose actions were right or wrong if you got caught in the middle and ended up dead. Of course, that didn't stop him from reminding me that he really needed all the latest collection notices typed and photocopied, in triplicate, by midmorning tomorrow so everything would make the afternoon mail pickup.

I appreciated his concern about my safety and quickly assured him I would finish my work on time. What I didn't mention was my concern over all the people who were getting injured by billy clubs or sick from tear gas in the parks and on the streets. I had managed to sidestep protestors who showed up in the Loop to obstruct traffic and generally create havoc. I agreed with the desire to stop the war and bring American soldiers home. But having grown up in a very small community, I had little experience with racial inequality. Considering the extreme circumstances now unfolding around me, however, I had to agree with my boss; observing from a distance and staying alive was sound advice.

* * * *

I continued to frequent the Chicago Public Library to hear the latest gossip, check out new mystery books, and peruse the current newspapers. In late September, I was pleased to learn that after Pigasus had been taken into custody by the police, the pig had been turned over to the Anti-Cruelty Society, accompanied by a Mrs. Pig and their piglet, who both had played a role in Yippies demonstrations during the convention. The well-tended porcine family was transported to a small farm in Grayslake, Illinois, an area known for its welcoming residents.

The protestors who made the biggest splash around town were arrested, labeled the "Chicago Seven" during a long circus of a trial, found guilty of various crimes, and then turned loose when convictions were overturned on appeal.

Meanwhile, the library had obtained several copies of Arthur Hailey's suspense novel, *Airport,* because of his popularity as an author and the novel's local setting. The plot unfolds during a snowy

16

blizzard, typical of winter storms that most Chicago residents have experienced. Disaster in the skies seems imminent. After racing through the heart-pounding novel, I compared the book's plotline to the Chicago riots, which also seemed to spell imminent disaster.

* * * *

Thinking back to those hectic days of August, I often focused on how I first learned of the Chicago Public Library's dual purpose as a cultural palace. With vivid details still fresh in my mind that the librarian had shared during one of my visits, I imagined myself standing on the Randolph Street sidewalk with a privileged group of citizens for the 1897 grand opening of the library. The Chicago Symphony Orchestra had regaled attendees with a rendition of Pietro Mascagni's music, the intermezzo from *Cavalleria Rusticana*, rustic chivalry.

I attended a moving rendition of the Italian opera at the Civic Opera House on Wacker Drive with friends over the holidays. I recalled how the music had aroused in me a strong awareness of events that had recently unfolded around me. Now, memories of the violins' emotional impact evoked thoughts of both sadness and pleasure.

Life was like that, I realized. Appreciation of the finer times, balanced with periods of discontent, allowed a person to experience the fullness of one's existence.

Dewey Decimate

by Brett Botbyl

"Write me a note, hon."

Gloria tore off a sheet from her dupe pad minus the carbon paper and slapped it on the table, along with a Bic ballpoint pen and a comically large, full-color menu. But at this time of night, she could usually do an order before even reading the chicken scratch. The old-timer in #11 was a regular, so this was an easy one. She stopped at the kitchen window.

"Toasted poppy bagel, Al! And give it a San Tropez tan, will ya?"

"That sounds familiar."

"Yeah, old Howard and his poppy with butter and jelly. At least he knows what makes 'im happy, I'll give 'im that."

The owner and head cook, Al Vasilatos, preferred the late shift, leaving the daytime hours to his greased-up brother Nikos. He and his tiny gold earring played the silver-haired set with just the right panache, but Al had always been a creature of the night. Besides, Gloria knew the unspoken truth. Going on thirty years, Al Vasilatos smiled every time she stepped through the front door.

Gloria had worked the late shift at the Olympia Diner for far longer than she'd ever admit. For a middle-aged woman, she was fast and nimble in her Zephyr work shoes. "Best you can buy," she'd tell the newbie waitresses when they started. Her husband, Hal, used to tease. "Ya spend a lot on those high-class waitress shoes, Glo. I better get a second job to keep ya goin'." Maybe he was right. But a second job would have meant even less time with him before the cancer took him down.

Gloria planted a fresh cup of joe in front of the old timer, then rounded back to the kitchen.

"George Hamilton poppy pickup, Gloria!"

Gloria chuckled. In his late-night diner cook way, Al was a charmer. His creative food names never failed to make her laugh.

"Nice one, Al! George Hamilton? Wow, there ain't a single kid in Sunnyside with a clue who *that* was."

Gloria threw three butter pats and two jelly packs into her apron pocket, then palmed the bagel plate. Her friend and fellow late-night waitress Lenore sidled up to her as she pinched a wad of napkins.

"What's wrong, Nor? You look like you're draggin'."

"Christ in a breadline, Glo. I am dead on my feet. Chrissy brought the baby over at the crack of dawn, 'cuz she caught Ryan suckin' face with that girl again."

"Jesus, Nor. She's gotta dump that deadbeat!"

"Sing me a song I ain't heard already a thousand times. But Chrissy? That girl's got her grandmother's genes. If I had it to do all over again, I woulda marched that baby into the GEN clinic as soon as I could walk and had her granny's man issues snipped out. Christ as my witness!"

A nearby crone in a woolen long coat and bedroom slippers turned her head just enough to bark, "Excuse me! Some of us are Christians here!"

Lenore waved her off. "Apologies, ma'am. Praise the Lord!"

Gloria flashed her best Christian smile, then whispered through her teeth, "Gotta watch that talk, Nor. Ya never know who's gonna turn you in for a few bucks."

Lenore nodded in agreement. "Glo, I'm deep in the weeds here. A kid just sat down in booth #3. Ya think you could please take him off my hands?"

Gloria smiled. Lenore was already teetering in her cheap waitress shoes. Gloria knew the woman had only about an hour left in her.

"Sure. Lemme drop off old Howard's bagel, and I'll take the kid."

"You're a lifesaver, Glo. I owe ya big."

Al's voice erupted from the kitchen. "Cut the love fest, ladies. That bagel's gettin' ice cold!"

Gloria rolled her eyes. "Calm down, Al! You wanna end up in Mount Sinai over a bagel?!" She plunked down the order, then patted old Howard's shoulder. "I'll get you a refill on my way back, hon." She snatched the dupe sheet off of the table and read the chicken scratch:

Toasted poppy bagel with two butters and jelly. Cup of coffee with sugar and ½ and ½.

* * * *

With a smile, Gloria arrived at booth #3. The booths were prime seating, especially after the clubs closed at 4 a.m. But since it was only 2:47 on the old Westclox Belfast over the door, the kid was good for an hour plus. Gloria plunked an Olympia menu down in front of the customer. Lenore said there was a kid in #3. She wasn't kidding. The boy had to be sixteen, maybe seventeen-ish.

"You all alone, kid?"

He smiled faintly. "Yes, ma'am."

For some reason, she had a soft spot for that one. It was March outside and a cold one for sure. That neck of the woods was hit with what natives called the Queen's Chill every winter. And that particular March wasn't going out like a lamb. The boy was wearing one of those white, short-sleeved, buttoned-up shirts. Institutional style, like the religious nuts risking jail to make a buck on the subway platforms. Then again, it almost had a hospital-patient feel. But short sleeves? Weird. His buzz-cut hair was wet and almost silver in color, with sweat, like he had just run a mile in August.

"Y'okay, hon? Can I get you something to drink?"

The boy looked up at Gloria. His face was sweet and pained.

She knew his pain. Every night at Olympia was like flipping through a picture book of humanity. Good, bad, and so much ugly. Gloria tore off a sheet from her pad and gently placed it on the table in front of the boy.

"I'll get you a large orange juice. In the meantime, take a look at the menu, then write me a note. Okay, hon?"

"Yes, ma'am." The boy smiled with a timid grin.

Gloria grabbed the coffee pitchers to make the refill rounds. The brown rim meant black and deadly, while the orange was decaf. After hitting up Howard and a half-dozen other tables, she went on the bring-it-home tour with checks all around. Heading back to the kitchen, she found Lenore half-sitting on a chrome counter stool.

"Ya gonna make it?"

Lenore stood back up and struck her best Wonder Woman stance. "Good as gold, Glo! I just popped two Tylenol. I'll be in fightin' shape in under ten minutes."

"Well, I just papered the house, so we'll get a little lull before the clubs spit up the mess," Gloria quipped.

Lenore started writing in her dupe pad. "I'll get these out, then meet you back here. Hey, how was the kid? Grilled cheese and a water?"

Gloria shook her head. "Nah, He's okay. I feel bad, though. He looks, I don't know… Somethin's not right."

Lenore gave one of her caring-mother smiles. "Well, it's almost three, and Bridget's on her way in. Why don't you get your tables outta here, then take a break? Maybe see what story your new stray has to tell."

Gloria nodded, "Yeah, maybe. Lemme get some food in him and a glass of OJ. The poor kid's all skin and bones."

A scoop of ice and a full draw on the juice machine and Gloria was ready to flip over the rock. She walked slowly up to the table so as not to startle the kid. "Here ya go, hon. Large orange juice."

She picked up the slip of paper but left the pen on the table. Something told her that the kid might need to write something else. "Okay, let's see what we got here." She stood at the tableside and read the note her customer had written. In careful, almost juvenile penmanship, the words sent a shiver up her spine.

"Before my time, before the previous time, back and back and back."

"Um…young man."

"Huh?" The boy looked up with little expression. "Dewey. My name is Dewey."

Gloria felt flushed, as if all the blood in her body had suddenly rushed to her head. "Um…Dewey. Where did you hear this?"

The boy bent a paper-thin smile. "From Burton. From your son."

Gloria put her hand on the back of the padded bench opposite Dewey. "I'm not sure who you are…"

"I already said. My name is Dewey."

Gloria's nails dug into the red vinyl fabric of the overstuffed banquette. "I know what you said," she spat, before realizing the sharpness of her words. She looked around the dining room, spotting Lenore moving from table to table delivering closing checks. Gloria sat down across from the boy for fear of fainting. Thoughts of her son raced quickly around anchor points of law and exposure and the very real calamity of arrest in New York City in 2041. She lowered her head, glancing lazily at the strange boy across the table as if to deny the importance of the conversation.

"Eyes are watching. Eyes are everywhere."

"Dewey. Honey. My son was killed over a year ago in a Wind-rail accident over the mainline. It was a horrible tragedy. Seventeen people died that day. I'm not sure what that sentence you wrote means to you. But I can assure you that my son, Burton, is gone."

Dewey locked eyes on Gloria. Not in a threatening or unwavering way, but rather with a childlike sense of knowing. He said, "There was a time when the world needed to know of his death. But now he is emerging with a truth made stronger by millions of silenced voices." He whispered, *"Voices from before my time, before the previous time, back and back and back."*

"Dewey. That is a quote from my son's favorite book when he was a teenager. *The Giver*, by Lois Lowry. But the book and all its quotes have been banned for a long, long time." Her voice was starting to quiver. Her son's death was a reality so bitter, so profound in the understanding that she would never again look her boy in the eyes. Her son. A scholar, a teacher, and a public nuisance. How swift the passage of time from that dark, rainy September morning when they came for him.

Gloria reflected. Rents were so expensive in the city. Even in Queens. Well, it just made sense to live with his mother. There was plenty of room since Hal passed. Sure, Burton had his pride. He had his hobbies, his father's love of whiskey and the unapologetic one-night stands with the working boys from the clubs. But more than anything, her son possessed a solid belief in the principles of an America long buried under piles of charred, hard history. An America that could never again be great. Or free. A time before the Red Hats, the alternate truths, the demonization of free thought, and the rampant banning and destruction of books. They came for him. Whistles and splintered wood. Screams and sirens and public display, tearing out the infected worm of rebellious, loud-mouthed homosexual agitation. Burton was a thought criminal, accused of speaking against the state and harboring information deemed contrary and dangerous to the welfare of the American people.

Gloria stood shakily to her feet. "I'll be right back, hon. Drink your juice. I'll get you another." Walking back to the waitress station, she felt disoriented. No one could have known the truth about Burton. Not some waif wandering into the diner well after bedtime with a quote from…

"You okay, Glo?"

Lenore was sipping her always-full Diet Coke from a bendy straw and tapping her foot to jump-start the circulation.

Gloria managed a grin. "Oh, yeah. Just…Yeah, the kid's just gettin' out of the cold."

Lenore leaned slightly to Gloria's left to glance toward table #3. "That's a strange one, Glo. That puppy is a runaway."

Gloria's eye twitched from the nerves. "What do you mean, runaway?"

Lenore just nodded with a touch of playful smugness. "Oh, come on, Glo. He's a tank baby."

Gloria was starting to uncover layers of possibility. *No one could have known the truth about Burton.* "Nah. I think he's just a local boy tryin' to get his head straight."

"Nope," said Lenore. "A tank baby. Didn't ya see the nipple on his neck? Right on the kid's albino skin. He was fabricated, not born. You better get him out of here, Glo. You don't want the Paladins marching through that front door."

Gloria swallowed hard. "The Paladins? What for? He's just a kid. And he's almost done anyway. Come on, Nor. Let's get the rest of these checks dropped before the next wave. Clubs are spittin' up soon."

Lenore nodded heading back out to the dining room. "We got this, Glo. Light at the end of the tunnel."

Gloria saw Al leaning against the counter. His face was absent of any trace of the usual midshift animation. "Listen, Gloria. You gotta get that kid out of here. Lenore called the Central Division while you were talkin' to him. She saw some kinda mark on his neck and she thinks he's a tank baby. You know, some kind of escaped test rat. We don't need any heat in here, Glo. Not after last Memorial Day and the fight out back. We got a yellow stripe and a code warning. Next stop, they'll shut us down."

"Jesus. She actually called us in because of some weird kid?"

"She's scared, Gloria. With her daughter and the baby, ya can't blame her."

"But Al, the kid is out on his own in the Queens Chill. He doesn't even have a winter coat, for God's sake. He'll freeze to death out there."

"It is what it is, Glo. But the clock is tickin'. The Paladins will be here in minutes. Even sooner if the boy's wanted for something. Look, you don't need this. What with your son…"

"Stop, Al. I appreciate your concern. I'll get him out of here." Gloria moved quickly through the dining room, waving off Howard and his bagel bill and a refill on #12. She slid into booth #3 across from the boy, now sitting before his empty juice glass. Gloria pulled a wad of cash from her apron, $20 or so, and slid it across the tabletop.

"Look, kid…um, Dewey, right?"

"Yes, ma'am."

"Dewey, this is all I can spare. You gotta leave right away. Out the front door. Walk as fast as you can down to the Baptist church on the corner and go around back to the shelter. Reverend Pike is an old customer and a good man. Tell him I sent you. Tell 'im you gotta lay low for a few days. That they're coming to arrest you."

Dewey looked up with a timid smile on his face, reading the name tag on Gloria's apron. "It's okay, Gloria. I know they're coming for me. I knew they would be when I left the facility."

Gloria's eyes began to tear. There was bad news coming, and her fight-or-flight instincts were on full alert. "No. You'll be alright, Dewey. Just go. Now."

Dewey shook his head. The kind of subtle gesture one makes when having to deny a loved one. His voice was soft and calm.

"Your son is alive, Gloria."

"No. You're wrong, Dewey. My son is dead."

"Gloria, I was created in a laboratory as a retention vessel. C-Barron-X3. LOT 5."

"Easy. Keep your voice down." She leaned over the table, her voice lowered to a near whisper. "What you're saying is dangerous. The Paladins are already on their way."

"I know, Gloria. Burton prepared me for this. All of this. I was born to store data. In my DNA coding. This was the grand experiment. I was created by the regime from the genetic fabric of their precious dynasty. My blood was meant to store the records of this mass empire of corruption and greed. Religion and law mattered less than their legacy. Democracy had collapsed and fear was sharpened to force the people to comply. To deny."

His voice was now barely loud enough to hear. Gloria could see customers beginning to quickly exit the diner. Lenore's warnings of the raid were clearly unfolding.

"Dewey, please…"

"Your son is the single greatest revolutionary of this terrible time. Because of him, rebel operatives infiltrated the facility posing as care and maintenance workers and read to me at night. Fed me. I was given data infusions. Nourishment of the mind. One by one, my genetic imprinting was overwritten. I became not a vessel of the history of oppression, but rather a repository of knowledge.

Digital copies of every book banned in the United States since the early 1950s are contained in the DNA of my blood. Gloria, I am the library of all that has been denied. The stories, histories, dramas, and truths. All denied as part of a strategy to make this country great again. Those in power feared that words would poison the blood of the American people. What a perfect irony that blood should be the antidote to this one supreme act of oppression."

He took a deep breath, then smiled sweetly. His face wore a profound resolution. "Your son is alive, Gloria. And I am the fruit of his sacrifice. I am the last library."

Gloria could no longer hold back the tears. "You have to go, Dewey. Please."

"No, it is *you* who have to go, Gloria. You know where to find your son. Disappear into the same mystery that took him in that accident."

Out in the street, the strobing blue lights of the Paladin vehicles ignited the shadows. Gloria stood, leaned over, and hugged Dewey, kissing him on the head.

"I'll never forget you, Dewey. Please take care of yourself." She could see Lenore out in the street as the dining room emptied of its last customers. Just seconds before they stormed the diner, Gloria turned to leave.

"Gloria?"

She turned around to find Dewey holding out a wadded white napkin in his outstretched hand. "Your tip. You can't forget that, Gloria."

Reaching out, she took the crumpled napkin from the boy. Tears were now running down her cheeks as she moved toward the kitchen. Passing the door to the grill station, Al stepped out and took her arm.

"They're here for the kid, Gloria. But you gotta go."

"No, Al."

"Listen to me, Gloria. The delivery van is parked out back next to the dumpster. It's got a full tank and a couple of crates of food for you and your boy."

She was caught off guard. "How did you know?"

With eyes welling with tears, he smiled. "I've been watching you, Glo. I've always watched you."

"Thank you, Al. If things ever blow over…"

"I'll be here. Waiting. Now get the hell out of here, Glo."

She could see the Paladin agents rush in through the front door, converging on Dewey in booth #3.

Gloria turned and slipped out the back door into the alley behind the diner. The beat-up van was exactly where Al said it would be. Next to the overstuffed dumpster, with a faded logo painted across the back panel: The Olympia Diner. Queens NYC since 1976.

She opened the door and hopped into the vintage, cracked, vinyl bench seat. Fumbling for the key, she placed the crumpled napkin on the passenger seat beside her and started the engine. In seconds the van was out on the main drag and speeding towards the Whitestone Bridge. Careful not to attract any attention, Gloria followed the flow of after-club traffic. The vehicles ahead bottlenecked at the toll booth just before the bridge. Stopping, she slid a simple lever on the dashboard to bring up the heat. That's when she remembered it. The napkin that Dewey handed her as she was about to leave. She cocked her head.

"Your tip," she said aloud.

Still unable to move ahead, Gloria reached over and unfolded the napkin. She noticed the blood first. Confused, she turned on the interior light and stared in disbelief. Almost gray from a lack of circulation, a pinky finger rested on the unfurled paper napkin soaked in blood.

She quickly rolled the finger back in the napkin and stuffed it into an empty coffee cup she found in the center console.

The traffic started to break, so she was able to pass through the toll booth. The auto license reader triggered a beep and a reassuring green light. Driving over the bridge, she recalled what Dewey had said.

"Digital copies of every book banned in the United States since the early 1950s are contained in the DNA of my blood."

With the flow of traffic moving freely, Gloria drove the rattling van, moving at a clip towards the Bronx, with New Jersey just minutes away. Back to her son. Back to Burton in a rustic little hideaway cabin in the Ramapo Mountains, far off the grid. Back to freedom, and the life of a revolutionary on the run.

"...back and back and back."

§

The Creaping Bottom Library Story
by Dawn Knox

Close down the library?

Over Petronella Asquelch's dead body.

She screwed the letter into a ball and aimed it at the wastepaper basket. Then, thinking better of it, she laid it on the library counter and smoothed it out. There was no ignoring it. The issue would have to be dealt with. And Petronella was just the woman to do it. She was the head librarian—indeed, she was the *only* librarian—in the tiny library in Creaping Bottom.

It was unusual for an English country village to have its own library. The inhabitants of other villages in the vicinity had to travel to the nearby town of Upper Chortle to borrow books. But during the last century, a rich benefactor had bestowed on the villagers of Creaping Bottom its own generously stocked library.

Petronella had been the head librarian for the last five years. And she was determined not to be the last librarian in Creaping Bottom. The ship would not go down on her watch.

Representatives from the local council would be visiting at the beginning of the coming month and Petronella would be required to demonstrate how popular the library was. But the truth was that library membership had dwindled over the last few years.

And worse—it was summer and the village cricket team was doing rather well. Players and their supporters were taking the game seriously and putting in lots of practice on the cricket pitch opposite the library, on the village green.

The Village in Bloom committee members had their eyes on the county prize, having been runners-up for the last three years. Accordingly, their preparations were underway to turn Creeping Bottom into a floral heaven before the judging took place.

All Saints' Church was organizing a fund-raising church fete and formidable Miss Twibbs, the churchwarden, had bullied more people into joining her bell-ringing team than she knew what to do with.

And even the village Knit-And-Natter Club had attracted new members to their weekly sessions.

It appeared that everyone in the village was too busy to read.

If only Petronella could lure everyone into the library during the next few weeks, she could make a case for keeping it open. But that prospect was looking increasingly remote.

Her morning's adrenaline rush on opening the council's letter had turned to despair by the end of the day. Only one book had been borrowed. Colonel Hodges-Snell had come in looking for yet another book for his wife. Strange how, when Petronella had met Mrs Hodges-Snell in the hairdressers the previous week and had reminded her the book she'd borrowed was due back, the good lady had professed no knowledge of such an item.

"Overdue books? No, I don't think so. I never have anything to do with books, m'dear. I don't have time to read." She peered at Petronella over the top of her glasses, her brows drawn together in disbelief. "Who'd run the Women's Institute and organize the annual gymkhana if I indulged in reading? It's a lot of self-indulgent nonsense, if you ask me."

Petronella didn't pursue the matter. She certainly hadn't wanted the formidable Mrs Hodges-Snell to win over anyone else in the hairdressers with her rather loud comments. So, who read the romances with the lurid covers featuring hunky, bare-chested men the colonel always borrowed "for his wife"? Not Mrs Hodges-Snell. But considering today's letter from the council, who cared as long as someone took books out and kept the library open?

As Petronella stamped the colonel's book, *The Sizzling Highland Fling*, she'd considered offering to find more books for him. Why take one when his membership card allowed him more? But as soon as she'd closed the book and slid it toward him, he thrust it into his bag and, with cheeks aflame, he fled.

Petronella gazed at all her neatly arranged bookcases. What would happen to all those books when the library closed? Would they be split up and sent to other libraries where they might become unneeded and unwanted duplicates? How would they feel about such humiliation?

Don't be ridiculous, Petronella! Her inner librarian's voice rebuked her.

And yet the atmosphere in the library had changed. There was an air of melancholy hanging over the bookcases as if the books knew their time together was drawing to a close.

Like coming to the end of a wonderful story.

But stories rarely finished on such a low point. Well, sometimes they did, of course, but not the memorable ones. The best stories concluded on a high. The heroine overcame all obstacles. The hero achieved his quest. Everyone except the villain was happy—or at least happy for now.

Why couldn't life be like a book?

An insubstantial thought like a bookworm wriggled into Petronella's consciousness. "Make life like a book," it said, or it would have said if it had been able to talk.

Easier said than done, thought Petronella sadly.

Or was it? She was surrounded by books. And books were full of ideas. Inside the library, she had access to thousands—no, wait—millions of ideas. And ideas lead to other ideas. Petronella's skin tingled with excitement. Her beloved books would attract people back into the library.

Exactly how? Petronella's sensible inner librarian voice asked.

To her surprise, the bookworm was still there, and he replied, "Well, a story starts by showing us the main character's everyday life. After that, comes the inciting incident, something that means life will never be the same for the main character. Then we need a climax, followed by a resolution. We've seen normal life for the library. It's deserted. So, to write the next part of the story, we need an inciting incident."

Petronella waited for more. An inciting incident? How thrilling. But what sort of inciting incident? The bookworm, however, was ominously silent.

* * * *

Petronella lay awake in bed that night. "Inciting incident" sounded intriguing, but it was like saying, "I'm going to shop for ingredients for dinner." Unless you decided what "dinner" you were going to serve, which ingredients would you buy?

She tossed and turned, rejecting idea after idea, but as dawn's insipid light filtered through her curtains, she gave up on the idea of sleep. She needed something theatrical, and she knew just the person to help.

Her cousin Rupert worked as a stage designer in a London theater. He'd understand her plight and her need for an inciting incident. After breakfast, she called him for help.

"Oh, you need a murder, darling. They always go down a storm."

"But I can't kill someone to save the library!" Petronella squeaked, slopping tea in her lap.

"No, darling. A pretend murder. With weapons and clues and things. Leave it to me. I know just the people. I'll send something over ready for Monday morning. Sorry, darling, I've got to go, *ciao*." He'd hung up before she had a chance to ask more.

How much was it all going to cost? Could she afford it? The library display budget was pitifully small.

You'll just have to cover the expenses out of your own funds if necessary. Think of it as an investment, she told herself. If she could secure the library's future, she'd still have a job. If she couldn't, the village would lose a valuable resource and she'd face financial ruin.

On Monday morning, she left home earlier than usual to get

to the library, ready to take delivery of the packages Rupert had promised. Expecting a delivery van, she was surprised when two police constables arrived carrying parcels. They introduced themselves as Brett and Sandra. After her initial shock at seeing two police officers in the library, she learnt they were actors in costume. Rupert had arranged for them to help her set up Operation Save Creeping Bottom's Library.

Actors? Rupert had sent actors? How much were they going to cost?

But she soon forgot the impending devastation of her bank balance as she discussed the organization of the day with Brett and Sandra over a cup of tea.

Under Petronella's direction, the two actors cut pieces of tape from a white roll and stuck them to the carpet in the shape of a body in front of the Crime bookcases. Then, taking a roll of yellow tape, they cordoned off the area. *Crime Scene—Do Not Enter*, the yellow tape proclaimed.

Perfect.

Meanwhile, Petronella sorted out the replica weapons Rupert had sent her and planned where to hide them. There were so many. Rupert's selection of literary weapons was awe-inspiring, although she wondered if he'd overdone it slightly. Well, she'd just keep concealing them until she ran out of space.

Harry Potter's magic wand and Tom Sawyer's catapult weren't too hard to hide in the Children and Classics sections. They slipped in behind the appropriate books quite neatly.

Luke Skywalker's light-sabre and Robin Hood's bow and arrow took a bit more ingenuity. However, Petronella was nothing if not ingenious, and finally, she'd secreted them in the Sci-Fi and Historical Fiction sections. King Arthur's sword slotted in neatly behind the Mythology books, and by pulling the Fantasy books forward slightly, she finally crammed Conan the Barbarian's axe in, too.

That left Chekhov's gun, Edward Scissorhands' scissors, Captain Ahab's whale harpoon, and Winnie-the-Pooh's honeytrap. She was quite exhausted by the time everything was concealed.

Now for the cards containing clues to the culprits…

Petronella had made six rounds of fortifying tea, and Sandra and Brett had eaten the entire month's biscuit allowance by the time the library was ready.

It was almost nine o'clock, but Petronella wasn't anticipating a rush. That would come after she'd posted her photographs on the village's social media page…Hopefully.

With minutes to spare, a serious-looking Brett and Sandra posed by the cordoned-off crime scene, and Petronella took photographs. She uploaded them to social media with the caption "An inciting incident in the library."

The church bell donged nine o'clock, and Petronella opened the doors, shivering with anticipation. Operation Save Creeping Bottom's Library had begun.

Within minutes, five people had arrived to peer at the outline of the body that was taped on the floor, asking what had happened.

Petronella shrugged. "I'm not sure. It's a mystery. The police are investigating."

People continued to come in throughout the day and many borrowed books. Six asked if they could join, and the social media pages buzzed with possible culprits and victims.

Petronella took a few more shots of Brett and Sandra "investigating" the murder amongst the bookcases, and they suggested they'd wait outside as if guarding the entrance. A good plan. The library was filling up, but it wouldn't hurt to attract more passersby. After all, not everyone regularly checked social media. There would still be villagers who were unaware of the inciting incident in the library.

By one o'clock, Petronella had begun to congratulate herself. Operation Save Creeping Bottom's Library was working like a dream. People came in, stared at the crime scene, took clue cards and hunted for weapons, marking them on their cards. Then they browsed and borrowed books.

She'd been so busy dealing with the growing queue at the library desk that she hadn't noticed the music. It was coming from outside. And not only music. People were whooping and whistling.

Petronella's heart sank. Had she incited a riot? No, surely it was nothing to do with her. It wasn't in the library, and that was the only place where she was responsible.

The party sounds had attracted people out of the library. Well, that wasn't in her plan. When she'd served the last person in the queue, she'd investigate. But suddenly, the line dwindled as people stole outside to find out what the commotion was.

Typical! Someone else had an event on and had poached her people! The cricket team with a jazz concert? The Village in Bloom committee members with a bring-and-buy sale? How annoying. If she'd known in advance, she'd have planned her event for a different day.

Well, whatever it was, she must stop it. She'd put in too much effort to save the library to let anyone ruin her plans. Petronella strode toward the doors and threw them open.

A strangled cry died in her throat and her knees nearly gave way. The two police constables were writhing—yes, that was the only word Petronella could think of to describe it—writhing to the music in a rather disturbing dance.

"Ooh, I say, isn't this scintillating!" said Miss Twibbs, the severe churchwarden. Her false teeth quivered with excitement. "I've never seen anything like it. And look at that male constable's muscles. Ooh, I say! I'm coming over all unnecessary!"

"Stop!" screamed Petronella as she realized what was about to happen.

* * * *

"This isn't London, Rupert. It's a tiny country village. I wish you'd warned me about Brett and Sandra," Petronella said later when she phoned her cousin,

"But you said you needed to make a statement. What speaks louder than strippergrams? I thought you'd appreciate them, darling. Didn't they add a little sparkle?"

Sparkle? When Petronella had first seen Brett and Sandra in action, the world had lit up with blinding light and almost seared her eyeballs. She'd frozen in horror. What would people think? Would they be shocked? Would there be a backlash? Should she resign immediately?

But, in fact, her scream had been so loud it had stopped the strippers before they'd removed any of their clothes. She'd apologized to the crowd and explained about the proposed library closure. People had voiced their dismay and congratulated her on her determination and the originality of Operation Save Creeping Bottom's Library.

Surprisingly, the day had been a great success. She would've patted the bookworm on the back if he'd had one—and if she'd known where he'd gone.

During the following few days, she was kept busy in the library as a constant stream of people borrowed books and returned them.

Miss Twibbs visited and asked if Petronella would organize a special children's reading event in the library over the weekend of the church fete. The Knit-And-Natter Club wanted to hold their weekly meetings in the room at the back. And the chairperson of the Village in Bloom committee had insisted all her fellow members carry out research in the Horticultural section since she'd found an unusual book about floral hydroponic displays that had inspired her.

Colonel Hodges-Snell had come in and borrowed three books "for his wife" and asked for Brett and Sandra's contact details for a soirée he intended to hold in the Manor. Even the cricket team captain had come into the library twice, although that was to arrange repairs to the window that one of the cricket balls had broken during training.

* * * *

At the council meeting, the members expressed surprise at the figures Petronella gave them to demonstrate that, far from rarely being used, the library was the hub of the village. Despite scepticism on the part of several members who'd intended to spend the money previously allotted to the library on their pet projects, the library's future was secured.

On the way home from the meeting, Petronella allowed herself an enormous sigh of relief. Thanks to an imaginary bookworm, she'd rewritten the library's story. She'd provided an inciting incident and Brett and Sandra had delivered a climax—albeit, one that still gave Petronella nightmares. But then what good was a climax if it went unnoticed? And now, the council had granted the library a favorable resolution. If not happy ever after, well, at least happy for now.

It was a well-written story and one that her imaginary bookworm would have given a thumbs up—if he'd had thumbs, of course.

Nine Lives Overdue for Return

By John E. Simonds

I guess we can blame this on Andrew Carnegie," the gaunt man with deep unflinching eyes and sharp-nosed profile pronounced to the others.

They sat about a round wooden reading table as they listened to him. No one had introduced them, but they seemed to know each other a little, though with only hints of why they were in a dimly lit village library, talking at night.

"Carnegie's money helped build this place and others like it," agreed a plumpish round-faced man in a wide-brimmed hat, peering above the rims of his round glasses as he spoke. In the darkness, a white notch contrasted with his black collar. "But why does that make *him* at fault for this group?" he asked.

The unsmiling man with edged features answered quickly.

"Carnegie may have invented modern steel, but he was known to experiment in mysteries of the mind and human behavior. He supported traditional education, but his deep interest in the science of the future gave new meaning to the term 'spirit of learning,'" the gaunt man declared.

A woman at the table, dressed in her 19th-century best, laughed aloud in an instant of recognition. "For a moment I didn't recognize you without your deerstalker hat," she smiled. "In fact, without it, you still look much like the actor Basil Rathbone."

"Yes, I get that a lot," said the weary detective of Baker Street. "A little like reality imitating art, or is it the other way around? None of us here is real, including you, Father Brown, a man who seeks to save souls and solve crimes."

"Stop changing the topic," said the woman at the table. "Back to Carnegie. He gave $15,000 toward the cornerstone in this quaint little fieldstone building under those spreading oaks and maples outside. Not much money now, but a lot then. Wasn't that good enough for us to be grateful?"

"Miss Sharp, you amaze me," said the smiling priest, gently looking over his rims. "I'm sure you've won sums that large in your days of tricking rich men in card games. Your reputation precedes you, but your kindly views of Mr. Carnegie give us all lessons in charity."

"That's not the point, Father," Sherlock Holmes jumped back in. "No one's disputing Carnegie's giving his money away. It's that, with it, has grown an idea that giant industries, machines, mathematical formulas can do our thinking for us—even replace our imaginations!"

A clearing throat from a quiet part of the large oaken table preceded a question. "Well, what's wrong with that?" he asked. The sound of an American voice caught some by surprise.

"That river just to the east of us is a place where I ran my first steamboat. The idea of lighting a boiler to drive a ship was considered insane. 'Fulton's Folly' is what people called it. Now look at it—so common it's considered old-fashioned, even on the ocean. New ideas need room to grow, but I'm still not sure what we're all doing here, like ghosts at a round table."

A tired-looking man with long hair and drooping mustache stirred in his chair before answering. "Well, I'm here for the story, real as I am, like Fulton here. Something about imaginary characters draws me in. Curious tonight about why our famous detectives are checking for Mr. Carnegie's fingerprints. As a fellow Scot, I marvel at his genius and generosity. But you sleuths are saying there's more to his influence."

"He was surely an influencer," said Holmes.

"Someday that may actually be a job title," Father Brown mused, "something people do for a living."

"Maybe sitting at a keyboard in front of a screen," said a heretofore silent man. "Sorry, couldn't resist. I got a little taste of wireless communication and can't stop with the fantasies. Some were sneering at it as 'Marconi's Madness,' but others called me the 'Wizard of the Ether.' "

"Wow," said Fulton. "Even I've heard of Guglielmo Marconi, and he was born nearly sixty years after I died."

"With all you interesting men at this table," Becky Sharp chuckled, "I feel like I should break out a deck of cards to see how much you can influence the fates in the luck of the deal."

"Probably the other way around," ventured RLS. "How much do the fates influence us? Look at my own life—adventure stories for boys, rhymes for children, travels to the South Seas—hard to explain my different experiences, how they clash in so many ways."

"Like Dr. Jekyll and Mr. Hyde," said Holmes.

"Elementary, you might say," Stevenson answered.

"Touché!" said Holmes. "But still, the real-life activities—whether fact or fiction—should be worth more than those products of machines and clever systems."

"You seem concerned, Holmes," Father Brown said, "that greater knowledge could be a threat to real creativity. Why not seize the moment to pursue its mysteries? See it as a challenge, as in 'the game's afoot.' "

Amid the general laughter around the table, Holmes rolled his usually piercing eyes and grumbled, "I get that all the time, too. I'm stuck with Conan Doyle and his clichés."

"But Sir Arthur was a believer in new possibilities, was he not?" Father Brown asked. "Communicating from the afterlife to those alive? That was bold. And my creator—pardon the reference, Lord—Chesterton spent a lot of time explaining how he could believe in both the Bible and evolution."

From deeper in the table shadows emerged a French accent

speaking in English. "Translation is the key," said the voice of a man calmed by years of experience.

"My work was in French, blocking its access to those of other tongues. Yet through translation, Edmond Dantes came to life for people of many lands, almost as the magic of his escape from prison transformed him into *The Count of Monte Cristo.*"

The surprise comment stopped the others. Marconi spoke up. "Interesting point, Dumas. It demonstrates that new ways of thinking can have the same effect as decoding, whether in language, reading music, or sharing signals for others to read—as soon as they figure them out and understand what's being transmitted."

The group could see Alexander Dumas nodding from the shadowy end of the table. Near him were two men, both still as statues in flowing white robes of desert attire.

"You'd think with all this magical realism, we could afford decent lighting in this place," Fulton snapped.

"It's okay," said Dumas. "I'm used to the dark. The transforming of identity seems as much a part of human change as the unlocking of what the mind can conjure as it develops new ways to expand its workings."

"Links have brought us together," Father Brown mused. "*How* is as difficult a question as *why.*"

"My guess on the *how* part," Marconi ventured, "has something to do with devices or systems that reorganize thoughts into plots through the use of energized data."

"Agreed," said Fulton, "using that power to propel likenesses of imagined theatrics—what we've seen here tonight."

"I've never seen such a curious assortment of men, even in my wildest nights," said Becky. "It's like the answer to an author interview question: 'What famous people would you like to have dinner with?' People usually pick Leonardo da Vinci, Charles Dickens, Queen Victoria, Albert Einstein, Oprah, or Taylor Swift."

"How interesting. Some of us seem to know of celebrities who arrived long after us," Marconi noted. "Whatever force brought us together seems to have given us a sense of fluid context. We're familiar with people and phenomena yet to happen in our own lives, yet somehow all around us now."

"How strange then," said Stevenson, "no one has mentioned the work of *Melvil*."

"Oh please," moaned Dumas. "Not another 'white whale' theory. Even in France we've grown tired of these floating symbols."

"No no! Wrong Melvil," said Marconi. "This is Melvil Dewey, inventor of the decimal system, the one that gives us all numbers so our books can be found on the library shelves."

"And in those small wooden drawers of cataloged cards," Holmes quickly added. "Yes, Father Brown and I are in the 843 group, along with Miss Sharp, for fiction, British fiction. Dumas is elsewhere in the 800 block. Scientists and inventors in the 500 to 600 shelves, Stevenson here with different codes—children's poems and grown-up stories."

"Understood," said Stevenson, "but connect the dots and dashes here, so we can figure out where we are with Dewey and his digital domain. Haven't libraries moved on from inking numbers on cardboard?"

"True in many places," nodded Fulton, "but Marconi's suggesting a lingering link to the old system somehow has assembled a random collection of borrowed numbers into a network of people, real and fictitious."

"Yes," said Marconi, "and the new analog tie-ins with wireless energy can deliver living visions of real and make-believe people with no particular connections."

"Unless," said Father Brown, "the numbers came to life from a pre-ordained pattern reflecting the life of a mysterious someone…"

"Or the reading choices shown by the titles and Dewey's code numbers on books that somebody borrowed!" Holmes leaped to his feet, waving his unlit bulldog pipe. "Brilliant, Father Brown! Consider this an *Aha!* moment I'm happy to share with you!"

"Not so fast!" came a sudden remark from a man in a turban and robes. "Please explain," the turbaned man said to the man next to him who was wearing a red-and-white burnoose and flowing white gown.

"I am Abner Meyers-Lee," said the turbaned man, "personal aide to Caliph Al-Mansur here, the designer and founder of Baghdad twelve centuries ago."

"Welcome," said Becky. "You've been so quiet and Sphinx-like, one might say, I wasn't sure if you were real—not that many of us are either—but why so silent?"

"As visitors, we were obeying the sign on the wall—the one that says 'No Talking,' " Meyers-Lee answered.

"Oh that," Stevenson laughed. "We forgot some libraries still have them, don't they? Sort of antique objects."

"Well, Al-Mansur and I are all about antique objects, having yielded many of them to your museums, but we're here to discuss other matters antique," Meyers-Lee said.

"It seems our favorite topic, 'Civilization in Baghdad,' was researched in this very library seventy years ago, but no books were borrowed for it. The work was done entirely here on those amazing 3 x 5 cards—a remarkable 19th-century offshoot of ancient Egypt's papyrus."

Meyers-Lee smiled as Al-Mansur held up a sample of a ten-lined card. "Mr. Al-Mansur speaks fluent English, by the way. He just prefers to use an interpreter, another 'antique' custom of diplomacy. He enrolled posthumously in the Berlitz of Baghdad program, but it became unnecessary with the new implosion of *instantly imagined intelligence* that brings us all here tonight.

"As Mr. Dumas noted earlier, we are immersed in a world of translation. Literal, digital analogous, whatever. Skills arrive intuitively and immediately, inviting all into the same loop. *Everything, everywhere all at once,* to echo the popular film title."

"Wait!" Father Brown injected with flat hands perpendicular in a T-shaped signal. "Are you saying there's more to this random linkage than the Dewey Decimal numbers in someone's borrowing history? What is the Baghdad connection?"

Meyers-Lee smiled again, enjoying the clerical sleuth's curious confusion. "Some of your earlier comments were on the right track,

Father," he said, "but our point is that we *all* are the real and fictional *imaginees*, as it were, of a library-user over the years in this little village place full of books, and now, of course, all these computers and other gadgets that fill the air with new energy."

"I think where we're going with this," said Marconi, "is right up my alley—that we're here in our seriocomic, pseudo-surrealist, expanded-awareness versions of ourselves because someone is revisiting a life of reading and research that involved us at passing stages."

"Add to that," said Fulton, "an advance akin to your wireless work, the new telepathic wrinkle that lets imaginers use brain waves to summon people to life in a time-travel context."

"Oh dear," Becky sighed. "This all seems so ethereal, so fragile. My guy Thackeray did this to me and the rest of our *Vanity Fair*-goers. He paraded us around to poke fun at folks in his own world, and in the end put us away like toys in a box. I hope our imaginer treats us better."

"Not to worry," said Father Brown. "We'll live on in our next lives in the minds of others who use their advanced intuition to signal us to the stage of their recollections."

Holmes had been unusually silent and nodded his head before speaking. "The new advanced intuition and aggregate imagining works both ways, enhancing my already well-publicized powers of deduction—though I let Conan Doyle think they were his," Holmes said, peering over a hand-frame of touching fingertips.

"Someone, somewhere, most likely an older man, is recalling his hours with novels and encyclopedias from this library, many years before our modern magic of moving brain-driven words and ideas through the air—*data transfer*, I think we first called it," said Holmes.

"Stevenson's poems for children, then tales of pirate gold and abduction; mysteries about Father Brown and myself; Dumas and his marvelous *Monte Cristo*; Becky's appealing deceits in *Vanity Fair*—a book our imaginer had to renew three times; papers he wrote on Fulton's steamboat and Marconi's wireless, and 'Civilization in Baghdad,' a freshman A+ in World History, written that Christmas while working mail routes for the post office there across the street."

"I won't ask how you know all this," said Father Brown. "Some things I accept as matters of faith. But you're right about reverse powers from the new brain-wave initiatives. I'm already sensing secrets from parishioners before hearing their sins in my booth. It's a test of patience to accept their filtered versions."

"Thanks to Mr. Holmes for including us in his analytics of why we're all here, assuming for now that we are," Meyers-Lee said. "Mr. Al-Mansur and I are men of few words but happy to join in the roles of *imaginees*."

"Ah, yes, Mr. Myers-Lee, sir, an intriguing emissary of Al-Mansur, the founder of Baghdad, once the world's largest city," Holmes began.

"Well, I can explain," Meyers-Lee started.

"No need," said Holmes. "The advanced intuition powers have confirmed my theory. Your family fled Germany in the '30s and settled in Shanghai, as did many others facing persecution in those years."

"Yes," said Meyers-Lee. "That's certainly part of it. Mr. Al-Mansur wanted someone to speak for him from a varied perspective. I later went to work teaching language in the Middle East—Iran, Iraq and Israel, my own Three Eye League, you might say. That's where I passed away a few years ago.

"I'm the only one here who's not famous, but my name wandered into the mind of our imaginer. It seems he's writing fiction about library life and needed a character of his own creation. He got my name from a book I wrote, *Put Your Memories to Work*, a combined memoir and coping manual. It sold a few copies. I did a talk show visit in Hawai'i, of all places, before returning to the desert."

"Real or imagined," said Dumas. "We are who we are, even when we're cast to play someone else. Dantes was a good guy, and I think I was, too. We both had revenge options against those who judged us unfairly, but we carried out getting even in civilized ways, I like to think…"

Others nodded. Dumas continued.

"Are we the 'stuff of dreams' or maybe the dreams of stuff," Dumas pondered, "scattered bits of mystery and history bouncing around in some old man's little-boy brain, now harnessed to high-powered recollection technology even he wouldn't understand, because it's been usurped by a self-navigating system that inspires and creates its own memorized scenarios?"

"A lot to process," said Fulton. "We seem to be occupying a new ether, alive with machine impulses that transmitted us here for reasons of their own, launched by a distant person rifling through the 3 x 5 cards of his aging mind."

"We could be back here again tomorrow," mused Becky, "unless the imaginer invites someone else to the table. But this is an 'unreality' show, not one of those where people get voted off the island."

"Unless," said Stevenson, "we're here to find a hidden treasure or some other secret stash."

"That seems so primitive," Holmes thought out loud. "Maybe the accelerated, augmented self-piloted system will invite Andrew Carnegie, so he can defend himself or Melvil Dewey to stand up for his decimals."

Father Brown laughed and shook his head, as Fulton and Marconi chuckled at each other.

"Sherlock," said the priest. "At the start of this you were complaining about modern science moving too fast."

"Yes, changing our world in ways we hadn't time to understand," said Fulton.

"Allowing words and ideas to spring into existence faster than the human brain could manage them," Marconi chimed in.

Holmes nodded with the faraway look of a man who'd reconsidered a hasty opinion.

"True," he began. "The mellowing of time and the wisdom of this group, real or imagined, have caused me to think further about my earlier concerns.

"And maybe," said Becky, "the brain waves of our thoughtful imaginer have influenced you as well. What if we characters conjured up an *imaginary imaginer's* mind to keep ourselves right here forever."

"Just think," said Stevenson, "the potentially endless life of the self-perpetuating, system-driven reminiscent mind cut loose from its moorings to generate infinite dreams, a sparkling of diamonds forever in our sky."

"This has all given new meaning to the term 'science fiction,'" said Meyers-Lee. "We're entering a world where machines can write future fantasies about today's humans."

"Inventors, authors, characters," Holmes said. "Ours is a table where science meets fiction, literally, and we can't be sure which is which."

"It's clearly time to shuffle the deck and start a new game," said Becky. "I'm not giving up on my cards, and I can hardly wait for the future to happen."

As though in a chorus, the group answered quickly, "It already has!"

To which the taciturn Al-Mansur replied when the laughter had stopped: "Somehow, I don't think I'm in Baghdad anymore."

The Library at the End of Time

by Bob Newell

I found myself in a bad part of a large city. Boarded-up buildings. Graffiti on every wall. Litter and broken glass. Scrawny weeds and stumps of long-dead trees breaking through the crumbling sidewalks. This wasn't at all what I had expected. Yet the narrow alleyway was exactly where the old monk had described. It looked dark and forbidding and for a moment, I was afraid to enter. Still, I had come this far, and I wasn't going to back away.

Even though it was midday, the shadows from the buildings made it hard for me to find my way without stumbling over loose bricks and other things I'd rather not think about. Rats scurried away at my approach. Yet, after about five minutes of cautious walking, I came upon a steel door at the end of the alley. Again, it was just as the monk had said.

The door was unmarked but I could see what appeared to be a doorbell. I pressed it a few times and heard a buzz from somewhere inside. Then the door swung open, noiselessly and smoothly, as if on well-maintained, well-oiled hinges. Standing in the entryway was a young man dressed in a blue suit with a white shirt and a matching blue tie. His hair was carefully combed back. "Mr. Gordon Richards," he said, "welcome. We've been expecting you."

"Um..." My voice faltered. "You know me? I don't have an appointment or anything..." I stopped when I realized how ridiculous

I must be sounding.

"No worries, Mr. Richards." The young man's voice was smooth and self-assured. "No one has an appointment. They just...come here. Not so many, I'm afraid. Actually, not so many at all."

"Is this The Library at the End of Time?" I asked.

"Yes, Mr. Richards, it is indeed. Your search is over."

* * * *

It all started when I was very young. I'll admit to having been sort of a prodigy, and maybe that had something to do with it. I grew up in New York City. My parents, who were devoutly religious, sent me to this parochial school where we were told that the purpose of life was to love and serve the Divine so that we could go to heaven later, which would be when our real life would begin.

I had a little trouble with this. So one day I spoke up and asked, "How come *this* life seems so real? I mean, if it doesn't count, if it isn't actually real, it seems like an awful lot of trouble to go to. Why not just cut to the chase and get on with—whatever it is?"

The teacher gave me a stern look. I had evidently crossed some sort of line. "Gordon S. Richards, come up front at once," she said. "I'll show you trouble. I'll show you real." I got whacked on the knuckles with a ruler and on the backside with a paddle, and then I got sent to the principal's office where I was summarily expelled.

I got another licking when I got home, this time from my dad, along with a lot of tears and threats from my mom, but I ended up going to public school, where you were allowed to at least ask questions.

The thing is, though, that my desire to know the meaning of life never left my mind.

Now, you won't be surprised to hear that I loved libraries. Books were my friend, at times my best and only friend. I went to the magnificent New York Public Library whenever I could. It was a place to hide away from the bullies, a place to lose myself in other worlds and to seek answers to my questions.

One day I discovered the philosophers and read Kant and Leibniz and Aquinas and Maimonides. Then I read Kierkegaard and

Sartre and even Alan Ginsberg, if you can call him a philosopher. It was fascinating, yet there were so many ideas, so many contradictions, and so much speculation. I wanted something solid, something clear, something that could be proven. So I read science. I read about computer models and parallel universes and the nature of time and space. Still no answers.

Time passed. I continued on in public school. My parents kept trying to urge me back into religion, though with less and less enthusiasm. Meanwhile, I found the means to visit other libraries. I went to the Boston Public Library and the Library of Congress. Somewhere, someone must have explained the meaning of life. I would just have to look hard enough.

When I graduated high school, I had the chance to go to Oxford. The great libraries of England and the Continent were now within reach. I searched the famed Bodleian Library. I took excursions to London to visit the Library of the British Museum. On vacations I traveled the Continent, seeking out the greatest libraries of France, Germany, Austria, Scandinavia, even Russia. I moved on from secular libraries to monasteries and cloisters and ancient abbeys. Then I sought access to the greatest collection of all, the Vatican Library.

Getting into the Vatican Library's inner sanctum isn't easy but I used some Oxford connections and got permission to visit for three months. The Vatican was both exhilarating and intimidating. Each day a stern-looking Swiss Guard armed with wicked-looking medieval weapons let me in. I could access only three books or manuscripts per day. To my dismay I was not given permission to view some items. No reason was stated, and there was no arguing over it with Vatican officials.

One afternoon toward the end of my stay, a cardinal happened to be in the library at the same time as I was. That wasn't at all an unusual thing. However, this fellow looked a little odd. His red robes weren't quite as resplendent as those of the other cardinals and he had a strange glint in his eyes.

It seemed that he was observing me, and sure enough, after a little while he came over to my table and, uninvited, sat next to me. He started asking questions about what I was doing. At first I was reluctant to answer; yet, despite his appearance, he had an engaging and even compelling manner. He said he was Cardinal Lin from some region in China that I didn't recognize.

We chatted for a little while and then, perhaps anxious to unburden myself to someone, I told him about my quest. He thought for a long moment and then said, "I believe I can trust you with this information. There is a book you must seek. If you find it, you will have all of your answers." He stopped and stared into my eyes, freezing me in place with a look the likes of which I'd never seen. "It is to be found in The Library at the End of Time. Go there and ask for the Book of Life."

I felt paralyzed and couldn't speak. I needed to ask him where to find this Library at the End of Time, but I was unable to utter the words.

And then he was gone.

I asked a Vatican official where I might find Cardinal Lin. He directed me to another official, who told me there was no such cardinal, nor had there ever been. But by the way the man looked at me, I knew he was not telling me everything. That evening I was notified that my access had been revoked and I was to leave the Vatican at once.

After my hasty enforced departure, I looked everywhere for information on The Library at the End of Time. I found little other than a few obscure references. Still, I pursued those, and that led me, at long last, to a monastery on the high plains of Tibet.

By now, I had learned to be circumspect, to not bring up the library at first, to just be patient and eventually make a casual mention.

It was a cold day with snow in the air when I reached this monastery, which I won't name. The sun was just a slight bright spot in a sea of clouds and the wind blew with some force as I pulled the bell rope at the old wooden entry gate. I was anxious to get inside. Perhaps there would be a cup of tea. I explained to the gatekeeper that I would like to see their librarian. The young monk was hesitant until I spoke to him in Tibetan and managed to convince him.

The monastic librarian was a very old man. He indeed offered me tea in his office, a room overflowing with books and scrolls, some of them clearly ancient, some of them quite freshly inked. Eventually, I found the opportunity to bring the conversation around to The Library at the End of Time.

The aged white eyebrows raised. "You ask of forbidden things," he began, in a voice that was barely audible. "But I am old and in my last days, and I sense your sincerity and understand your yearning and even your weariness after so many years. So I will speak now of that which I have never before spoken." He paused for a moment, as if finalizing his decision in his mind. "There is a reason knowledge of this library is kept secret," he continued, "for if you find it, your questions will be answered."

I offered the view that this was a good thing, to have one's questions answered.

"What you do not realize is that few who have been there have been prepared for the answers. Most never returned. I, and just a small number of other living people, have made the journey and come back, and only by realizing that some questions are best left unanswered."

But I was insistent. "Where may I find this library?" I asked. "I am ready for whatever may come."

The old monk gave out a brief sigh. "Are you really?" he asked. "You know not of what you speak. But never mind, if this is what you truly wish, I will tell you." He told me, and then made me swear to never tell another person, to never tell how I had learned this secret, or even let on that I was in possession of it.

Although I have already broken some of this oath, I'll keep the main part, and not reveal more than I must.

And so I journeyed to The Library at the End of Time.

* * * *

The young man gave me a brief smile and repeated his affirmation. "Yes, Mr. Richards, this is often called The Library at the End of

Time, although there are other names. Unimportant. You have questions and we need to get about responding to them." He hesitated a moment and added, "If that's really what you want."

But before I could reply he said, "Follow me, please." He set off down a short corridor with steel walls and ceiling and a concrete floor. In contrast to everything outside, it was spotlessly clean and modern in appearance. At the end of the corridor he opened a door that led to a flight of stairs. I followed him. The door closed immediately behind me. The stairs were wide with polished wooden treads, not showing any signs of wear.

We descended what must have been several stories. It was hard to say exactly. The young man didn't say a word the whole while. Suddenly, we were at the bottom of the staircase, facing another steel door.

"I must leave you here," the young man said.

And then he simply disappeared.

I stared at this new door for a long moment, but then, like the door up above, it too swung open in an eerily smooth and silent manner. I stepped forward into a large, brilliantly lit room populated by perhaps six people. The walls were of rich, dark wood paneling and the ceiling was of carved plaster. Persian carpets covered the floor.

A man dressed in a tweed suit was at the front of the group. "Welcome, Mr. Richards," he said, and proffered a hand. I shook the hand and then he went on, "As our greeter Jonathan has told you, we've been expecting you for some little while, ever since we learned that the librarian in Tibet told you of us."

I was quite surprised and asked, "How did you know about that?"

"Oh, here we know everything," the man said. "But never mind, never mind. You may call me Mr. Eternity, perhaps, for I am the Head Librarian and this is indeed The Library at the End of Time. Sadly, or perhaps fortunately, we have very few visitors any longer. You're the first in…how long, Miss Hours?" He had turned to a tall woman in a long formal dress, who replied, "Oh, decades at least. I think it was back in the days of…"

"Yes, yes, surely so," Mr. Eternity interrupted. "In any case, we've assigned Mr. Future, my assistant, to work with you during your visit with us." He now indicated still another relatively young man, dressed in casual office attire, who stood just behind him. "Mr. Future hasn't been here all that long. I don't even think it's three centuries yet, is it? In any event, he has thorough knowledge of the library and will be glad to help you."

Three centuries? The fellow looked to be about twenty-five at most. "How long have you been here, sir?" I asked Mr. Eternity.

"Oh…an eternity!" He smiled. "But now we'll leave you to it. Mr. Future, please take over."

Suddenly everyone but the young man, who maybe wasn't young at all, simply wasn't there any longer, and we were now in a tiny, cramped office that looked like it dated to the 19th century. Mr. Future was sitting behind an old wooden desk in an old-fashioned office chair, and he bade me take the seat in front of the desk.

"Let's go over your questions now," he said. "Tell me of your quest in your own words. Of course we know all about it. However, it's for the best to have you tell it yourself. In complete detail, if you will."

I began, and slowly but surely I told him everything, from my troubled youth to my long search for answers, to finally learning about The Library at the End of Time. It must have taken a long while.

"Well, very good, it's all as we thought," Mr. Future said when I was done.

"Why don't I feel tired?" I asked. "We've been talking for hours."

"Oh, have we? I suppose you would think so. Don't worry. Of course you're not tired. No one gets tired here." He said no more than that.

"So what happens now?" I asked. "How long am I allowed to stay? How will I do my research? I've heard there is a special book…"

"There certainly is a special book," Mr. Future said, his expression brightening. "Yes, yes, a special book just for you. And you won't have to worry about research. We'll take care of everything for you. As to how long you'll stay, well, that's not really up to us, now is it?"

"I don't understand any of this."

"You'll see. You'll find out. At once, in fact. Well, not *quite* at once. But soon enough. We just have some walking to do. Rather a lot of walking, actually, so, sir, if you'll please just follow me?"

Without waiting for a reply, Mr. Future started walking. Once again it seemed like the scene shifted. Instead of the small office, we were now in a huge vaulted room such as I had encountered in the old libraries of Europe, but much, much larger. The ceiling was incredibly far overhead, in fact so high up it was little more than a blur. I didn't see any walls either, or windows, yet there was a natural light that illuminated endless parallel rows of immense bookcases. It wasn't apparent where the rows began or ended. There were little archways at intervals to allow passage between the narrow stone-floored corridors that separated the rows. The bookcases had to be a good hundred or more feet tall, and I noticed black wrought iron spiral staircases on wheels, which must have been how the upper levels were accessed.

Mr. Future stopped and turned to me. "This is the main room of the library. Here we'll find what you're looking for. Now, tell me once more, what is your full name and date of birth?"

"Um...sure. Gordon Samuel Richards, May 15, 1995."

"Thank you, just double-checking. We can't have mistakes, you know! Please continue to follow me. We have quite some distance to cover."

He set off once again at a rapid pace and I needed to hustle to keep up. We walked for a very long time. It must have been hours and hours. It was hard to read the labels on the shelves at such a rapid walking pace. Eventually I was able to see that they were all marked with a year, month, day, and time on their engraved brass markers. Mr. Future darted confidently in and out of the various archways without the slightest hesitation.

Finally, as I now had begun to anticipate, we came to an area whose markers all began with May 15, 1995.

"Mr. Richards, do you happen to know the time of your birth?"

I only knew it approximately. "Around 7:30 p.m., I think."

"In what time zone?"

"I was born in New York City."

"Oh, GMT—Greenwich Mean Time minus five. Very well then. Allowing for Daylight Saving Time, that would actually be 1:30 a.m. GMT on the 16th, not the 15th. That will leave us a little more walking to do."

We walked for another extended period until we came to the May 16 markers. We continued on and found the 1:30 GMT range.

"If only you knew the exact second..." Mr. Future said, more or less to himself. "But never mind, we'll find your book."

It took another twenty minutes. Somehow I still wasn't tired when by rights I should have been dropping from exhaustion.

"Here we are at last!" Mr. Future said. He wheeled over one of those mobile staircases and began to climb. Up and up he went until he was a mere dot in the upper reaches of the bookcase. But soon he came back down, bearing a leather-bound book. "This is it!" he exclaimed. He handed the book to me.

The cover was stamped in gold letters that stood out on the maroon leather.

GORDON SAMUEL RICHARDS
MAY 16, 1995, 1:30:15.4482
NEW YORK CITY, USA, EARTH

"I'm sorry," Mr. Future said, "that the book is as thin as it is. Most of them are a good three times this size. You'll see why in a moment. Well, you might. It all depends."

"On what?" I asked.

"Why, on you, of course."

I took the book from his hands and started to page through it. It seemed thick enough to me, a good eighteen-inches, and it was extremely heavy. It was the entire story of my life, in every detail, starting with my own birth.

I was flabbergasted. "How...how..."

"Take your time, you'll soon understand."

I continued to turn the pages, but then I grew impatient. I wanted to see how the book ended. With some difficulty I turned the book over so I could open the back cover and look at the last page.

"Er, Mr. Richards, I'm rather sure you don't want to do that quite yet."

"I went through so much, for so many years, seeking to learn the meaning of life," I said a bit testily. "If this is the book of my life, I want to find the answer, and it can only be on the last page."

I opened the back cover. I exposed the final page. I began to read. The text spoke of my visit to The Library at the End of Time. It told of my long walk through the library's corridors in the company of Mr. Future. It described his fetching this book and handing it to me. It said that I read for a while, but then anxiously skipped to the very end, unable to wait any longer to discover the meaning of life.

And then it said I read the last lines on the last page:

GORDON SAMUEL RICHARDS
MARCH 19, 2024, 18:06:19.7521 GMT
LIBRARY AT THE END OF TIME
*** LIFE SIMULATION COMPLETE ***
*** PROGRAM TERMINATED ***

§

The Book Dragon
by David W. Jones

"What is that disheveled pile of books doing in the back corner of the Obscure Histories of Obscure People section?" the head librarian demands when you arrive for work that morning.

She is prim and proper in her full-length skirt and white long-sleeved buttoned-up blouse. Her black hair is tied back severely in a bun. She does *not* approve of anything even remotely disheveled or unorthodox. Such as tattoos. Or, you're sure, your love life.

She's very conservative. You doubt she *has* a love life. So you wear your hair in a bun and wear a similar skirt and blouse to work. It wouldn't do if she found out what you're really like. *Would not do!* You'd be out of your internship in an instant.

And this might be your last chance.

You carefully consider your answer to her question. You've learned so much from the knowledgeable head librarian, including her perfectionism, her exacting standards, and her lack of tolerance. She's also very spiteful and quick to bite your head off. Sometimes you think of her as a dragon, but you keep very quiet about that!

"Ma'am, I wasn't in that section yesterday. What pile of books?"

"Then, in the future, please check the entire library before you leave for the day," she snaps. "And they call people like you *library science students*."

She draws herself up to her full six feet in height, and standing ramrod straight, peers down her nose at you. One foot shorter, even wearing four-inch heels, you puff out your chest. Your boyfriend and girlfriend both insist you're the perfect height, but by the end of a workday, straining to appear taller in those high heels, you're exhausted and need a lie-down, while your boyfriend gives you a back rub and your girlfriend massages your feet.

Their love, and your hoped-for-someday MS in Library Science, is the only thing keeping you glued together since meeting the head librarian.

You follow her into the main library. Miss Smith, the assistant librarian servicing a patron at the checkout counter, smiles sympathetically.

The librarian marches into the stacks. You must scurry to keep up with her long strides, but fortunately, you've learned to scurry quietly, so she doesn't hear you racing. You're so practiced you don't even arrive out of breath.

The librarian points. "*This* disheveled pile of books."

You see books heaped randomly—different sizes, shapes, colors. Large hardbacks piled shakily on mounds of paperbacks. Obscure histories? No, all sorts of books, all sorts of genres, even CDs brought here from the far other side of the library.

And, worst of all, someone left one of the newspapers on its long wooden rod, lying across the pile.

A single step beside it might be enough to cause a bookslide.

"Ma'am, I have no idea who made this mess."

The librarian looks down on you and sniffs. "You need to become more observant. Both I and Miss Smith have heard scurrying in the library. We have vermin!"

"Vermin!" You sound horrified. No librarian worth anything tolerates vermin. Vermin chew on books, damage maps, leave behind droppings and urine smells. You refuse to become the first librarian to tolerate vermin.

But what kind of vermin could gather so many big books together? And why?

"Vermin," the librarian says and nods. "So you will begin by cleaning up this *pile* and tracking down the vermin responsible." The librarian appears to grow taller and looks down at you. "Although you are merely an intern, I delegate you full *librarian authority* to eliminate the vermin. *Do not make me regret it.*"

She abruptly turns and marches away.

You study the pile. You scurry back to the workroom and collect a cart, which you place beside the pile while you decide how to dismantle it.

Then you hear a small voice come from atop the bookcase beside you.

"Please don't take my treasures," it says, sounding scared and sad. "I worked so hard to gather them together, and will just have to do it all over again tonight while you're all gone."

Startled, you look up and step back. Vermin large enough to haul heavy books around is one thing, but *talking* vermin? Horrors!

Looking down at you, its six-inch-wide head at the end of a scaled neck, is a dragon. A drab, short-fanged dragon with wings that flutter nervously behind it. Two large gray eyes watch you.

You step back again. As a library science student, you've learned about the kind of vermin found in ill-kept libraries: ants, cockroaches, mice, rats. Worst of all, silverfish: loathsome creatures that eat paper and glue in books. But this?

The little dragon, or lizard, shuffles nervously atop the shelf. It's maybe two feet long. You relax. For some people, a two-foot long lizard would be a horror from the pits of hell, but your boyfriend studies reptiles, so you can cope.

"A talking lizard?"

The dragon draws its head back in a huff. "I am not a lizard. I am a book dragon!"

"A book dragon?"

"You're a librarian, surely you know about book dragons."

"Uh, I'm not a librarian yet. I'm just an intern." Then you seize the confidence of your *authority*, switch to your best stern librarian whisper and step forward firmly. "But I have *full librarian authority* from the head librarian herself to remove this pile of books—"

"Pile? That's my hoard!"

"—to remove this pile of books AND eradicate the vermin behind it. Meaning YOU."

The lizard puffs itself up, then suddenly droops. Tears seemingly of blood start from its big eyes. Like horned toad tears.

"No, no!" it whimpers. "I'm too young to die! Don't hurt me. I'll find a better hiding place for my hoard, I'll go away and you'll never see me again."

Before you can respond, the lizard runs to the end of the shelf with a dry, rustling sound and flies off with a barely audible whisper of wings. Then it's gone, its drab colors perfect camouflage in a library.

As you neatly stack the books on the cart, you think. Dragons aren't real, and you've never read of a dragon hoarding books, so it can't possibly be a dragon. Just how do you go about getting rid of a lizard that size?

A lizard that can apparently fly. And talk.

You consider telling the head librarian about it. But something inside you quails. She'd assume you're too weak to deal with the usual library vermin. Or sneer at you for not knowing something *real* librarians have known about for years. Or call you a coward for not killing the lizard with your bare hands.

You roll the cart back through the library, visiting each section where you need to re-shelve something while avoiding the head librarian. By the time you return the empty cart to the workroom, you'll surely have decided what to say to the librarian. She expects a full report. An excellent report.

"I'm doomed," you mutter to yourself as you return to the workroom. No matter how much you delayed, and how long you spent in the restroom, you still don't have a suitable report for the head librarian. Yes, you re-shelved the material in the pile, and nothing in it had been damaged.

But the vermin is still at large. And nowhere to be seen.

Back in the workroom, you line the cart up precisely in its spot by the door. The head librarian likes precision, as if that will help.

You almost feel her glare boring into you through the glass wall of her office.

But no. She's not there.

"Oh God, she's in the stacks looking for me," you moan involuntarily. "I'm dead, my internship is dead, I'll never get my degree."

"Oh no, she isn't looking for you," says Miss Smith, the assistant librarian behind you. You swallow an involuntary shriek that becomes a coughing fit. "Are you okay?"

You gulp. "I'm…I'm sorry. I'm a little stressed right now."

Miss Smith studies you, then nods toward one of the workroom tables. She leads you to the table and pulls out a chair at one corner for you. "Sit, before you collapse." Then she sits in a chair next to you rather than in the usual confrontational across-the-table separation. "So…the head librarian is not having her assistant fire you. Maybe you can relax a little? Now tell me what's going on."

"I…I can't, it will—"

"Suffering a nervous breakdown and collapse in the library certainly won't help."

You start to panic. "But someone needs to be at the counter. I can do that so you can have lunch—"

Miss Smith smiles slightly. "I've already had lunch. You've been here long enough to know that this is our daily slow time. That's one reason why our head librarian schedules her lunch and meetings with the regional director for these two hours." Miss Smith gestures quote signs around the word "meetings."

You give her a big-eyed *Huh?* look.

"Oh, interns are so precious." She laughs. "I've seen enough of you in my years here." Then she becomes serious and concerned again. "But you don't seem precious. You seem terrified. What happened earlier?"

"I…No…I can't tell you. You'll just tell *her* and—"

"No. And she can't make me tell her anything either. I know you're afraid of her. But when it comes to seniority in the library system, she's way behind me. I was offered the head librarian position before her."

You goggle at her. "Huh?"

"Oh, the director asked me if I wanted to be promoted to head librarian. And I certainly thought I did! Who *wouldn't* want the job?"

"Why didn't you take it?"

"I didn't want the baggage *he* came with."

"Baggage?"

"He took me to lunch to discuss the promotion. Then he concluded by putting his hand on mine, looking deep into my eyes and saying, 'May I call you Maggie? I think you're very beautiful and could go far with the right man in your corner.' When I replied, 'Don't you mean *in your bed?*' he abruptly broke off the lunch and never spoke another word to me except when he announced to the library staff our new head librarian as my boss."

"That kind of crap happens *in libraries?*" you ask.

Miss Smith arches an eyebrow. "Well, yes, it can happen anywhere. *And she knows I know about it.* That's why we get along. We *understand* each other. So…back to what happened out in the stacks this morning? I saw you talking with her. You looked like a deer staring into oncoming headlights."

"There was a pile of books in the Obscure Histories of Obscure People section. I guess she thought I left it there."

"No, she knew you hadn't. She knew all about the pile." Miss Smith sighs. "It's been a long time since I was in college. What do they teach about vermin these days?"

You glance down, embarrassed. "The usual, I guess. Ants, cockroaches, silverfish, termites, mice, rats. Pigeons that sometimes fly in through open doors and get trapped inside."

"So they don't teach about book dragons?"

You look up. "No. They only teach facts. Dragons aren't facts."

"But you met one this morning."

"Well, I met a big lizard and my imagination took over—"

"And you frightened her horribly. Her name is Inanna. She thought you were going to kill her."

"YOU KNOW ABOUT THE DRAGON?"

"Hush, dear, this is a library, you know." Miss Smith says gently.

Your shoulders sag. *You want to be a librarian but you shout in a library? Ugh.* "You know about the dragon?"

"Yes I do." Miss Smith pauses. "So does the head librarian. She set you up to fail, you know, giving you *full librarian authority* to eradicate it. She knows the best we can do is re-shelve the books, and force it to find a better hiding place."

"You can't eradicate a book dragon?"

"They're dragons! Do you think you could take on even a baby dragon?"

"But it's only two feet long!"

"Oh, you really need to learn about book dragons."

You saw its claws over the edge of the shelf. And it had fangs.

"Venomous?"

"Very! One bite, you fall into a trance, your mind filled with book after book of stories, never-ending stories, and you never wake up."

"Then why was the lizard, er, dragon, terrified of me?"

"Because she's a baby. How would you act if something that outweighs you a dozen times threatened to take the treasure that you *instinctually must have*, and kill you?" Miss Smith smiles nostalgically. "I remember the first book dragon I met. He was very shy, even for a book dragon. Yes, they're very shy. After I helped him find a secret spot for his hoard and told him how to pick books nobody would miss…" She sighs. "He was so sweet. After a while, he would find lost books and quietly bring them to me so I could re-shelve them. We solved many a lost-book mystery there!"

"Then what happened?"

"I transferred here as an assistant librarian. The head librarian at the time knew all about book dragons, although we didn't have one. Then he retired, and now we have our present head librarian. Our book dragon arrived after that, practically fresh from the egg, and has been traumatized ever since."

"Oh, the poor thing! The head librarian's awful! How can you stand her?"

Miss Smith smiles. "It just takes a little imagination. She's a good laugh!"

You both giggle, then laugh, imagining the head librarian going at it with the regional director.

You finally catch your breath. "Thank you, Miss Smith."

"Oh, you can call me Maggie. I was named after a bird that likes to hoard things, so I completely sympathize with our book dragon!"

"What kind of bird is a 'maggie'?"

"My original name was Magpie. I changed it as soon as I was old enough. You do not want to grow up being named Magpie. 'Sing for me, Magpie!' 'You trying to steal my pencil, Magpie?' But the students weren't the problem. It was my parents. They named me for the first bird they saw after I was born."

"Ugh, how could they? That's like being named after the first car they saw in the parking lot."

"Or worse, the car you were conceived in."

"What kind of car do you think the head librarian was conceived in?" you ask, giggling. Miss Smith roars in a quiet librarian way.

"She wasn't conceived in a car. She was conceived up a stick!"

You two laugh together again, then you say, "So what can I do about our book dragon? And the head librarian?"

A stern voice comes out of the head librarian's office. "What is so funny?"

You freeze before her glare. She has come in through her office's private entrance. "You, what's your name, intern? Why aren't you working? That children's section won't re-shelve itself, no matter what Miss Smith might have told you."

Your eyes widen, feeling like they'll swell right out of your head. Like a bird staring at a snake.

"Well? Do you really want to become a librarian or just stay a useless, worthless, *ordinary person?*"

Maggie strides fiercely over to the head librarian, and stops with her own angry expression just six inches from the librarian's sneer. "Stop this right now, and start behaving properly toward our intern."

"How dare you! I'll have you both out of here so fast—"

"*Right now.*"

"How—"

"For the rest of her term with us, you will behave professionally and politely. At the end of her internship, you will write her a fair, accurate, constructive evaluation of her internship work."

"As if! She has no business being a librarian, leaving that disheveled pile of books behind last night!"

Maggie smiles sweetly. "She knows about the book dragon. They don't teach that in school anymore, you know. So you can't blame her for that."

"I'll write what I want about her! She's a disgrace. I know she has tattoos!"

"I have them, too, Ursula. Just not in places that are so visible. What do you hide under your long sleeves?" The head librarian's lips flap at the shock. "And I'll write my own evaluation of her, too."

The head librarian laughs. "The regional director will just throw yours out. He and I are very close. He understands me!"

"Oh, I won't just send it to him, I'll send it to her professor directly. But…" Maggie pauses, then turns aside and looks at you. "*She* also knows about your close relationship with the regional director, and how you're not the first woman he used that trick on."

The head librarian's mouth snaps shut, her face pales.

"I think you understand me," Maggie says sweetly. "Men who treat women that way don't keep their positions very long. Yes?"

The head librarian backs away, shaking her head slowly.

"Yes?" Maggie repeats, following the librarian until she backs into the counter. "Yes? Or—"

The librarian nods. Her shoulders sag. Her tall body droops. "I knew I shouldn't have accepted his offer. Please don't tell anyone else," she whispers. "Please! I love him. His wife doesn't understand him. When they get divorced, he says he'll marry me."

Maggie merely shakes her head sadly. "Well," she asks you. "Is that good enough for you?"

You glance at the pathetic head librarian. "Please, Maggie, just one last thing. Could I do my internship work under you?"

"Of course you can, *Myfanwy*—a good Welsh name! The Welsh have always loved dragons. I'm on good terms with our book dragon. I'm pretty sure you will be, too, after we find her a better place to keep her hoard."

Long Story Short

By Michael Little

Call me crazy, dear reader, but even on the most perfect of Saturday mornings in paradise, Hawai'i's version of it anyway, I often find myself indoors, in the local neighborhood library. Surrounded by books, flying solo from one library section to another, I am Columbus, I am Magellan, I am, well, just a guy who loves getting lost in the stacks. Sometimes I also make use of the library's free computers. You never know what strange land you will discover. So here's my latest discovery: the word "drabble"—a word I had never heard of, even as an English teacher. I wondered, Is it a person, place, or thing? Animal, vegetable, or mineral?

When I began to look into the history of the drabble, I came upon a startling discovery. My Google search included a reference to an article dated 2030. Surely a typo, but once I clicked on the link, there was the date again, June 11, 2030. The article was titled "The Evolution of Short and Shorter Fiction." Everything was rising. I knew all about the rise of the modern novel in the 18th century, the rise of the modern short story in the 19th century, and so on to the short short story, which arose with the advent of television in the middle of the 20th century.

So what new craze in fiction was rising in the late 20th century? Turns out it was the drabble, an invention of science fiction fans in the UK in the 1980s, and taking its name from Monty Python, as described in the group's 1971 *Big Red Book*. A drabble is a short work of fiction of precisely 100 words in length. 100 words? Surely that was the end of the miniaturization of fiction. But the writer of the 2030 article asserted that there was an even shorter form called "55 Fiction," which limited a story to fifty-five words.

The drabble grew in popularity during the rise of the Internet, cable television, and smart phones, which competed for attention with the old-fashioned fiction books. The article claimed that by 2025 the drabble was wildly successful.

In the midst of this drabble mania there arose a young man with a new idea. His name was Anthony Shorter. He was a graduate of the famous Iowa Writers' Workshop, and he loved the classics. He bemoaned the shrinkage of fiction and feared that only a few would still read the classics. Shorter found a place as an intern at a small publishing house in Iowa. It was there that the clouds parted one day, and the angel choirs sang. That same day he pitched his idea to his editor.

He called it "Long Story Short" or LSS for short, combining the drabble with the classic novels. The LSS Series was soon born, and the LSS trademark made Anthony a rich young man. His idea was rather simple. If someone wanted to read *War and Peace*, for example, but didn't have the time or inclination to read all of Tolstoy's 1,225 pages, why not read the LSS version? Just 100 words and you're done. Long story short. Then you can move on to Dickens and *A Tale of Two Cities*. It was the best of times, it was the worst of times. But for the average reader, it was the shortest of times. No need to plow through it for thirty-eight hours and forty-six minutes, just read the core story, 100 words.

"Ladies and gentlemen, step right up! Don't be shy. Behold the greatest invention of the 21st century. Now you too can read *War and Peace*, and have lots of time left over to spend with the family. What's that you say? Always wanted to read Shakespeare but couldn't find the time? Just make a one-time purchase for the LSS version of *The Complete Shakespeare*. Read the LSS versions of all the comedies the first night, then move on to the histories, and, finally, the tragedies. By the end of the week you'll be able to jump right in the next time your friends are talking about Shakespeare around the water cooler or down at the pub."

Long story short, Anthony Shorter was able to retire at thirty. One of the young ladies at the publishing house caught his eye. Long story short, they traveled the world together. In the evening, they enjoyed reading 100 words to each other, leaving lots of time to enjoy other romantic pleasures. Long story short, they had three handsome children, and lived happily ever after.

Learning about drabble and LSS is just one of a thousand reasons why I love my neighborhood library.

§

Ancestors by the Book

by Gail M Baugniet

Fraternal twins Rob and Lenny sat across the table from each other at the local library. A pile of books lay jumbled between them. Their seventh grade final English assignment instructed them to write a short story called a "drabble" about their ancestors. A drabble is a story containing exactly 100 words. With a generous two-month advance notice, along with weekly writing exercises during English class, their teacher expected everyone to hand in a neatly written and entertaining story. Most of their classmates hadn't even known what the word *ancestor* meant. Sister Veronica explained that children were considered *descendants* of their parents, and relatives of earlier generations were called *ancestors*.

Lucky for Rob and Lenny, their mother had researched some of their family's history over the years. At the supper table on Saturday evenings, everyone took turns relating something interesting they had done or learned during the week. Their mother often shared her latest discoveries about long-deceased relatives. Some of their ancestors had been in the business of building and moving houses in their village farther north, using tree trunks as rollers under the jacked-up houses. A great uncle had almost been smushed when the moving truck hit a pothole and one of the tree trunks slipped out from under the house.

Baseball practice and after-school games against neighboring schools often got in the way of homework, though. Not to mention fishing and trapping with their dad on weekends. And now that the city council had changed the zoning laws for their farmland on the outskirts of town to residential, their parents were discussing plans to build a new house right next door as the latest family project.

But when their mom overheard them discussing the assignment deadline for their stories and realized her sons had been delinquent in their homework, she assigned them her own ruling: "No matinee movie this weekend!"

So…the Saturday afternoon before the English assignment was due, the boys didn't get to root for Kirk Douglas and Walter Brennen in a heart-stopping shootout among the foothills of the Old West. Instead, Rob and Lenny sat in the reading room of the town library on 16th Street. Not the original 1891 building, but a mission-style replacement partly funded by a grant from Andrew Carnegie. Each boy stared at blank pages in their opened notebooks. Rob slowly tapped his fingers on the tabletop while Lenny kicked the table leg in rhythm to Rob's tapping.

"Mom said to make a list of ancestors we thought sounded interesting," Lenny said, whispering so the librarian wouldn't reprimand them for loud talking and disrupting other patrons in the library. "Who do you have on your list?"

Rob only shook his head, lifting a blank page to show Lenny the whole lot of nothing he had written. "We should be able to remember some of the stuff Mom told us about the ancestors, though. The book topics on the list she gave us to check out are supposed to link to their lives somehow."

Lenny picked up one of the library books from the pile spread out between them, a book about Baltic amber. Their grandfather had told them stories about an ancestor who lived in Prussia and fished the Baltic Sea. One of his stories focused on amber that had been discovered there and how it had been created. He told the story to each of his grandchildren on their seventh birthday. Lenny and Rob had heard the amber story when they were in second grade, five years ago. The best part of the story was a fairy tale that was meant to explain how amber ended up at the bottom of the sea. But Lenny didn't think it was the kind of story he wanted to submit for his final seventh grade English assignment.

Rob rummaged through the pile and pulled out another of the books, one about a devastating fire in Peshtigo, a town in far northern Wisconsin. He held it up for Lenny to see.

"Mom said this book has something to do with our ancestors who lived north of us in Kewaunee. A huge fire broke out up there around the same time as that one in Chicago." Rob often thought he would like to become a fireman after he finished high school. That or a professional trapper, like the ancestor who trapped for a living in Quebec.

"This one looks interesting, too," Lenny said, holding up a story about the Knights Templar. "Mom mentioned an ancestor of Dad's who had been a knight in Belgium."

"Fine," Rob said. "You browse through that book, and I'll check out this one. Then we can share notes and decide what to write about in our short stories."

Lenny nodded, slumping down in his chair. As he opened the book about knights, he said, "Hope it's got lots of pictures."

As Rob opened his chosen book about fires up north, he silently hoped there were no pictures at all.

On the hour, the librarian made a walk-through of the library. She checked that no patron had wandered over from The Corner Bar, the tavern's actual name, for a quick nap under a table or, heaven forbid, a high school couple who had taken license to smooch in a dark corner. She gave only a cursory glance to the two boys seated at the reading table. Their mother had explained the situation to her about the looming deadline and asked that they be left alone as long as they didn't get rowdy.

Both boys appeared to be in their own little world, staring off into space. The librarian wasn't pleased that they had removed so many books from the shelves and stacked them haphazardly on the table. But she understood the dilemma, how these boys had waited until the last minute to begin their research. Having two grown sons of her own, she knew quite well that boys will be boys. She left them to their burden and returned to her other duties. Lord knew she had enough on her own plate, especially with her husband being one of those wandering patrons from The Corner Bar. Today, at least, she knew his whereabouts. He and both sons were cheering on the Braves at County Stadium in Milwaukee, urging the twenty-one-year-old Hank Aaron to add another home run to his season record.

Neither Rob nor Lenny noticed the librarian making her rounds. They continued to stare off into space, each struggling for an acceptable story idea.

Lenny daydreamed of knights with sharpened lances. According to his mom's genealogy records, one of the ancestors on his father's side had been a Belgian knight. He was known as Baweegnee of Meeffe, a knight born in the year 1215. But the photocopied records were in some ancient language, French or Dutch, Lenny thought, with no details that he could use to write a story, even one only 100 words long.

What he did remember liking about Belgium was the little bronze statue of a young boy that everyone seemed to favor. Belgians even fought over the statue's ownership and made a game of stealing it. That's the story he would write about, Lenny decided, using both hands to stifle his laughter over thoughts of the boy's naughty public display. He glanced up at his brother, planning to tell him about his decision, but saw Rob staring at the long stacks of books and decided not to disrupt his thoughts.

Rob, meanwhile, had been weeding out options for his own writing assignment. He had decided that life-threatening fires were too depressing to write about in a short story. But his dad had once told them about some uncles in Bavaria. They had worked in the salt mines there until deciding to make their fortune in America by moving to Kewaunee where, rumor had it, a gold mine had been discovered. With their mining experience, they figured they would surely be rich in no time. Rob knew the story about gold just waiting to be mined in an eastern Wisconsin farming community. It didn't end well, but he did like the idea of writing about salt mining. He looked over at Lenny to tell him of his decision. But to his dismay, Lenny was already furiously writing in his notebook. Rob grabbed his pen and started writing the story he had imagined, not wanting Lenny to beat him by finishing his story first.

* * * *

When their mother tapped the library table to attract their attention, both Rob and Lenny were startled by the sudden intrusion. They had each completed writing their stories and had reread them to their own satisfaction. They had then exchanged notebooks and were in the process of reading each other's stories when she arrived.

"Finished, boys?" their mom asked.

Both nodded, holding up the notebooks filled with scribblings as evidence.

"Good," she said. "Then gather your things. Dad is waiting outside the library by the picnic tables. I packed a picnic basket full of goodies for us to munch on while you each read your story aloud. We don't leave until your assignment is complete and parent approved."

Nervously, the boys gathered their stuff as the librarian approached.

"I'll return all these books to the shelves," she said, knowing the boys had diligently focused on writing their stories for the past couple of hours. As she ushered them out the back door, she added, "Good luck with your homework assignment."

The door snapped shut and a loud click of a lock signaled that the librarian was closing the library for the weekend. No further research would be available to the boys if their stories didn't receive parental approval. They spotted their dad sitting at a picnic table near the far end of the patio. A picnic basket lay open on the ground. Paper plates of celery sticks with dip, sliced peaches, and cold chicken were spread out on the table, along with a small bowl of apples. All finger food, so no utensils were needed. Little red napkins and plastic cups filled with juice added a festive color to the display.

"Okay, boys," their dad said, his "Army" voice suggesting he was delivering an order. "Which of you wants to read your story first?" When no answer was forthcoming, he pointed to the notebooks each boy clutched in his hand. "Let's try this then. Hand your notebooks to me. I will place them behind my back and your mother will pick one to go first. How's that sound?"

Nodding silently, Rob and Lenny handed the notebooks to their dad. He made a big show of mixing them up behind his back before facing their mom and motioning for her to pick one. After biting into a stick of celery coated with cream cheese dip, she pointed the celery stick toward their dad's right hand. With a flourish, he withdrew the hand, which proved to contain Lenny's notebook.

Rob blew out an audible sigh of relief while helping himself to an apple and a cup of juice. Meanwhile, Lenny slowly opened his notebook. Dry-mouthed, he asked, "Can I have some juice to drink before I read, please?" Then, with his thirst quenched and the mostly empty plastic cup settled on the picnic bench next to him, Lenny stood stiffly and read his 100-word assignment, a drabble entitled ***Many Costumes For A Naughty Boy***, skipping over the crossed-out words.

In Brussels they ~~onor~~ honor Mannekin Pis with a statue on a back-street corner. Nobody knows why the statue is there. He just decorates a ~~founten~~ fountain where people in the Middle-Ages came to get ~~fetch~~ fresh water. Going back to the 15th century, it's been hidden to protect against bombs of invading armies or theft by ~~bad people~~ others claiming to have the oldest statue of a peeing boy in Belgium. This statue of a little boy doing just what the name implies has over 654 costumes from around the world. The best costumes are of Santa Claus, a Zulu Warrior, and even Elvis.

Lenny took a final gulp of juice from his cup, made a sweeping bow, and helped himself to a handful of peach slices. Celery with peanut butter was a favorite snack of his, but the cream cheese ones tasted kind of yucky to him. He was pleased to hear his mom and dad clapping and to see the wide smiles on their faces. Rob hadn't clapped along with his parents. Instead, he had given his brother a nod and a thumbs-up, which was about the same as an Olympic score of a perfect ten in Lenny's eyes. Their parents always treated them equally, so they never felt any outside pressure to compete. Only during games of Monopoly or lawn croquet did they sometimes need a referee. In baseball, competition was always against the other team. And with fishing, the goal was always to increase their own catch, in count or size, whether it was bass, rainbow trout, or hand-sized perch, which was their mom's favorite for pan-frying.

"That's an interesting tale, Lenny," his dad said. "I remember seeing that little fountain when I was in Brussels. It really is just a small statue, of little significance in itself, but the history of wars and stories of attempted thefts that surround its existence make it an important part of our Belgian history."

Everyone helped themselves to more snacks and refreshed their drinks except Rob. He took only a handful of potato chips while wishing he had used the library restroom before the librarian locked up for the weekend.

"And now," their mom said, as though making an introduction to a large audience, "we will hear a story by another young author."

Reluctantly, Rob stood. After wiping the salt off his hands from the chips and tossing his apple core into the paper garbage bag, both stalling tactics, he retrieved the notebook from his dad, cleared his throat, and began to read his story, entitled *Salt Mining in Bavaria.*

> *Herman worked the Bavarian salt mine since ~~early~~ spring. His brother ~~didn't start until~~ started after harvest. Following morning roll-call, they adjusted their helmets before sailing down a metal track on a saddlecloth cushion into the mine below. To avoid docked pay, they ~~always~~ marked ~~all there~~ their arrival and ~~exit~~ departure times. Muscles bulging, they chiseled salt from walls. The salt was turned into brine, heated*

in a horseshoe-shaped pan hanging overhead in the salt house, then dried in ovens. Baldwin was content. ~~But~~ Herman craved more. Soon they were sailing the Atlantic toward a gold-mining future. Baldwin was grateful his brother always allowed him to tag along.

Rob lowered his notebook and waited for a response to his story. He was a bit sensitive to the opinions of others, but when it came to his mom and dad, their approval meant everything to him.

The silence seemed to stretch out until it became unbearable. But it was only a few seconds before his mother enthusiastically clapped her approval and his father joined in. Lenny followed with a short whooping cheer, meant as support for his brother but also to relieve tension.

"Well, Rob," his mother said, "you have chosen interesting ancestors to write about. They were two brothers who were also brothers to Renata, a great-grandmother of mine. Herman, the older boy, was a dreamer, always devising some brilliant idea to add excitement to his life. The younger boy, Baldwin, tagged along, willing and eager for the next adventure his brother drummed up. You captured that dynamic between them quite well in your tale."

While his mom talked, Lenny watched his dad clear the picnic table, stowing everything back into the picnic basket or tossing stuff into the trash barrel by the flagpole. At first, he had felt cheated when his mom said he and Rob couldn't attend the Saturday matinee today. The punishment seemed overly harsh considering they still had Sunday to write their stories. But now he realized how much he had enjoyed sitting in the library, dreaming up his story, and then quietly writing out his thoughts. That alone was fun. But having a picnic with his parents on the library's outdoor patio, and having their full attention as he and Rob read their stories, was worth more than any ol' cowboy movie on any Saturday afternoon. It even meant saving this week's allowance. Soon he could buy a new fishing rod. Smiling, he thought about the ancestors who fished the Baltic Sea. Maybe he would write down more of the stories he had heard from his grandparents.

"What are you smiling about?" Rob asked, noticing the grin on Lenny's face. "Are you glad we finally don't have to worry about writing short stories anymore?"

Lenny nodded, but wondered if Rob would disagree that writing down stories about other ancestors was a brilliant idea. When their dad cleared his throat for attention, Lenny was relieved by the interruption.

"Well, boys," he said, "your mom and I agree that you've both done a fine job writing the stories, even if you did wait until the last minute. But you do still have to copy them to a clean sheet of paper before handing in the assignments."

Both boys groaned but couldn't argue. One requirement of the assignment was a neatly written story.

"However," their dad continued, glancing at their mom for final approval, "you do deserve a treat, so hop in the car and we'll head over to the Outdoor Theater on Memorial Drive."

"And," their mom added, "that's after we place our orders for ice cream cones at the Custard Stand."

This time, both boys whooped in relief. Not only had they received a day's reprieve from rewriting their stories, but they would also see a double feature with singing cowboys and lots of adrenaline-charged gunfights.

Texts, Tomes, and Murder

By Larry and Rosemary Mild

Hearing of a calamity that affects someone in your own town is distressful enough—more so, if you recognize the victim's name. But when you learn it's your own teacher, someone with whom you've exchanged personal dialogue on a weekly basis, it's a whole other emotional experience.

My name is Cal Finley and I was thirty-two years old in 1963. I was an electrical engineer at a major corporation. My wife, Sammie, was twenty-nine and an editor at a medical publishing company. Despite our demanding jobs, we launched ourselves into an off-the-clock adventure: as writing partners—specifically, as wannabe fiction authors. We took two semesters of creative writing classes from Ella Fraise, a well-known local novelist in Baltimore. The Johns Hopkins University offered these excellent noncredit classes at its Homewood campus in the Odyssey lifelong learning program.

During our classes, eighteen of us huddled together in Clark Hall, room 204. We wrote and Ella critiqued, sometimes with stinging expertise. She drilled and we wrote some more. She rarely sat. Her hefty, large-boned body stood in no-nonsense flats, her eyes level with my shoulder, and I'm six feet tall. She always came to class swathed in a cable-knit sweater stretched over her broad bosom and extra-wide pants. Her bobbed hair stopped at her ears—blonde hair laced with an appealing pinkish-red color. Straight bangs covered her forehead, calling attention to dark, serious eyes. Her vibrant personality matched her imposing physical presence, captivating us with her insights and humor.

Ella gave us homework: challenging exercises, such as "Describe a lake as seen by a man who has just committed murder. Do not mention the man or the murder." We wrote from other unorthodox points of view, like an animal in a dire situation or an inanimate object projecting emotion. After completing the two semesters, Sammie and I decided we wanted more individual attention, so we engaged Ella for ten personal sessions to help us with our first novel. The three of us met from 6:00 to 9:00 every Wednesday evening in the Milton S. Eisenhower Library. Milton was the brother of President Dwight D. Eisenhower and president of JHU for twelve years.

Ella had ID passes made for us because we weren't full-time JHU students, and left them at the desk. We exchanged our Maryland drivers' licenses for these passes each time we entered the library and retrieved them upon leaving.

The Eisenhower library is Federal Period architecture. The building features six square white columns with red brick façades on the right and left. Sammie and I managed a five-minute glance into the awe-inspiring main reading room. Awash in a golden glow of lighting, the room rose six stories high with a glass-paneled ceiling. The six floors of book stacks were open on the sides facing the reading room, separated by columns with grillwork railings. The library is almost entirely underground, due to a campus building-height limitation imposed by a major donor's conditions. The structure enchanted us with its unique design. *What a privilege*, I thought, *for Sammie and me to be able to learn in such an environment.*

But we never had the opportunity to use the glorious reading room. Instead, we traveled in an elevator downward into the bowels of the building, where we had been assigned to a small, glassed-in conference room. Floor-to-ceiling bookcases overflowed with fragile literary relics. Most were in foreign languages such as Greek, Arabic, and Latin, as well as many exotic ancient languages. The only furniture was the ten-foot table with six armchairs and a dictionary stand in one corner. The room was air-conditioned with special temperature, humidity, and dust controls. At least it smelled that way—a faint pleasant odor.

We had finished eight worthy sessions, and they weren't all literary. Ella had a congenial side and freely shared moments of her home life. She was married and the mother of three-year-old twins. She complained to us that her husband, a salesman currently between jobs, refused to babysit the kids while she was at work, so she had to take them to her sister's place. "Claude's a good guy most of the time," she protested. "Anyway, that's why I love teaching. Not just for the income, but it's my escape from eternal home entrapment."

* * * *

That fateful night in November, already dark at 5:45, felt vicious—a punishing downpour with high winds. The library was a ten-minute walk from the parking lot. But no walking that night. My agile wife sprinted ahead of me in her red trench coat, ponytail flopping as she skirted puddles. "Yikes!" she shouted as a sudden gust flipped her umbrella inside out.

Still dripping, we picked up our ID passes and elevator key, then headed to the elevators. Only one went down as far as we needed to go, and it required the key. I pushed the DOWN button, inserted the key, and the two of us arrived six stories underground. The elevator doors opened, and we stepped into the main aisle thirty feet from our conference room. Oddly, I didn't see any other students around. Usually, they were hunched over their studies in the carrels, the partitioned booths so popular in libraries.

Immediately, I felt something was wrong, like a bit of static electricity ramping up ready to discharge. I couldn't tell whether my brown-haired, hazel-eyed wife felt this same edgy thing or not. A few steps ahead of her, I cautiously approached our meeting room. It was dark, but the overhead lights in the corridor cast a shadow on a figure seated at the table. Stepping inside, I flicked the light switch on—and saw Ella slouched forward with her head bent over on the table. As I inched closer, my stomach lurched and my breath caught in my throat. Strands of her blonde hair were soaked in blood. A huge hard-cover book leaned against the left side of her head. It was the dictionary that Sammie and I often consulted when Ella challenged a word in one of our chapters. Blood pooled everywhere—on the light-grained oak table, around her face, on the spine of the book, and trickling down the back of her white sweater.

I swallowed several times to teach that night's supper to behave, then stopped, spun around, and Sammie crashed into me. Wrapping my arms about her, I tried to shield her from this horror, but she propelled herself on tiptoe to see over my shoulder. She screamed, "Oh my God!" She pulled out of my embrace and moved to get a closer look. "Oh no! Cal, is she dead?"

"Pretty…damn…sure."

"Don't you think you should check? We owe her that much, don't we?"

Careful not to disturb the crimson puddle at my feet, I braced myself by gripping the top of the chair with my left hand. Trembling, I bent over to touch her neck with two fingers of my right hand. Her flesh was still warm. I prayed that she was still alive. I pressed down on her chubby neck, seeking any positive response from her carotid artery, and was deeply disappointed. Pulling back quickly, I wiped my fingers off on the leg of my jeans even though there was nothing foreign on them. But I had touched a dead body. Wasn't that a taboo or something?

I turned away and my eyes landed on the dictionary stand in the corner. One of the two volumes was missing. Morbid curiosity drew me to the stand. ***Webster's Third New International Dictionary OF THE ENGLISH LANGUAGE UNABRIDGED, 1964, VOLUME II.***

Dear Lord, I thought, *each volume is over 1,200 pages and probably weighs at least six or seven pounds.*

Someone had used Volume I as a weapon to bash Ella's head in and crush her face down on the table, breaking her nose. "Sammie," I said, my voice quavering, "I'm guessing that such a mighty blow to the back of the head caused a fatal concussion. Volume I was undoubtedly the murder weapon."

"Oh Cal," she cried. "Shouldn't we report this to the police or at least to campus security?"

"Of course, but I have to find a phone first."

"There's one on the wall to the left of the door," said Sammie.

I whipped my head around and saw what looked like an in-house phone for library users. Putting the handset to my ear, I heard the dial tone. It hummed. I pressed zero.

A young soprano voice said, "Main desk, how can…"

Abruptly, the line went dead—no voice—no tone—nothing. Until that point, I had stubbornly assumed the killer would have fled after his terrible act. Wouldn't that have been the logical thing for him to do? Fear must have carved its image into my face. Sammie couldn't help but notice.

"What's wrong, Cal? You look strange."

"A librarian answered, but the phone went dead. Sammie, I think somebody just cut the phone line. Which means the killer must still be in the building."

"Cal, I'm scared. What're we going to do?"

I peered out through the glass wall to the corridor and caught a glance of the elevator. The doors were still open. I mulled over our desperate situation. *Apparently, no one's called it into service since we used it. Is he hiding close by and eyeing us right now? Will he try to make it to the elevator before we can stop him?*

I steeled myself to talk in a normal tone. "Hey, Sammie, I have an idea. If I could get to the elevator and turn it off before either the killer or someone else calls for it, there would be no way out of here for him."

"But that means there'd be no way out of here for us either. What about the fire exit?" she asked. "Couldn't he escape that way?"

"He could," I replied. "But he'd have to climb six steep flights of stairs to get to the ground level while the alarm blasts and announces his getaway."

"What alarm?" she snapped. "You haven't turned one on. And isn't it even more dangerous for us to be locked in the same space with a desperate killer? We don't have any kind of weapon to fight him with. Besides, Cal, how can you be sure the killer's a man?"

Cal shrugged. "You're right, baby. Just assuming. Maybe it is a woman, but she'd have to be a helluva strong one to wield that heavy dictionary as a weapon. But I don't think the killer is armed. I get the idea it was a crime of passion. He chose a weapon of convenience when he picked up Daniel Webster's finest. If he'd brought a weapon to the scene, he would have used it on her. I'm going to the elevator now to turn it off and take the key."

"Cal, are you crazy? No matter what you're doing I'm coming with you."

"Sammie, no. When I leave this room I want you to push the table up against the door. It opens inward. If he tries to get in, push against the table from your end. Friction—its weight on this carpet added to your pushing against it should keep him out."

"Dammit, no, Cal!" A flush suffused her freckled cheeks, and behind her horn-rimmed glasses her hazel eyes flashed with anger and fright. "If you think I'm going to stay in here all by myself, you're nuts. Besides, that huge table is much too heavy for me to move."

It was time for my plan B, and the more I thought about it, the better it sounded. I didn't know whether the killer was watching us or not. Hoping he wasn't, I took Sammie's hand. We stole out of the conference room and tiptoed to the elevator. As I stepped inside, Sammie's body huddled so close to mine I could feel her breath on my neck. For that moment I didn't protest her being with me. I found the brass elevator control plate. Above the two columns of floor buttons and indicators was an alarm button and a round-barreled key. In plan A, I would have rotated this key a quarter-turn to the OFF position and pocketed it, thus sealing off any elevator escape for the killer. But also shutting off any escape for us, as Sammie had reminded me. Plan B would be a surprise, even to her.

I hit the elevator's Help-Alarm button and heard the alarm re-sound in the elevator shaft. I foolishly thought, *No one's going to listen to that infernal noise for long without responding to it.* Sure, enough someone upstairs did respond—by simply resetting the alarm from the main level. I hit the button a second time and, true to form, it got reset again. Well, I thought, the third time would be a charm. How wrong I was—silence reigned. I put plan B into motion. The elevator doors were still open. I pushed the Main Floor button and started stepping out into the hall.

"No!" my wife shrieked, grabbing my arm to pull me back inside. Sensing my body moving over the threshold, the doors re-opened. I shook her hand off and darted out. "Get help, baby!" I shouted. The doors closed with her inside, just as I wanted. I heard the loud hum of electric motors as the car rose to the main floor where I knew my wife would be safe.

Now for my plan C: an ugly game of chess. The players? The killer and me. I didn't know how aggressive my opponent would be, nor what strengths he'd bring to the table. The big question was: Could I keep him in check long enough for help to arrive and checkmate? Our playing board? Thousands of square feet laid out in aisles and rows like a chessboard. I wondered how much of an advantage his desperation granted him. My key stratagem: Don't let him get away. Which was pretty naïve, considering I no longer had the athleticism spawned in my college wrestling days. Sammie and I played tennis and walked several miles a week, but that was puny stuff, not rigorous training. *What if I have to tangle with the killer mano-a-mano? Jeez, I'd better find a weapon.*

In a nearby corridor, I came across an impressive display: a series of ancient maps and prints suspended from one-inch-thick wooden dowels about the length and breadth of a common broom handle. At the far end of the display, I spotted several empty dowels just lying in their brackets. I selected one and tried it out for size. A spin in both directions and a forward upward lunge convinced me that this was a viable weapon, a Japanese-style fighting staff, reminiscent of the *aikido* and *bōjutsu* conditioner training we took as college wrestlers.

I decided against searching for the killer in this vast space. It was too risky—he could come out of the darkness at me from any direction. It was best to let *him* be the player of the white chess pieces—allow him to make the opening move. Time was on my side, because Sammie would eventually bring the cavalry. Could his desperation force that opening move? Or would he lay his king down and quit? I knew he needed to escape, and there was only one way out: the fire exit, even though he would have to climb six flights to leave the building. I planted myself in front of the fire exit door. And waited.

The silence was broken only by the flow of air blowing in from the cooling system. It was the kind of quiet where you could hear your own heart beating. I hate waiting for anything—I'm the impatient type. And worst of all? I had no idea what the killer looked like, or which direction he would come from.

I heard leather soles slapping on the tile floors as he approached. He made no pretense of sneaking up on me. My first impression? Tall and gangly with a wild mop of wavy brown hair, a hawkish nose, long chin, and a sour expression. He wore a black windbreaker over a black turtleneck and khakis. Escape was now his first priority and the fire door his goal. He carried a weapon—also a dowel! He'd beaten me to the punch on that one. He continued to walk toward me, stopping about ten feet in front of me—to size me up, I supposed.

He charged at me, swinging his pole wildly one way, then the other. I parried his pole to the left with a hard whack of mine, and sidestepped to the right. As he tripped past me, I shoved the end of my pole into the small of his back. He nearly folded in two as he fell to the floor on his face. He gingerly rolled over and rose to his feet. Again, I stepped between him and the fire door. He sprang back into action, this time poking the pole at me as soon as he got close enough. Luckily, his short, punishing-style jabs didn't make it to my body. I kept batting them to one side or the other, and those that I missed, slid past me, barely grazing each of my elbows. He soon slowed, tiring. I took advantage, driving him backward and sideward with a few well-aimed pokes in the ribs and a bash to the side of the head. A follow-up slam to the left shoulder knocked him off his feet. I stood over him with my pole pressed tightly to his chest. To be cautious, I pinned down *his* pole using my foot. His knuckles got caught underneath so painfully he had to release it. I kicked his pole a good distance away. Each time he tried to roll away, I bore down with the pole I held to his chest. He finally gave up. All the fight had gone out of him. Sitting up on the floor, he began to sob. He was an emotional mess. I decided to satisfy my curiosity and do a little interrogation before the police came.

"Who the hell are you?" I asked, "And why did you kill Ella Fraise? What did that brilliant, talented woman ever do to you?"

"My…my name is Claude Fraise. Ella was my wife."

"Your *wife*? Damn it! You've got two kids. Why on earth would you want to kill the mother of your children?"

"She was an unfaithful bitch. Every Wednesday evening she was gone for three or four hours. Told me she was teaching a class, but when I looked in the catalog, there was no such class. Even the university registrar hadn't heard of it. Yeah, I got two kids. They're screaming or fighting all the time. I hate children. I'm a lousy father."

"Where are they now?"

"Like always, Ella took 'em over to her sister's place. Then I followed her here. Hey, are you the homewrecker she's having an affair with?"

"You're insane, man. My wife and I hired Ella to privately teach us how to improve the novel we're writing. We paid her handsomely for ten of these Wednesday evening sessions. Tonight was to be the ninth one."

"Your wife wasn't in the room *last* Wednesday when I looked in on you."

"You mean you spied on us *last* Wednesday too? Damn you… you murdering creep," I stammered. "My wife went back to the car to get a previous chapter we'd forgotten to bring to class."

"What the hell? You weren't having an affair?"

"Of course not, you asshole."

"She was telling the truth all along? Oh dear God, what have I done?"

"What made you think your wife would be here tonight?"

"Same as last week. I followed her and saw her sitting at the table in that glass room. I thought she was waiting for her lover. If you're telling the truth, where's your wife now?"

"She went to get help," I said. "She'll be coming back with the police. By the way, Claude, how did you manage to get into the library without passes?"

"I filched a couple off Ella's desk," he mumbled. He then went silent, knowing the worst was about to come. The elevator doors slid open. Two uniformed officers and three plainclothes detectives sprang into our space with their weapons drawn.

"No need for guns, gentlemen," I told them with my hands in full view. "Your killer is sitting on the floor here. The situation is under control."

Claude's body was wracked with sobs. "I didn't mean to kill her," he sputtered. "I saw the dictionaries in the corner and picked one up and hit her with it just to teach her a lesson. But it was so god-awful heavy."

He held out his hands to be cuffed and was helped to his feet afterward. The two uniforms led him to the elevator.

Sammie had been told by the officer to stay in the back of the elevator until he gave the all-clear. Hearing my voice, she just couldn't wait any longer. She leapt out of her confinement and pushed between the officers until she had her arms around me.

"I was so worried about you, hon. I know now sending me off alone in the elevator was the right thing to do. But you could have been hurt—or killed! How dangerous was he, anyway? What actually happened while I went for help?"

"I'd like to hear those answers myself," said one detective, who identified himself as Sergeant Finnegan. He was a white-haired gentleman with a round, red face dressed in an ill-fitting brown suit. He told us the crime lab technicians were on their way.

His colleagues were tending to the body in the room, while I explained the gruesome events preceding his arrival. He collected our names and address and added a few detailed questions, which we answered to his satisfaction. He then told us we were free to leave.

In the elevator on the way up to the main floor, Sammie blurted out: "The Strawberry Blonde Murder."

"What?" I asked.

"*Fraise* means 'strawberry' in French," explained Sammie. "Coincidentally, Ella's last name was Fraise, and she had blonde hair with reddish highlights. So, you see, it's a strawberry blonde murder."

"Oh. Okay," I replied.

In the months that followed we wrote our first mystery novel, *The Strawberry Blonde Murder*. We substituted the names to protect the family. In those same early months, we read about Claude Fraise's trial and Murder One conviction, resulting in fifteen-to-twenty years of incarceration.

§

Authors' Disclaimer: "Texts, Tomes, and Murder" is entirely a work of fiction. The plot and events are of the authors' imagination and invention. All characters are fictitious and any resemblance to persons living or dead is purely coincidental. A few real spaces have been altered to accommodate the story. As far as we know, a murder was never committed in the basement of the JHU Milton S. Eisenhower Library.

Jimmy Chan and the Library Looter
by Bob Newell

It was about three in the afternoon on a Monday in late September. The weather was still quite warm, and of course the air-conditioner in my office wasn't working. It actually hadn't worked in quite a long while, but replacing it would cost more than I could afford, as business was pretty slow.

I'm Jimmy Chan, and I'm a private detective, and if you ask me if I've got anything to do with that other Chan—that Charlie guy—you're asking to get your lights punched out. Not that I really would, but it gets pretty tiresome answering that same stupid question over and over again. No, Charlie Chan was in novels. I'm a real guy, thank you.

I've got what amounts to an office in the Wo Fat Building in Honolulu's Chinatown, two small rooms with some old furniture. I'm in the back room and Jasmine, my assistant, is up front. She stopped me as I was about to leave and go find a cold beer at a nearby bar.

"Hold on there, boss," Jasmine said. She was originally from Taiwan. She was slim, trim, and…well, I better not take it any further than that or I'd be likely to get myself into hot water.

"It's a miserable Monday," I said, frowning. "Let's close up and go home. Or for a beer."

"No can," she replied. "You've got an appointment in, like, ten minutes. And before you gripe, as usual, we need some clients. No clients, no money. Funny how that works."

She was right, of course. We were barely making enough to keep the doors open and let me go for that beer once in a while. Once in a while wasn't going to be now, it seemed.

"Who's coming in?"

"The librarian I told you about when you weren't listening, and don't you dare say 'What librarian?' to me."

"Uh, yeah, the librarian." Actually, I had no idea. "Why did you schedule her so late in the day?"

"She said she didn't want to miss more than an hour of work. Now get your tail back into your office. I think I hear her coming up the stairs."

I groaned. One of *those* types. Likely very demanding, very particular, very stingy, and standing between me and a nice cool bottle of Longboard Lager. But I did as I was told.

No sooner had I sat back down at my desk when I heard the entry door open and Jasmine saying, "Good afternoon, Miss Kirkbridge. Thank you for coming. Mr. Chan has been expecting you."

"Given that I have an appointment, he ought to be." The voice was shrill and deep at the same time. Quite the trick and not a good omen. "And by the way, I had to park in a disgusting parking lot and I expect you to validate my ticket."

"I'm sorry ma'am, but we don't..."

"Very well, then, I'll deduct the cost from whatever fees I may be asked to pay."

Jasmine ushered her in. She was middle-aged, nothing you could call attractive, and dressed in a manner that even I could tell was unfashionable. Like something out of the Forties. I quickly stood up, trying to look in control, but the springs in the chair squeaked and the back made a loud snapping sound. Another thing to fix one day.

We shook hands and I could see she was not impressed. After she had taken a seat, I said, "Well then, Miss...uh...Kirkbridge, how may I help you?"

"I'm from the State Library," she said, "and, in fact, I am the Head Librarian."

I waited a moment. "And?" I said.

"I thought your secretary had filled you in on the details. Must I repeat everything?" She sniffed loudly.

"Uh, yes, if you don't mind."

"I *do* mind, but if I must…Well, there has been looting at the library. Valuable books have gone missing."

"You mean theft? Like, rare books?"

"Call it what you will. I prefer looting. And, Mr. Chan, *all* books are valuable whether or not they are rare."

"How many are missing?"

"Twenty-four books."

"How much money are we talking about?"

"The total worth of the books is $876.88. As you can see, quite a lot of money."

"Seems like a small amount to me. Have you notified the police? This hardly seems like a case for a detective."

"No, I did not notify the police. Do you want me to cause a scandal? Do you want the public to believe that they can loot the library at will? Besides, it isn't the dollar amount, it's the principle. Only the lowest of the low would loot the State Library."

"So…um…how can I help you?"

She sighed and crossed her legs, in the process showing me her sturdy-looking and not especially clean work shoes. "Why, find the looter, of course, and recover the looted items. What else?"

"Why me?"

"I've heard of you. I've heard that you are…inexpensive. Actually, I'm expecting you to take this case pro bono, for the benefit of the library."

"Well, ma'am, I can't exactly afford to work for free. I have the office to keep up, I have Jasmine to pay, and I want to have a beer once in a while."

The minute I said "beer" I knew it was a mistake.

"Beer? How pedestrian! And surely an office such as *this* doesn't cost much. From the looks of it, it ought to be free. Well, if you can't donate your services, I'm prepared to pay you up to one hundred dollars—provided, of course, that you successfully complete your work."

A hundred? That was my hourly rate. Well, almost; five hundred a day plus expenses. But maybe I could build some goodwill in the community, and there was nothing else going on at the moment.

"Okay," I said. "I'll do it."

"See that you do."

* * * *

We met at a downtown coffee shop the next morning. She didn't want me at the library for "security reasons." I told her I'd have to investigate on site and ask questions, but she was adamant. Finally, she said, to my dismay, "I'm not looking for a Charlie Chan. I'm looking for a Nero Wolfe. He solved all his cases without ever leaving his home."

"He had Archie Goodwin to do his legwork for him," I replied. Over the years I've become pretty familiar with the literature.

"Nevertheless, do not come to the library unless you must. By all means, do not look for me if you should be there. We must maintain total secrecy, as I told you quite clearly."

"I know. No hint of a scandal. I get it. Okay. Give me a list of what's missing. Another list of likely suspects. Video footage if you have it. The works."

Miss Kirkbridge harrumphed but said she would see what she could do.

* * * *

The next afternoon Jasmine brought an envelope into my office. "Someone dropped this off," she said. "And given that it's in a State Library envelope, it's got to be that info you asked for from Miss Kirkbridge."

"Hey, you're quite the detective now," I said. "Maybe you've solved the case already?"

"For a hundred bucks? Not worth *my* time." She pranced out of the room with that look on her face that meant for the millionth time she just couldn't figure me.

I opened the envelope. There were a few sheets of paper, nothing more. No thumb drive with video files as I had hoped.

I glanced at the first sheet. It was that list of missing items, mostly book titles.

Love Lost and Found, Romance in Romania, Sarah's Stolen Kisses, Passion and Passionfruit...

The list went on. All romance novels by a bunch of different writers with names like Lauren Kwan and Clarice Peterson. Probably all pen names. But the real question was, who would steal stuff like this when they could just check it out and read it? Surely reading it once would be at least enough.

But then I looked at the rest of what Miss Kirkbridge had sent me. She had looked up the checkout records for all the missing books. There were a few names in common among the records, but only one person had, at some time or other, checked out every single book: a certain Wally Miller.

It didn't take much looking online to get Wally Miller's address and phone number.

This was going to be easy. And somehow that bothered me.

Miss Kirkbridge could have easily figured all of this out on her own, and I'd bet she probably had. So why come to me? It just didn't add up. I had a growing suspicion.

* * * *

"I'm going to the State Library," I told Jasmine as I exited my office. "Don't call me there. You know how much they like quiet in a library."

"As if I'd have any reason to call you. Got a sudden love for books now?"

"Yeah, I'm really into steamy romance novels."

Jasmine just shook her head as I headed for the stairs and the little alley where I parked my car.

I was at the State Library in a few minutes. Finding parking there was another thing; that took more like fifteen minutes and

95

quite a bit of change to feed the meter.

I stopped at the information desk and asked where I could find Miss Kirkbridge. They told me and asked if I had an appointment. I said I did. A little white lie, but I was on the trail of something.

I found the office easily enough. It being marked "Laura Kirkbridge, Head Librarian" didn't make it very hard. I knocked on the door and heard a female voice say, "Come in."

I opened the door and entered. Sitting behind a modern-looking desk was a tall, attractive blonde, who was probably about fifty years old. She was slim and well dressed in a definitely stylish manner.

"Oh, sorry," I said, "I was looking for Miss Kirkbridge."

"Excuse me?" she said. "I'm Miss Kirkbridge. Just who are *you*?"

It took a little explaining. She was pretty frosty at first, but she quickly took an interest when I told her that someone had impersonated her and sought my services.

"So there were books stolen?" I finally was able to ask.

"Oh yes," the real Miss Kirkbridge replied. "A number of books. That happens all the time, no matter how hard we try to prevent it. My concern is for the books stolen from our Hawaiian collection. There were four of them. They are extremely valuable and completely irreplaceable."

"Wait a minute," I said. "You mean the thefts weren't limited to about two dozen romance novels?"

"Oh no," Miss Kirkbridge said. "We did lose those, to be sure, but that was relatively minor. As I said, books go missing. This was different. It's the first time we've lost such precious items."

"Have you contacted the police?"

"Not yet. We didn't want to..."

"...cause a scandal."

"Exactly."

"Well," I went on, "I can't promise that it won't leak to the public at some point, but I'm pretty sure I know who the thief is."

"You mean that fellow who stole the romance books? The one

you identified from library records?"

"Maybe." I didn't want to say any more until I looked into it.

* * * *

I left the real Miss Kirkbridge's office and called the police on my cell phone. After all, I hadn't made any promises not to. I reached Lieutenant Morrison. He was normally no friend of mine, but I told him the story and for once he actually listened.

"Look, Chan," he said. "That librarian of yours really should be the one to call it in. We can't do a lot except question this guy without someone official swearing out a complaint. But we'll go talk to this Miller and at least see what he can tell us, okay? Now I'm busy. Don't call me, I'll call you."

Later on in the afternoon, Morrison actually did call me back.

"Interesting," he said. "The uniforms saw books all over the place at Miller's apartment. He stole those romance things all right, and he admitted to that and a lot of other book thefts from different library branches, and even a couple of bookstores. But he didn't know a thing about the Hawaiian items. Or at least so he says. I think he's lying and trying to get off easy by pleading to a string of petty thefts. Anyhow, we'll keep grilling him. And I won't call your librarian until we wrap it up."

Morrison hung up the phone. I was now more convinced than ever of being on the right track.

"You might want to see this, boss." It was Jasmine. She had entered my office quietly after I got off the phone and had one of those grins on her face. The grin that told me she'd been busy.

"What've you got? Something for which I'll have to give you a raise first?"

She laughed and crossed her arms over her chest. "Hah! A raise? How about I just get the back pay you owe me? No, look. You know that woman that was here? The fake Miss Kirkbridge?"

"Yeah."

"Something didn't seem right about her."

"No kidding."

"It was her shoes."

So Jasmine had seen that, too.

"They weren't the kind of shoes someone in such a high position would wear to work. And she said she was coming here from her office. They were work shoes, and they were scuffed. Didn't seem right. So I managed to get a photo of her without her noticing, and I've been doing face matches online. Well, I got a hit on Facebook. Here."

She handed me a printout and, sure enough, it was her. But her name was Patricia Patson, not Laura Kirkbridge.

I gave a low whistle. "Good detective always looks for something unusual."

Jasmine groaned. "Enough with the Charlie Chan movie quotes," she said. "Get yourself back to the library, like now. You know, chop-chop?"

It was my turn to groan.

* * * *

Miss Kirkbridge—the real one—was in her office.

"You're back?" she said after I knocked on her door and was admitted.

"I've got something, I think," I replied. "Have a look at this photo."

She stood up from behind her fancy desk and clack-clacked her high heels around to where I was standing. Yep, high heels, not work shoes. I showed her the photo of Miss Kirkbridge that Jasmine had taken. "Familiar?" I asked.

"Vaguely. Seems like someone I might have seen around here. Wait! Let me make a call."

She clack-clacked back to her chair and picked up her phone. "Keahi? Know anything about a Patricia Patson? I'm looking at what's supposed to be her photo here."

Supposed to be? Could anyone doubt Jasmine?

"Sure," she went on. "Come to my office right away."

She turned to me. "That was Keahi Robins from our Hawaiian section. He says he knows who we're talking about."

A few moments later a slim, tall man of about middle age came in. He looked to be native Hawaiian and had quite a scholarly air about him.

"Keahi, this is...what did you say your name was? Charlie Chan?" Miss Kirkbridge actually laughed.

"Jimmy Chan," I replied, and I wasn't laughing at all.

But Miss Kirkbridge was on a roll. "Mr. Chan is, not too surprisingly, a detective. He's been looking into our problem with stolen books. Mr. Chan, show Keahi the photo."

I handed it over. He took a close look, handed it back, and said, "Yes, that's her. She worked in the Hawaiian section for a while. Just recently we had to let her go. She wouldn't maintain a professional appearance. Always wearing dirty old work shoes. And she wasn't careful with the items in our collection, some of which are very fragile. Not sure why she was hired in the first place."

"Probably had a really good fake resume," I offered. "But I think our case is solved."

"What do you mean?" Miss Kirkbridge asked.

"This was all a setup. Patricia Patson, working in the Hawaiian section, would have known about your rare books and what they were worth. But she was clever. She had stumbled upon the guy who was obsessively stealing romance books. She figured she could steal a few valuable items and get it all blamed on this Miller. Then to make it look good, she came to me with enough evidence to let me put the finger on Miller. She'd be in the clear, and she would have never shown her hand to anyone but me. It worked—up to a point. Morrison is still questioning Miller, thinking he stole the valuable items, too."

"You call that clever?" Miss Kirkbridge said. "I call it foolish, going to Charlie Chan, renowned for his acumen...Oh, right, you're *Jimmy* Chan." She laughed again and this time I almost—but not quite—said something.

"I'll go back to my office and call Morrison," I said as calmly as possible. "He needs to get a search warrant."

* * * *

About fifteen minutes later I put in my call to Morrison. He wasn't

99

there. I left a message and then made what was probably a dumb decision. See, the thing was, I was kind of afraid that Morrison wouldn't be able to get that search warrant after all. Sure, Patson had mounted an elaborate deception. But there was just no evidence at all that she had stolen the valuable Hawaiian items, even though it was a logical conclusion.

So I figured I'd go explore on my own. If I could turn up a little evidence, even if it turned out to be inadmissible, it might be enough for Morrison to get his warrant and act. I could have just dropped the whole thing. There wasn't going to be any money in it, and I didn't really have a horse in the race. But the thing is, I hate to be played, and I kind of wanted to settle the score.

I quickly told Jasmine where I was going. I was in a rush so I barely heard her saying, "Boss, you might not want to..." and the rest was lost as the door closed behind me.

* * * *

One of the things Jasmine had dug up was that Patson lived in one side of a duplex, but it was all the way out in Pearl City and it took me a little while to get there. Honolulu traffic just gets worse all the time and, as usual, H-1 was moving slower than molasses on an iceberg. But I finally arrived.

The duplex was in a typical Pearl City neighborhood, kind of down-scale, and the building was old and needed paint. Probably needed termite fumigation, too, but what else is new?

I knocked on the front door, actually kind of hoping she wouldn't be in. It would make things a lot simpler.

No answer. I had a couple handy little detective tools in my pocket. With a few quick glances around to make sure no one was looking, I picked the lock and opened the door. I entered and quickly closed it behind me.

I was in a living room that was kind of messy. There were old pizza boxes stacked on a cheap coffee table, and the carpets looked like they hadn't been vacuumed since vacuums were invented. All of the furniture looked pretty ratty.

I assumed that Patson would have the books in her duplex

somewhere, figuring no one was going to suspect anything. She'd know enough to keep them in good condition if she was going to try to sell them on the black market, which I guessed was her endgame.

It didn't take long to find a carefully wrapped box on the top shelf of a linen closet. I took it down and was surprised by the weight. I undid the wrappings and looked inside.

Bingo.

Four books that looked so valuable I hesitated to even touch them without gloves. And at that point, my own endgame changed. I didn't really care if she went to jail or not. I did care about returning these culturally important items to the State Library, where they belonged, to be preserved as a part of Hawaiian history. So forget the warrant and arrests and charges. Patson wouldn't dare try to get me for breaking and entering. I'd just take the books back to the library and that would be the end of the case.

It all would have been great, except the front door opened and in came Miss Patson.

"You!" she said when she saw me. "How did you..."

"Never mind how," I replied. "Just get out of the way. These books are going back to where you stole them from. Don't make any trouble and you'll stay out of jail. I'm not going to the cops with this."

"Yeah, seeing as how you broke into my place, you're not. And I'll make double sure of it."

Before I could react, she reached into her purse and pulled out a .45 automatic. "Don't move," she ordered. I heard the safety flick off, and she chambered a round. "I'm going to have to get *you* out of the way now. So put those books down. I'd hate to have to shoot you while you're holding that box. Might damage the merchandise."

"No way am I putting it down," I said.

"Okay, fine. I'll just shoot you in the head. I'm rather good with this weapon. Now, put the box down." She raised the gun and aimed it directly at my forehead.

I put the box down.

"Stay right there." Never letting the gun waver, Patson walked over to the couch and picked up one of the soiled, tattered cushions."

"Improvised silencer," I said. I was hoping her attention would waver so I could dive at her legs or make a run for the back door—there had to be a back door, right? But she was too alert.

"Okay, Chan, on your knees."

"Really? You've watched too many movies."

"Do it or I shoot you now."

I started to bend down when a shot rang out and the gun flew from Patson's hand.

There in the doorway, in a perfect two-handed firing stance, was Jasmine, holding the Sig Sauer that we kept in the office. She had shot Patson's gun hand right in the center.

* * * *

Some while later, Jasmine and I were at Mei Sum. I was treating her to soft-shell crab as kind of a thank you for, you know, saving my life and all that. The books had gone back to the library and Patson had gone to jail after all. Morrison hadn't said a word about my breaking and entering.

"I warned you, or tried to," Jasmine was saying. "I dug a little deeper and found that this Patson gal had a record, everything from shoplifting to—guess what?—illegal possession of firearms. She was on a suspended sentence for that. She was *dangerous*, Jimmy."

"I kind of found that out, I guess."

"So I followed you. Would have been there sooner except for the darn H-1 traffic."

I ordered a couple more plates of crab before I asked, "Where did you learn to shoot like that?" Now there were a lot of things that Jasmine didn't talk about, like what she had done back in Taiwan. All I really knew was that she had learned a lot of pretty unusual things somewhere along the line.

Jasmine just smiled. "A girl has to know how to look after herself."

"Man never born who can tell what woman will, or will not, do," I said.

"*Charlie Chan in Reno*, right?" she asked. "Cheesy."

She reached out with her chopsticks and took another crab from the serving dish.

§

Pixilated in a Public Library

by J. T. Page Jr.

Despite my infirmity, I grew up believing things like magic and miracles were possible. But I never thought something of that nature could ever happen to me.

My name is Christopher. I'm twenty-five, an only child, and I was born with a malady called congenital kyphosis. In simple terms, that means I entered life as a hunchback. My parents were loving and supportive, but they could not always protect me from the taunts of other children as I grew up. Even later, as I entered into adulthood, because of the cruel hump on my spine, I could always see or sense people averting their gaze, turning away, or avoiding me. Due to my condition, my face was almost buried in my chest as I walked along. I suffered frequently but, over time, learned to quietly accept my fate.

With the generous help of my parents, I completed college, where I developed an interest in writing. My focus was on history. That later led to a desire to write historical fiction while I completed a graduate program in creative writing. I quickly learned that writing historical fiction required as much research as writing about history itself. My vocation demanded that a great deal of time be spent in the local public library. That's where I first met Nancy, the librarian. She had recently finished her master's degree in library science, and I became one of her first regular patrons.

Nancy and I connected almost immediately. She was as friendly and helpful as all the librarians I've encountered, but there seemed to be some sort of constant sadness about her. However, I felt a special kinship as we easily communicated with one another and were quickly on a first-name basis. She always treated me as well as anyone ever had and, if she was repulsed by my deformity, I never felt it.

One day a major storm was due to arrive in our area. We had been warned about it for the past week by all the radio and television news shows. The rain and wind were getting really nasty and most people wisely started to stay home. We figured it would be short-lived but were mindful of the necessary precautions.

I was at a critical point in my research. Because the local public facilities remained open, I decided to take my chances on continuing my efforts at the library. And, as I had hoped, Nancy was there as well.

It was late afternoon in the middle of the week. Besides Nancy and me, there was only one other group of people in the library. They looked to be grandparents with a young child. Loud thunder started threatening the calm atmosphere and one could see the first drops of rain fall outside. The family quickly found a book for the child, checked it out, and departed. That left just the two of us in the library. After a short while, Nancy strolled over to the table where I was sitting and asked to join me while we waited out the storm. I quickly agreed and chivalrously started to rise as she motioned for me to sit. We launched into some small talk about the weather as conditions worsened outside.

Nancy chatted pleasantly. She looked directly at me, which was something I was not used to experiencing. I lifted my head as high as I could from my chest and looked at her eyes as my head nodded slightly. Her attention and warm smile were welcome and appreciated.

Suddenly, there was a large thunderclap and all the lights in the library died. We both reacted a bit, but immediately settled into a calm moment together without any particular sense of unease or worry.

Then something totally unexpected happened. As best as we could later remember, both of us fell fast asleep at the table. Some amount of time must have passed and I suddenly awoke.

"Nancy…Nancy! Are you okay? Are you awake?"

Her head lifted as her shoulders heaved back and her eyes widened.

"What happened?" she asked.

"It looks like we both somehow fell asleep. I think we were out for a half hour or so. I can't imagine how we both could somehow fall asleep at the same time."

Nancy looked around and said, "Yes. It is quite the mystery."

"Do you want to talk about it?" I responded.

The lights suddenly came back on and Nancy shook her head. "I think I should lock up so we can both go home. Will you visit the library tomorrow?"

"Yes, I plan to be here," I replied as I gathered my things to leave. We bid each other a good evening and I departed.

As I walked home in the rain, I tried to reflect on what had happened in the library. I wanted to make sense out of the stupefyingly bizarre dream I just had. I hesitate to say so, but it featured what appeared, of all things, to be a fairy. But then I quickly corrected myself. The tiny creature actually identified herself as a pixie as she darted and hovered over Nancy and me. I could not remember every detail, but there was something said about a book. Yes. I must get a book on fairies to learn more about them. The stores were now closed so I had to wait until tomorrow. I was almost home and I knew it was time for a much-needed and deserved drink. My rarely used bottle of Hennessy cognac awaited my arrival. Ah, I thought to myself. A French cognac created by an Irishman. One of life's happiest marriages.

* * * *

The next afternoon, on my way to the library, I stopped at a local bookstore and bought a copy of *Fairies: Real Encounters with Little People* by Janet Bord. For some reason, doubtless prompted by my dream, I had a desire to buy a book on fairies. I tucked it into my briefcase and departed. As I walked towards the library a few blocks away, I noticed that the weather started to appear threatening again. Storm clouds filled the sky and a sprinkle of rain started to fall as I reached my destination.

Upon entering, I went directly to the main counter area to greet Nancy and see if all was okay with her. She was busy checking out books for a few young adults. I waited off to the side and noticed a book lying on a chair behind the counter. It was next to what I imagined to be Nancy's purse and umbrella. When I saw the cover, I had to look twice. There was a picture of a fairy. I focused a bit more on the book and saw the title: *The Fairies in Tradition and Literature* by Katherine Briggs.

"Wow!" I thought to myself. "What a surreal coincidence."

A few moments later, Nancy walked toward my end of the counter and greeted me. She smiled, but seemed a bit more serious than usual.

"How did the rest of your evening go last night?" she asked.

"Just fine," I responded. "Are you doing okay?"

"Yes," said Nancy. "But the bad weather kept me up a bit. It looks like we are about to have a repeat performance tonight."

I nodded and then spoke. "Can I ask you a question?"

"Of course," she replied.

"While I was waiting just now, I noticed a book on the chair behind you. It looks like it's about fairies."

"Yes," she said. "I just bought it earlier today on my way to work."

I paused for a moment and then continued. "I don't mean to pry, but was there any special reason you bought that particular book?"

"I can't really explain it," Nancy replied. "I simply had a sudden interest in fairies."

I nodded in both agreement and interest. "May I show you something I bought on my way here today?"

Nancy's expression seemed to concur while her eyebrows raised in curiosity.

Reaching into my briefcase, I pulled out a book still in a paper sack. I reached into the sack and slowly exposed the cover with perhaps a bit more drama than necessary.

Nancy stared and her eyes widened. "Really?!" she gasped. "A book on fairies?!"

"What are the odds?" I flatly stated.

The young people left with their books and there was only one other person, who was working at a computer. Nancy and I were silent for a time as was the library. Low rumbles of thunder could be heard in the distance and the natural light outside grew darker.

"Nancy," I began. "Can we talk a bit more about what happened last night?"

She hesitated and wasn't sure what to say. I decided to seize the moment.

"I'll start," I said. "I had a dream when we fell asleep and the strangest things happened."

As I spoke, my memory seemed to open up and I suddenly remembered more particulars with perfect clarity.

"My dream involved a fairy-like creature." I paused and smiled sheepishly. "Actually, she identified herself as a pixie," I said with a nervous laugh.

"It's not possible!" injected Nancy just before a huge clap of thunder occurred. *Whack!* We both jumped. The library lights began to flicker and suddenly all the electrical power died.

The person sitting at the computer swore a brief four-letter oath as his work was lost. He stood up, paused, and asked us to forgive his outburst. He hurriedly put on his raincoat and said, "Sorry, sorry. I'll try and come back tomorrow." He and his umbrella left the library with a flourish.

Nancy and I were now alone in the dark…or at least we thought so.

"I have a flashlight handy," said Nancy.

She quickly found it and turned it on next to us. "That's a bit better," she said. "And now I have an idea."

Nancy produced a small piece of paper and a pen. She wrote something on it and turned it over so it was hidden from me.

"Christopher…by any chance, did your pixie have a name?" she asked.

I had so many things buzzing around in my head about the previous evening, but found I could answer her question easily.

"Yes," I responded. "Her name was Sasa."

Nancy's eyes widened again and she slowly turned over the piece of paper. Written on it was one word in all caps…SASA.

Both of our jaws slackened and we stared in astonishment at each other.

"Sasa said her mother was a Seelie Court fairy named Kick," I injected.

Nancy immediately responded, "And her father was a leprechaun named Pedro."

We were both stunned into silence as we realized we had somehow shared the exact same dream.

The lights came on suddenly and snapped us back into reality.

"Can we keep talking this out a bit more?" I asked anxiously.

"I think we need to," replied Nancy. "It's almost closing time. I can lock the front door and we can have some privacy. Will you stay a while longer?"

"I'm in no rush and would love to compare notes. We need to figure out what the heck is going on."

Nancy excused herself to lock the front door. She turned off most of the library lights except for the area we had shared the previous night. I moved to my usual table and sat down. Nancy joined me almost immediately. We stared at each other, took a deep breath, and started to share our experience.

The more we spoke, the more animated we became. We were able, time and again, to confirm the precise similarities of our mutual dream.

We agreed that Sasa was from the pixie community of fairies. She said she normally lives in a garden or in the woods of her native Ireland. But, like others in the various fairy communities, she does like to travel from time to time. She looked to be about four or five inches tall, but had lovely humanlike features. Her head was a bit oversized for her body. She had a delicate nose and pointy ears. Sasa also had wings that fluttered rapidly like a hummingbird's and seemed to change color whenever she spoke. She was rather scantily dressed in a green-colored fabric which accented her unique overall appearance. Nancy readily agreed with me that our pixie could easily be described as gloriously charming.

Nancy and I also learned that the fairies who travel to remote places are especially fond of libraries because of the preponderance of books. Sasa taught us about what she called "Book Travel." We were amazed when she disclosed that many members of the fairy community can magically travel in real time. They have to simply place both little fingers on the word "Fairy" or "Fairies" on any book cover title. They then close their eyes and say aloud a single word like "home." One of the most common words she learned to use is "library," which is how she arrived at our location. But, unlike "home," most other words put her in an unknown destination. Sasa volunteered that it made the Book Travel experience more of an adventure. It would be hard to disagree with her.

According to Sasa, this singular ability of fairies to travel had actually been going on for over 1,000 years. She emphasized that it all started with the *Book of Kells* in the 9th century. But, in fulfilling their unique sense of adventure, fairies using Book Travel are allowed to spend "no more than a fortnight" (i.e., two weeks) at any single destination. If they don't return home by then, they must remain forever in that location.

In Sasa's case, after she arrived in this library, the lone book on fairies had been checked out a few days later. She only had a short time left before she would be forced to stay and never return home again.

A book on fairies was needed in the library so Sasa could travel back to Ireland. She volunteered that she had been observing us for a few days and noted that we treated each other kindly. She confessed she had no choice but to seek our help to ensure that one or more books on fairies would be available soonest in the stacks.

The thunder boomers started rumbling heavily outside and lightning flashed.

"Well," I said, "it looks like we should get our new books and put them out so Sasa can return home."

"I'm a bit ahead of you on that," said Nancy. "I already prepared a new catalog number for the book I bought. It's in the 398 series of the Dewey Decimal System. If you are willing to donate your book, I can catalog that as well."

"Absolutely! Let's do it!" I responded.

We walked back to the main counter and Nancy finished cataloging the two new books. As she walked them over to their new home in the stacks, the rain began falling harder and harder.

I went back to the table and Nancy joined me. The rain was now coming down in sheets as the lightning and thunder resumed.

Probably in an effort to get our minds off the last twenty-four hours and the bad weather, Nancy looked at me and started to speak.

"Christopher, we haven't known each other very long…but I feel a positive connection and that I can trust you. Can I share something personal with you?"

I smiled and nodded as best as my bowed head allowed. Nancy continued.

"My life has been difficult for the past year. I moved here from another state after I found this library position online. I was in a relationship while attending graduate school and it really went sour. It became unbearable and I knew I had to make a change. I think I've always been a happy person, but that experience made me sad, even bitter." Tears began misting her eyes. "I just feel the need has come to share all this with someone else. I really hope you don't mind."

I reached across the table and placed my hand on top of hers. "Thank you for trusting me with this, Nancy. I think you can believe me when I say that I have fought disappointment and bitterness throughout my life because of…my condition. From my view, your decision to make a fresh start was correct in every possible way. Please know that you can talk to me anytime with the certainty that I will respect your privacy and always wish you nothing but the best."

Tears fell down her cheeks as she placed her other hand on top of mine and smiled. I reached into my briefcase with my free hand and pulled out a travel packet of Kleenex that I always carry with me. She took the packet and withdrew a single tissue to dab her eyes as I slid back both of my hands.

It continued to pour outside and I briefly turned toward the hard rain splashing noisily on the library windows. When I looked back at Nancy, I saw her head slowly drop as if she was going to sleep. Before I could say or do anything, I thought I saw a small figure hovering over us and sprinkling something that looked like sparkling dust. I felt myself fading out faster than the library lights.

Some time had passed before I came to my senses. I was out probably as long as a decent power nap. Nancy was still asleep. I took a moment for myself and realized I had experienced another dream. But this time it seemed a bit different since I recalled a direct discussion with Sasa.

She thanked me for the fairy book and, in appreciation, said she would try to grant me a wish. Without much hesitation, I told her that I wished she could take away the sadness from Nancy and restore her gentle heart to complete happiness.

"For your kindness," spoke Sasa, "I will grant your wish and also share with you my knowledge of the basic essence of love. It is simply to wish the best for someone else. All fairies know this but not all humans." She then said something I was sure was in the Gaelic language, and I was later able to translate it. I'm quite certain it was "*Go raibh mile maith agat.*" (Pronounced "GUR-uv mee-la MA ah-GUTH.") It means "May you have a thousand good things."

With that, Sasa giggled loudly and disappeared. That's when my dream ended and I awoke.

Nancy began to stir and rubbed her temples as she returned to a relative state of normalcy.

"I think this time I had a private dream with Sasa," she said.

"So did I," was my reply.

Nancy seemed anxious to continue. "Sasa thanked me and said something else I didn't quite understand. It was some other language. But she also granted me a wish." Nancy paused, looked at me, and suddenly became very emotional. "And it looks like it came true!"

"Are you happy now?" I asked. "Is your heart full?"

"Oh yes," said Nancy. "I don't think I have ever been happier. I can see clearly that my wish came true."

"I don't quite understand," I asked. "What is it you see."

"I see you as healthy and strong," replied Nancy. "That was my wish."

"I still don't understand. What do you mean?"

Nancy stood and took a step toward me. She cupped my face in both her hands and asked me to stand. I stood and realized that my head was off my chest and that I was suddenly quite a bit taller than Nancy. Her hands slid evenly down my neck and across my shoulders. I placed my right hand on my bad shoulder and realized that the hump was gone. I quickly checked the other shoulder and that was normal as well. I started to laugh and then cry. We hugged each other tightly.

Nancy had wished the best for me, as I had for her.

The rain suddenly stopped…and we both knew our lives had restarted.

* * * *

I hope this story of mine was worth your precious time. It is up to you, dear reader, to decide if it be fact or fiction. Miracles can indeed sometimes happen and you can be certain that Nancy and I wish the best for you. But be further assured of one more thing… books can transport us, mind and soul, to other places. It doesn't seem too far-fetched that books can manage to transport actual fairies as well.

As a closing thought, the next time you visit a library, you might want to check out the stacks using Dewey Decimal catalog number 398. You never know what you might discover…or perhaps even dream!

§

A Rose from the Dead

By D.V. Whytes

I shook the wet from my slicker, like a wet dog.

"Hey," said a man, as he skirted past me while brushing the rain from his sleeve. He acted like I had drenched him with my waggle.

"I didn't get you that wet," I said, a little too loud. Nonetheless, he just grumbled, and hurried off into the bowels of the Boston Athenaeum Library. Miffed, and no longer dripping on the floor myself, I dashed off in another direction. The weatherman had promised an approaching squall within the next few hours, so there wasn't much time.

Without delay, I gathered several of Graham Greene's books in my arms, and as I turned to leave, a book fell. I picked it up, and realized I had read it before. Therefore, I set it back on the shelf. When I got to the fourth floor reading area, I found myself nearly alone. "How marvelous," I said, while noticing that my favorite spot next to the window was available. I set the bunch of books on the table and removed my raincoat. As I draped it over the back of my chair, a book fell again.

"What a butterfinger," I said aloud, and with a big sigh, bent over to retrieve it. But to my surprise, it was the same book I had placed back on the shelf, *The Power and the Glory.* Following a shrug of my shoulders, and thinking myself to be a bit scatter-brained, I laid the fallen book aside, sat down, and opened *The*

Quiet American.

The rain began to pelt the window a bit harder. As I gazed out, a man passing by bumped into my table, causing that same book to fall to the floor once again. Annoyed, I bent over to retrieve it once more. That's when I noticed a piece of paper sticking out from underneath. It looked important, so I called out, "Hey, hey mister, you dropped something." But, no one was there.

I unfolded what appeared to be a telegram. In our days of smart phones, iPads, emails, and instant chats, I thought the communication form somewhat obsolete. Yet what was even odder, was that it was addressed to me. Unsure what else to think, I read the message, and it was just as peculiar.

> "A PICNIC AND LOVELY WOMAN MISSED MOST STOP MEET OCTOBER THIRD CORSEAUX CEMETERY STOP TEN AM STOP SKIES GRAY WEAR GREEN SHAWL STOP BRING PICNIC STOP RESERVATIONS CONFIRMED HÔTEL DES TROIS COURONNES STOP PROMISE YOU'RE PLEASANTLY SURPRISED STOP"

It was signed GG.

My mouth fell open and I shook my head. Hmmm…I had to read it again. Corseaux, Switzerland. Three days from now. Truly, I was intrigued. How could I forego such a unique proposal? Immediately, I booked a flight to Geneva and made arrangements to rent a car. The drive from the airport to Corseaux would be about an hour. I found that accommodations had been made for me in Vevey, just as the telegram had promised. To top it off, it was only about fifteen minutes from my destination.

I began to pack, and pulled out the green shawl that I had purchased only a week ago; fortuitous or a coincidence? Whatever… into the suitcase it went.

My flight was uneventful and the drive to Vevey beautiful. My trek along Lac Leman was on Route One, probably better known to the locals as Route de Suisse. I stopped to purchase various items for our picnic. And since I was in Switzerland, I chose a fruity, yet light-bodied Gamay wine, along with some black olives, grape tomatoes, prosciutto, sausages, brie and Stilton cheeses, and fresh bread.

Surprisingly, I was rather calm that night. I held no anxieties about my blind date the next morning. Sleep came sweet and I awoke fresh and enthusiastic. Coffee and a small omelet helped start my morning.

The day was sunny and breezy, and my drive to Corseaux was both scenic and pleasant. I parked the car near the cemetery, grabbed my basket full of goodies, and strolled through the gate.

My green shawl was tossed around my neck like a large scarf and it snapped in the breeze. Soon I was immersed in reading the headstones as I went. It wasn't long before I spied the spot for our picnic. To my right, between two tombstones, was a very short fold-up table with a single red rose in a small vase and two large floor cushions alongside. I set the wicker basket down and leaned over to smell the rose. That's when I first heard his voice.

"So you got my telegram? How did you know I'd be here?"

I turned, and there he was; Graham Greene, seated on the top of his very own headstone. He held a burning cigarette in his left hand, and offered a sly smile.

"Where else would you be?" I replied.

"Hmmm..." came his response. Pensively, he drew deeply on his Chesterfield, and then blew a whiff of smoke into the air. It dissipated quickly into the wind. "We all want to be comedians. Now, you wanted to talk. What about?"

I poured the wine, and handed him a glass. "Yes, I want to talk. But how did you know?"

He chuckled. "It was a rainy day. But then you'd be surprised what I know, especially now. So, why choose me?"

"You intrigue me. You were a brilliant writer, and yet so..."

"Troubled? Tortured?"

"Yes...you're bipolar, isn't that right?"

"And what does that mean to you?"

"I thought I was the one who got to ask the questions."

"Nothing is sacred anymore, is it?"

"You were also a spy. Nothing was sacred then, was there?"

"And yet, there is so much more to this life...enough for the common as well as the holy."

"Then you believe?"

"Once I did. But that's not what's on your mind, is it?"

"You wrote because you were tortured, and found it therapeutic. For the most part, it helped. You wrote about all that bothered you; religion, politics and war except...sex. I understand that when you were young, you were sent to a school where homosexuality abounded. You were even bullied there. Writing didn't help you. Instead, you became obsessed. I heard you had over forty prostitutes as well as many affairs with married women."

"Well, one can't write about sex—not really. Not then. And not very well today either. Of course you can describe the event and even expound on the emotions, but not the soul of the matter. You must understand...sex is so much more than just sex. And I should know."

"So it would seem."

"If sex is simply sex, then rape would be no more than physical abuse. Yet it is so much more. It's far more than the fear...the cuts and bruises. It brings enough suffering and sorrow to last a lifetime. You're less then you once were, as if part of your soul had been filched, or fallaciously stronger, simply because you are more determined. But being determined does not make you whole. You're still missing the necessary element of self-warmth. Either way, it's tragic."

"And why do you think that is?"

"Quite simply because it's rarely experienced within the boundaries of marital bliss, of course. And I do emphasize bliss. For that's when love watches over you like a protector, who is a giver, granting the birth of a renewed love within. It nourishes."

"But outside of these borders..."

"Without its guardian, sex always steals, even if it was good. The ripples are felt for years to come, literally changing your life. It has stolen from me countless times. I still feel the harm—and the loss. Yet we stubbornly keep trying to refill that loss, the very same way we lost it. This is what I was talking about in *The Quiet American*.

He looked up and after taking in a deep breath, referenced his work, "You see, suffering is not worse because of how many are involved, but rather by the depth by which just one undergoes its torment."

Casually, as if we had just discussed nothing more significant than the weather, he began to empty my picnic basket. He tasted the Stilton between bites of prosciutto and sausages with a sense of pure pleasure on his face. He swallowed and then paused. Looking at the delectable chunk still in his fingertips, he said, "Umm, simply wonderful. I'd almost forgotten how enjoyable dining could be."

"So you want me to get to the point, then."

"We only have an hour," he said.

"You saw things, didn't you? Things that no one else saw or knew. Some of your writing was almost prophetic."

"Oh, how so?"

"How about your piece on organized crime? *J'Accuse* was all about organized crime within the highest levels of government in Nice, including police corruption. Because of this work, you received threats and mysterious phone calls. You even carried a canister of gas around in order to protect yourself. And then there was that lawsuit for libel, which I believe you lost."

"Yes, but Médecin was tried later. In fact, he was found guilty for corruption."

"But not until after you had died. And only the mayor? What about the others?"

"There are always others."

"I believe that was in '94. And you also received Britain's Order of Merit for this work."

"Yes, in '86."

"There was also the Paddington Trunk murder. It happened shortly after you published "It's a Battlefield," a story where a bus driver knifes a policeman, who he thought was going to strike his wife. It was said that the details between your work and the actual case were so similar that you feared arrest."

"Your point being..."

"Tell me. Tell me about seeing. How you saw things. How did you know what would happen? You wrote it all in novels, but there was much truth there, too, wasn't there?"

He chuckled. "All novels hold truth. That's what captivates the reader. But it's not really about seeing things differently. It's about not filtering out that which you don't like or don't want to see."

He took a sip of wine and nibbled on the olives and a little tomato. I remained silent. I didn't want to fog the issue at hand, or allow him to go off subject.

"I won't go off subject," he said, suddenly.

"How... how..." I stammered.

He laughed.

"It's all about being willing to see things as they are. To hear the truth set before you in the *now* moments of life. Not to ignore something because it soils your ideology of life or your belief in an individual. Don't get me wrong—this takes courage. For when you take things as they are, you risk the business of offending others. Offending those who still want to hide or close their eyes, believing in what they want, rather than the truth."

He paused here to finish his Chesterfield, and then let the butt fall to the ground, merely to smash the dying embers with his foot.

I pressed on. "Let me quote to you again, this time from *The Heart of the Matter*. 'You see, simply because a thing is in your heart, does not necessarily mean that it is right. Every heart possesses a ruthlessness, because it's prepared to see others suffer, as long as our life and our loved ones are happy.' "

I closed my eyes and knew he was right—too right. Alas, we do seem to base our decisions on the happiness of those we love, even when our choice is not the best. We allow our assessment to lean toward short-term satisfaction versus the more difficult options that stimulate long-term interests. "So," I began, "in other words, you recommend that we just take off the rose-colored glasses."

"Yes, but it's not that simple. Nothing is. You must have a genuine love for the truth. Truth must take a priority in your life, whether you like it or not, for it's a part of our soul."

"Another reference from *The Heart of the Matter*?"

"Why yes. Not only must you have read the book, but it must have meant something to you as well."

"The depths in which you write inspire me. You make one think about what they've read, leaving each reader less shallow than before. This is why I wanted to talk with you."

"I'm touched. Really." He finished his glass of wine, poured a second, and then lit another cigarette. After a few deep puffs, he smiled and said, "Ah. I miss these, too. Please, have a drink," and he handed me a fresh glass.

I ate a little of the Stilton and olives, washing them down with the Gamay. "Tell me, how does anyone know if they're even wearing rose-colored glasses?"

His eyes lit up like a Christmas tree.

"Hmmm...I do believe you're starting to get it." He rubbed his hands together as he thought. "Well now, let's see. You know those times when you replay an event in your mind, about an incident you weren't happy with? You tweak it into something more acceptable, going over the circumstances again and again. The glasses are on. Oh, and then there are those little twinges you feel when you ignore or breeze by a certain fact or situation. This is sure proof that you're hiding from the truth."

"How so?"

"You wouldn't overlook or discount something you liked or approved of, would you? No, of course not, you'd rave about them. People do tend to overlook what they find distasteful. We could list the reasons, but basically it's because we don't want to find ourselves face to face with the unpleasantries of truth."

"Such as?"

"Such as when your opinion of someone you favor is tainted or spoiled. God has given us free will. It is a gift. It is a curse. Now I know this is a cliché, but little Johnny must be held accountable for what he has chosen to do. But that's what we hate to see, isn't it? That cute little face behind bars."

I let the last of the wine slide slowly down my throat and thought of how, I too, had fallen into this trap. Like the time I saw an old friend pilfer a bracelet. I had kept my mouth shut because I didn't want her to get in trouble.

"Why do we do it, do you think?" I asked.

"Well, I would say that it's rather obvious…"

The truth in the case of my friend was that I really didn't want to hear her call me a snitch, or think poorly of me. My silence had not been for her benefit. I wonder what she's up to now.

Following my contemplative pause, he continued. "For one, we hate to be deceived or embarrassed. We prefer control. So we decide to keep secrets, hoping it'll offer up some type of escape rather than exposure. Yet when an opportunity arises, those secrets we've discovered we exploit in order to get what we want. This leads us to the bottom line."

"Which is?"

"That we allow the evils about us, simply because we fail to love the truth."

At this point, I thought about how sorry I was that I had asked him about how he saw things. How he was able to write profoundly, almost prophetic, because now I had to make my own decision. I continued to mull over what he had said. We could love the truth or become a hider, a keeper of secrets. If I heard him correctly, the effects of all our choices were simply that significant.

I sighed. I could no longer allow the things that I knew were wrong to continue on in silence. There were many reasons. For one, I would fall prey as a victim from my own choices one day. And for another, this behavior wasn't love, not if I wasn't pursuing truth, even if I meant to choose what may be problematical, awkward, or troublesome.

"That's correct," he said, and smiled at me.

I shook my head. Had he read my mind again?

"It's not like that," he said.

"Like what?"

"One does not read another's mind. If you are quiet enough and pay close attention, you can see what someone is considering." He chuckled, and then said, "And now, I see that you're beginning to understand. Therefore, you must choose to love truth."

This time he sighed. "Sadly, you will lose friendships. It is inevitable. There are always those who will choose to allow evil."

"You have done me harm by what you have told me."

"Yes, but you will be the better—and actually, the happier for it. Tell me, what is your musing about these new smart phones and chat rooms? Do they make the world any better?"

"They too come with a choice. Sometimes too much information is bad. Either we don't have the full story, or we simply don't cope properly with what we have learned."

"Is that all?"

"Since we are rarely face to face with anyone, we deceive ourselves with a false bit of courage, once we realize we can hide behind doing what we normally wouldn't."

"So, they are a bad thing. No good comes from them?"

It was my turn to pause and reflect for a moment. "Yes, they do have a good side. People learn things and much evil is diverted. But the ugly of it all is that too many are losing their interpersonal skills, resulting in uncomfortable or offensive interactions."

"Ah yes, I see." He seemed to drift into a moment of contemplation.

I broke off a piece of bread and chewed ever so slowly, while giving him a puzzled look. In his silence, I cleared my throat to bring him back to the here and now.

Startled by the noise, he took in a deep breath and said, "Then what I wrote in *The Heart of the Matter* is true. Friendship is a thing of the soul. And now I understand that when a story is incomplete, it can appear as something it is not. The only conclusion one can make then is a wrong one, a false one. Only evil will follow."

We were both silent for a few moments, ruminating on all that had taken place.

This time Graham broke the silence. "Our time is over," he announced.

"Yes...and I wish that it were not so."

"Are you pleased with our morning together?"

"Pleased, yes. But somewhat burdened."

"That need not be."

"How so?"

"Because you can trust in the truth."

I smiled and reached for the rose, plucking it from its vase, and twirled its stem between my fingertips. Pulling it close, I took in a deep breath to enjoy its fragrance. It was then that I heard a slight whisper, one that seemed to float on the wind: "Truth."

The murmur echoed in the distance for a moment and then suddenly began to grow stronger, "Ahem, ahem…"

I awoke from a nudge to my shoulder.

"You're snoring."

"Huh? Excuse me? What did you say?"

"You were snoring. Time to get up, we're closing." As he walked away, he added, "And smoking is not allowed here...you're welcome."

What was he talking about? I rubbed my eyes and looked out the library window. The rain had stopped, but there on the window sill was a smoldering Chesterfield—and a solitary rose in a small vase. He was gone. Or was he? I looked around only to find myself alone. Smiling, I thought how his work had always moved me, but it never touched me as deeply as our time together today.

Eartha and Milly,
"Book Worms" Extraordinaire

by Gail M Baugniet

Eartha and Milly were two very eager book worms, who enjoyed inching their way around the books at the local library. As best friends and avid students of nature, their interests bore especially deep into the variety of soils found within the layers of their tropical island. Handicapped as they were by their youth, not to mention the iron-clad curfews of overprotective parents, they spent an inordinate amount of time weaving through the stacks of the library's Hawaiian reference books to satisfy their insatiable appetite for all things related to soil.

Eartha was most fond of soils located around volcanic structures and *heiaus*; Milly leaned more toward sandy beaches and hiking trails. Their parents allowed them to visit the library every Saturday as long as they arrived home in time for the evening meal, a deal they stuck to faithfully. But the exhilarating idea of hopping a bus to sites of their favorite research topics remained the two young book worms' closely guarded secret. After perusing the pages of a book on the creation of Leahi, more popularly known as Diamond Head, Eartha had decided the volcanic crater located at the far eastern end of Waikiki Beach would be a perfect place to begin their field research.

Volcanic Tuff at Diamond Head

Eartha and Milly walked from the bus stop through the tunnel that led to Diamond Head Park. From there, they crossed the parking lot to the admissions booth, where they showed their student identification for entrance to the grounds.

According to their library research, the Koolau Volcano had long been dormant before it awoke in violent eruptions of volcanic ash and cinders to form the towering cone shape of Leahi. Eventually the ash and cinders joined to form tuff, a type of rock made up of compacted volcanic material.

With Eartha leading the way, she and Milly followed the winding trail up Diamond Head. Because they weren't allowed to climb unattended past the first lookout of the crater, they quickly collected a small amount of soil along a wall facing away from the ocean. Eartha figured there was less chance of salt water contamination that way. Milly agreed, but neither had any idea if the soil was originally tuff rock. It was definitely soil from Leahi and to them that's what counted.

Returning to a small park area near the trail entrance, they removed granola bars from their backpacks and sat at an empty picnic bench near a row of bougainvillea bushes. Doves and a few red-crested cardinals hopped around in anticipation of being fed, but posted signs said "No feeding the birds." When a mongoose stuck its head out of the bushes, Milly pointed and squealed with delight.

"Do you think it would eat some of my granola bar?" Milly asked.

"No," Eartha answered. "They like rats and snakes and worms. But rats sleep during the day. The mongoose sleeps at night."

"And everyone knows there are no snakes in Hawai'i," Milly added. "So they must eat an awful lot of earthworms."

"Bird and turtle eggs, too, unfortunately," Eartha said, scrunching her nose in disapproval. Then smiling, she lifted the small container of soil. "But we now have our first soil sample."

* * * *

Not wanting to be outdone, the following Saturday at the library Milly chose a reference book about hiking. She announced to Eartha that they would hop a bus to the trailhead at Paradise Park, where they would check out a variety of forest plants and trees along the hiking trail. Afterward, they could head up to Manoa Falls and cool off by the pool before heading back.

Rainbow Eucalyptus and Manoa Falls

A short distance from the trail entrance, they came across a bunch of bamboo trees that formed a welcoming start to their hike. Farther along the trail, they spotted a grove of rainbow eucalyptus trees, also known as *koa haole,* or foreign *koa* tree. Milly had read that their deep roots stabilized the soil and prevented erosion. She squatted near the root of one towering tree to dig up a bit of soil for their collection, proudly labeling the sample "Manoa Koa."

Milly noticed there were lots of silk trees, quickly recalling that their correct name was Albizia. She thought they were rather pretty with their feathery leaves, but also knew they were considered an invasive species.

"Have you noticed that there's an awful lot of invasive stuff taking over native plants and animals on the island?" Eartha asked, then didn't wait for an answer. "The Albizia tree was supposed to control erosion in Hawai'i because they are fast-growing trees. But after the sugar cane business came to an end, the tree spread across the empty cane fields. Now they're everywhere."

When they arrived at the falls, several other hikers were milling around the roped-off area of the pond. "We cannot go into the water," Milly said. "It's contaminated. But we can sit near it to enjoy the breeze and any spray from the falls."

Eartha agreed to the plan and they unpacked their snacks. None of the other hikers made an attempt to swim in the pool either. After a fifteen-minute rest, they gathered their belongings and headed back.

As they exited the trail at Paradise Park, Eartha and Milly were greeted by a confident peacock, who swished its long flowing tail feathers right and left to attract their attention. The cocky bird slowly lifted and spread its glowing white train until it had fanned out in all its glory. Responding to their encouraging exclamations, the flamboyant bird turned a full circle to display the majesty of its extended fan. After lowering its feathers, the peacock then strutted off, displaying a spectacularly indifferent attitude.

Eartha and Milly Stuck in the Library

The first Saturday after midterm finals in English and Arithmetic, Eartha and Milly decided to lie low at the library, not wanting to arouse suspicion about their clandestine bus excursions around the island. Their mothers would surely insist they take their grubby younger siblings along.

At the library table, with several research books opened to articles on Hawaiian soil, Milly whispered to Eartha, "Where should we take our next bus trip so we can check out the reddish soil?"

"Red dirt is more like it," Eartha said. "And it's all over the island. Auntie Fetida lives near Red Hill and says the family is always getting red stains on their clothes. We'd better stick to books for our research of red soil. Here," she said, handing a reference book to Milly. "Read this about iron and other oxides in lava."

"Wow," Milly said a few minutes later. "I guess it makes sense that red soil would come from red-hot volcanic eruptions. But then why isn't all the soil here red in color?"

Resigned to a day of indoor research, Eartha shrugged. "Maybe the stuff that shot out of the volcano in the beginning just faded after a while. Sort of like how my Auntie Cutty's hair turned from that shiny dark brown color to a drab gray."

* * * *

Once they were sure no one suspected their soil research expeditions, it became routine for Eartha and Milly to take turns picking out a favorite book at the library each Saturday, planning a bus trip, and then spending the day exploring deep into the soil around their chosen site.

By the time summer vacation rolled around the year they graduated from junior high, both Eartha and Milly had a long list of reference books and corresponding sites they wanted to explore. After Eartha double-checked her notes against information in a reference book about *heiau* locations on the island, she replaced the book on the library shelf. The main thing they would look for at the site was the different colors of soil. At the corner of Beretania and Punchbowl, they caught a bus heading up to Haleiwa and their destination of Waimea Falls Park.

Sacred *Heiau* in Waimea Valley

Exiting the bus, they hiked up to *Puu O Mahuka Heiau*, intent on inspecting the soil around the outer edges of the sacred site. At first, they were distracted by the view from high above the Pacific Ocean. The sun glimmered off the azure water and white-capped waves, creating a scene of such contentment that neither one could speak. When a stiff wind chilled them, they finally snapped out of their reverie and got to work.

Each girl carried a small plastic shovel to gently lift a section of loose ground. After waiting for some creepy bugs to scurry away, they verified the color and texture of the soil. The top layer was a sandy texture in a shade of dark brown; a bit lower they dug into a yellowish-brown silt. They quickly replaced the dirt and tamped it down as a bird flew overhead and settled on a tree branch.

"Oh, look at that mynah bird," Milly said. "It's the same color as the soil, brown and yellow. Isn't it cute?"

Eartha wrinkled her nose. "I guess. But you know they're not native. They were brought here to control the army worms, and they've become sort of invasive."

"They're still cute, though," Milly said, her voice sounding a bit defensive.

Nodding in agreement, Eartha led the way back down to the highway. Knowing they had a long wait for the next bus heading back to Honolulu, they caught a local bus into Haleiwa. There they each ordered a mango-pineapple "shave ice" at Matsumoto's store, adding a request for adzuki beans.

Hawaiian Monk Seals on Waikiki Beach

The girls missed Saturday's library research day. Milly was going to her cousin's birthday luau. The following Saturday, they walked *ewa* with renewed focus from the Duke Kahanamoku statue on Waikiki Beach. They were headed toward the beach fronting the military hotel Hale Koa, where a Hawaiian monk seal had been sunbathing over the past few days. Milly wondered if the seal was pregnant and had come to give birth to a monk seal pup. The last time a seal had taken up residence on Oahu was at Kaimana Beach in Waikiki.

The mother seal had given birth on the beach, then fiercely protected the newborn, departing only after the pup had been weaned. Monk seals, endemic to the Hawaiian archipelago, did much of their birthing on the island of Kauai. Having one choose Oahu was a privilege everyone appreciated. Daily visitors continued to enjoy the pup's antics, causing some concern that the baby seal might not learn to adapt to ocean life. It had eventually been moved to an undisclosed location to cavort with other young seals until it safely ventured out on its own.

After the girls passed the army museum, they spotted people milling around some orange cones and a roped-off area on the beach. "That must be where the monk seal is," Milly said.

"Come on," Eartha said, starting to run. "Let's check it out."

When they got closer, they slowed to a walk and made their way along the surf line of the water until they spotted the monk seal basking in the sun. Each time a wave floated to shore, the seal languidly lifted its snout a bare inch. Then its head lazily lowered again in rhythm with the subsiding wave. Eartha and Milly overheard someone say the seal was only taking a tourist-style break, not there to give birth or to be rescued after swallowing a hook on an errant fishing line.

A bit disappointed that the seal wasn't there to give birth, but relieved to know it was healthy, they decided to take a short dip in the calm waters of the Pacific. Afterward, Eartha and Milly walked barefoot along the beach toward Hilton Hawaiian Village. Sugar-fine white sand flowed between their toes and stuck to the moisture on their calves.

Milly collected a small amount of sand in a glass jar, knowing the grains of sand had been created by waves breaking down corals from the many coral reefs that surrounded the island. The ocean's constant wave action aided in turning volcanic rock into stone and pebbles before pulverizing it into sand. Unfortunately, there were no black sand beaches on Oahu to explore. The island had formed over the volcanic hotspot millions of years ago. Any coastal lava rocks had likely been broken down and washed away eons ago.

"I suppose," Milly said to Eartha, "it isn't likely that any of Waikiki's sand came from the volcanic eruptions of Diamond Head when it was formed."

Eartha scooped up a handful of the finely worn sand and let it flow through her fingers. As it trickled down onto her toes, she giggled. "Well, for sure it isn't as hot as anything that erupted over four hundred millenniums ago."

* * * *

The next Saturday, before they left the library to catch the bus for Hanauma Bay, Eartha asked Milly to read through a short article about corals. That coral reefs were made up of living things had been a new idea to Eartha and she wasn't confident she could adequately explain corals to Milly.

Coral Reef in Hanauma Bay

Once on the bus, they discussed the general concept of corals. They decided that the living corals at Hanauma Bay were the kind that released something called calcium carbonate. The corals used it to make external shells for themselves.

"That explains why coral is so hard," Eartha said.

"And after the shells harden into limestone," Milly said, "they sort of clump together to make a coral reef. But is there some type of soil that the reef sets on?"

Eartha smiled. "Actually, that's the cool part. I don't know if it's considered real soil, but when some of the coral breaks up or fish graze on it, it forms carbonate mud, which is like soil."

"Will we have to go snorkeling to see the soil in the bay?" Milly started to fidget. "You know we're not allowed to snorkel without adult supervision."

"No, but we should be able to get a good view of the reef from one of the hiking trails near the shoreline. Even if we did snorkel up close, we wouldn't be allowed to take a soil sample."

Once they arrived at Hanauma Bay, Eartha and Milly walked down the paved entrance path to the beach. They hiked along the shore to the far side of the curved bay, then followed a narrow dirt trail that led toward the eroded end of the volcanic crater.

"What are we going to do now?" Milly asked, once Eartha stopped walking. 'The water is clear enough to see marine life from here but not to check the soil."

"It's a great view of the entire bay, though," Eartha said. "Especially the darker masses of coral reefs. And one more thing."

Milly waited for her to explain what the one more thing was. She finally noticed that Eartha was pointing to the ground several yards in front of them. Two turtles were sunning themselves in the short grass just off the trail.

"I think those are green turtles," Eartha said. "They have a greenish tint to them."

"But green turtles aren't really green," Milly said. "Only their fat has a green tint to it. The turtles lounging in the short grass have a kind of raptor-like beak, so they must be hawksbill sea turtles."

Eartha squatted down on the path to get a clearer look at the reptiles. Milly followed suit and asked, "Do you think they are in the grass to lay eggs?"

After giving the question some thought, Eartha said, "No. They would be much better hidden if they were laying eggs. And they lay eggs on sandy beaches. Once the eggs are laid, the mama turtle goes back to the ocean. Maybe these turtles aren't even mamas."

"Or," said Milly, "one might be a male and the other female. Mr. and Mrs. Sedwick Hawksbill, if you please. And maybe they're working on starting a family."

Suddenly, their giggles had them rolling on the ground, hands covering their mouths to keep from drawing attention to themselves. Once they got control of their laughter, they stood, brushed themselves off, and headed back to the beach.

Dole Pineapple Plantation

The library had several books on growing pineapples in Hawai'i, but Eartha and Milly were unable to make heads or tails out of the fertilization process. They caught a bus to Dole Pineapple Plantation, hoping someone there could explain how the soil was treated to grow such sweet-tasting pineapples. Upon arrival, near lunchtime, nobody was around. They walked out to a barn behind the main building. A man dressed like a *paniolo*, a cowboy, was holding the reins of a saddled horse. They walked toward him.

"Can I help you with something?" he asked. "Are you here for a tour?"

"Actually," Milly said, "we would like to know how you treat your soil to grow such sweet pineapples."

"You mean the fertilizing process?"

"Yes," Eartha answered. "Hawaiian soil doesn't seem to be very good for pineapples."

"You're right." The cowboy tossed the reins of his horse on the ground and directed Milly and Eartha to follow him. Inside the barn, he walked over to a wall of shelves.

"The soil on the plantation needs help before it's any good for growing pineapples." He pointed to a stack of bags. "It needs to be more acidic, so we add sulfur and some organic matter, like compost or manure."

Milly wrinkled her nose at the idea of manure being added to the soil to grow sweet pineapples.

"It's sort of a complicated process," he continued. "But does that answer your question?"

"We're studying different kinds of soil around the island," Eartha said. "But it sounds like the soil you use for growing pineapples isn't actually Hawaiian soil by the time you use it."

"I guess you've pretty much hit the nail on the head," the cowboy said with a chuckle. "We don't offer horseback rides here anymore, but if you'd like, I could saddle up a couple of gentle rides and take you back to a small waterfall. How's that sound?"

Because the cowboy looked so much like their grandfathers, both agreed that his offer sounded great. Once the horses were saddled and he had assisted them in mounting, the three of them trotted down a well-worn path past eucalyptus and flowering plumeria trees. Soon they arrived at a medium-sized waterfall. With the cowboy's assistance, they dismounted and walked over to the grotto. He cupped his hands, took a drink of the flowing water, and signaled for them to do the same.

Milly and Eartha were both surprised at how cold the water felt and how delicious it tasted. They were also pleased when the cowboy handed them each a plumeria blossom that he'd gathered from the ground. "Now place the blossom behind your right ear," he told them with a smile, assuming they weren't married women.

The ride back to the plantation barn ended quickly. They thanked the cowboy for the information he had given them and for the generous horseback ride. They also offered a heartfelt *mahalo* for the flowers tucked in their hair.

During the bus ride home, they decided it was finally time to tell their families about their excursions around the island. It would be so much fun to share tales of their adventures.

* * * *

Interest in topics such as soil samples and erosion waned slightly after Eartha and Milly entered high school. Boys became a bit more interesting than sand and dirt. The research with boys involved became even more fun.

Their parents noticed the subtle shift in activity, the less frequent Saturday visits to the library. They understood the sudden interest in boys. They were especially pleased about the lack of sand, mud, and red soil that Eartha and Milly had constantly dragged into the entrance hall after their Saturday "library" sessions.

134

But to no one's surprise, when the two eager book worms eventually headed off to college, they both majored in soil science. Bolstered by their parents' belief that they would become outstanding in their field, Eartha and Milly planned to one day assist in maintaining a healthy *aina*, Hawaiian land.

The Library Steps

By Larry and Rosemary Mild

The smallish town of Farmingville, Georgia, prided itself on its impressive library. Gracing the public green across from Main Street, the one-story white brick structure had a faux marble, pearl-gray façade and four white wood columns. Six genuine marble steps led up to the double front doors.

Inside, over the entrance, a large mural greeted visitors, depicting Johannes Gutenberg and his movable-type press. The librarian's desk sat proudly next to the entrance. A wood railing, just beyond, guarded a flight of steps that led to the basement. The library owed its popularity to its surprisingly large collection of books for all ages, from the children's section to its voluminous reference aisle. Ellen Wainsworth was one of the library's most faithful borrowers.

Her son Buddy sat alone out front on the marble steps. The red-headed youngster sat, knees to chest, over to one side so as not to block anybody going in or coming out. He wore khaki shorts, a red Georgia Bulldog T-shirt, untied sneakers, and a Band-Aid over his left knee. Restless in the scorching August sun this Thursday afternoon, he invented a little game for himself. As each car passed on the street in front of him, the eleven-year-old took aim with his imaginary slingshot. He never missed a *zip-boing* or a *zip-bing-a-bong* sound on each targeted vehicle. Buddy mouthed the *zip* part as he drew back the stiff elastic band. *Boing* was a direct hit and *bing-a-bong* was a ricochet.

"Hey, Buddy, whatcha doing sitting up there?" asked a voice from down on the sidewalk.

"Oh hi, Mitch. Not doing anything. Just waiting for my mom. She's inside swapping off last week's books for some new ones. She's always reading. I bet she's already read half the books in the library."

"Wow! That's a lot of books," said Mitch Butterman. Climbing the steps two at a time, he plopped down next to his sixth-grade classmate. The stocky but nimble boy wore faded baggy jeans and a striped polo.

"Sure as heck is," agreed Buddy.

"Say, it's a whole lot cooler inside the library," said Mitch. "Why don't you wait inside where it's air-conditioned? Like my mom says, 'It's hot as Hades out here this time of day.'"

"Can't."

"Why not?"

"I've been banned," replied Buddy. "Old lady Pritcher, the librarian, told me I can't put one foot inside her library for three whole months."

"Hey, she can't do that—it's a public library," said Mitch.

"My pa says she can," said Buddy. "She's in charge. He told me, 'The poor woman has to keep order in the place.'"

"What did you do to upset the old lady, anyway?" asked Mitch.

"You know those humongous reference books on the corner table?" asked Buddy.

"Yeah!"

"Well, I dropped one of 'em, dead weight, on the floor to see what kind of a booming sound it would make. I also wanted to see how high everyone would jump. I waited until the whole library was ultra-quiet."

"And what happened?" asked Mitch.

"Everyone jumped and then laughed about it, except old Pritcher. She banned me for a whole month. I think she jumped a foot out of her chair."

"But where did the three-month ban come from?" asked Mitch.

"Well, after my one-month ban was over, I tied Maryanne Bunyan's long braid to her chair. She had no idea until she tried to get up and then she let out a scream that was twice as loud as the boom. The effect was perfect. Maryanne didn't know who did it, but right away eagle-eyed Pritcher laced into me. She kicked me out for three months this time."

"Why do you keep aggravating the old lady, anyway?" asked Mitch. "What's she done to you?"

"She's a mean old grouch, always dictating the rules to us, and I aim to keep her on her toes. Besides, it's too much fun to give it all up."

"Hey, you're not cooking up another prank to pull on her when she lets you back in, are you?" asked Mitch.

The freckles on Buddy's fair cheeks danced as he flashed a lop-sided grin. "Well, now that you bring it up, I do have a plan."

Mitch scrunched up his face under his Atlanta Braves baseball cap and thought for a minute. "Hey, Buddy, whatever it is, are you sure? You could get banned from the library for life!"

Buddy scowled. "So what? It'll be worth it."

His friend's brow furrowed. "What are you talking about?"

"Mitch, you're gonna help me. It'll be fun. What if we could sneak inside the library this Saturday night when everyone's at the town hall meeting at the high school? We could raise a bunch of funny business with old lady Pritcher's desk and all her stuff on it and in it. Mess it all up. She wouldn't know what hit her."

"Hey, wait a minute, Buddy. That's pretty serious stuff. The old lady's a grouch, but she's never done anything to me. And what if we get caught?"

"Mitch, you don't have to worry. She's gonna know right off it was me and goose up the punishment plenty. But she won't suspect you. Listen up. I've got this really cool plan. I know the perfect way to get in. There's a broken window in the basement around back of the library next to the fence. There's only a piece of cardboard covering the missing pane. We peel off the cardboard and we're in.

Nothing to it."

Mitch lowered his head, hunched his shoulders, and stuffed his fists into his jeans pockets. "I dunno, Buddy. What you're saying is pretty scary."

Buddy scowled and ran his fingers through his tousled red hair. Suddenly, his green eyes brightened and he said, "Hey, Mitch, I can get you some really neat baseball cards for your collection. Would you come then?"

Mitch's anxious expression faded, but he still cocked his head with suspicion. "How would you manage that?"

Buddy sensed he was getting warm. "My brother has a ton of 'em. He won't miss a few. I'll even get some of the Atlanta Braves ones if I can. So, are you in?"

Mitch's stubborn stance melted. He loved his baseball card collection. "Okay, I'm in. Hey, here comes your mom." He hopped down the steps to the sidewalk. "See you Saturday night."

Buddy tingled with excitement, but kept sober-faced not to betray his emotion to his mother. "See ya, Mitch."

* * * *

Nine o'clock Saturday night came around quickly, too quickly for Mitch. For all his bravado, he hadn't quite made up his mind whether to go through with the break-in or not. The youngster sat on his bed tossing a baseball from one hand to the other, trying to decide what to do. He wasn't a hardened criminal without a conscience. But when Buddy rang the doorbell of the ranch house, Mitch bounced up and out the front door, suddenly sucked in— wooed by thoughts of adventure, especially after Buddy slipped him a fistful of baseball cards.

They had agreed to wear black pants and black T-shirts—Buddy's idea for being less visible on the street. Good logic, except that both tees bore flamboyant graphics. And Mitch had had another moment of guilt pulling on his black pants. His mother had designated these exclusively for Sunday School.

They trotted the six blocks to the library and ran around back. At the broken basement window, Buddy pried off the cardboard with his jackknife. He reached in, unlatched and pushed the window frame out of the way. They slipped inside, dropped down onto a wooden crate below the open window, then slid to the concrete basement floor. Surrounded by a sudden darkness thicker than nighttime itself, they couldn't see a thing. Momentarily, they stood still, clutching each other, their hearts pounding.

"Did you bring a flashlight?" asked Mitch.

"Sure thing," said Buddy. "You think I'm a dummy? But it's a heck of a time for you to be asking about it." He flicked on the beam and swung it all around. "So where are the stairs? All I see is stacks full of old, dusty books down here—boxes, too. Doesn't look like anybody's been down here in a while."

"The stairs are in the front of the building," said Mitch. "They come up to the first floor right behind her desk. I remember seeing the railing there. Follow me."

The boys found the stairs easily and climbed to the main floor. The reading room was dimly lit with an array of low-wattage night lights, creating eerie shadows among the stacks. The boys reached their target, Laura Pritcher's oak desk, and laid the flashlight on top of it. All her daily work items were lined up neatly along the back of the steel desk: a stapler; several rubber stamps hanging from a rotary holder; a large ink pad; and a bottle of ink.

Mitch reached into his deep pants pocket—and slowly lifted out a squirming, complaining little bullfrog, ribbiting away.

Buddy's mouth dropped open. He gawked at the small amphibian—about four inches long with a green head and back and yellow belly. "Man oh man, where'd you get 'im?"

Mitch felt quite puffed up making his special contribution. "Scooped 'im up at Grady's Pond a few days ago. This is Barney. I keep him in a jar with holes punched in the cover." Clutching the throbbing bullfrog in his right hand, with his other hand Mitch pulled open the librarian's largest desk drawer, the bottom one on the left. He set the bullfrog down in front of a lineup of file folders. "There you go, Barney, Now you can scare the panties off old lady Pritcher."

"Yikes!" Buddy sputtered. "Won't he smother inside there?"

"Nope," answered Mitch. "I'm leaving the drawer open a crack. He'll have plenty of air."

Time to get going with the plan. Buddy removed the top drawer on the right and dumped the contents onto the top of the desk. He then turned the empty drawer upside down and slid it back into place. Mitch emptied the librarian's stapler and threw the staples into the middle top drawer. Buddy changed the month, day, and year on her date stamp and interchanged all the labels on each of her other rubber stamps hanging on the rotary hanger. The labels easily slipped out of their channels. Mitch added a tad too much ink to the inking pad so it would squirt out when pressed or pounded. The ink bottle with its eye dropper top was just too handy to be denied.

"That ought to do it," said Buddy. "That'll teach her to mess with the masses." *Whatever that means*, he thought. He'd read it somewhere. "Now let's get out of here."

"What was that noise?" asked Mitch.

"What noise?"

"Someone's at the door," said Mitch. "Quick, hide in the stacks."

They bolted for the stacks and wound up in separate but adjacent aisles. They heard a rattling of the library's front door. Fearing they'd be caught in the act, the boys cowered between the stacks for several minutes—the only sound being the second hand of the electric clock on the wall. Tick, tick, tick…Quite a few clock ticks after the rattling of the door stopped, the boys came out of hiding.

"It must have been the cops checking to see if the front door was locked," whispered Mitch. "I guess they do that every evening about this time."

"Let's get out of here," said Buddy. "Something doesn't feel right about this whole thing."

"Yeah," said Mitch. "The town hall meeting's going to be breaking up soon, and I'd better be home when my folks get there, or I'll be grounded for life."

The two prowlers retraced their path down the stairs, across the basement floor. They used the same packing crate to get high up enough to shinny through the open window out onto the ground. Carefully, Mitch replaced the cardboard to cover the empty window space. At this point they parted, each setting out for his own home.

* * * *

All day Sunday passed without a hitch. But around the supper table that evening Buddy learned some disturbing news. He was finishing off two scoops of Rocky Road ice cream while his mother washed the dishes and his father dried. His parents were conversing as they worked. Buddy was only half-listening until he heard the librarian's name. He perked up his ears and tuned in.

"Gertrude Plumber told me, in confidence, that Mrs. Pritcher's husband is facing surgery for prostate cancer," said Mom. "Quite advanced, too."

"Oh boy, that's rough!" replied Dad. "Say, didn't they just lose their only son in the Middle East fighting?"

"Yes," said Mom, "and they just received some medal for his heroism as well."

"Now that you mention it," said Dad, "I remember seeing it in the paper."

Buddy was so taken aback that the spoonful of ice cream on its way to his mouth melted sufficiently to slide off the spoon and plop onto the floor. His eyes widened and his stomach lurched. He felt sick. *So that's why she was so grouchy to everybody and mean sometimes. She had every right to be. Oh my God! Our pranks. We were the real mean ones. We've got to undo the pranks. She really wasn't so bad. Pa was right—she just needed to keep order in the reading room. I need to talk to Mitch and undo everything.*

* * * *

That night Buddy hugged his mom and dad goodnight and went to bed—but stayed in his shorts and T-shirt. He waited until eleven o'clock, when he was sure his parents were asleep. Then he pulled on his sneakers, grabbed his flashlight, and slipped out the first-floor window to the ground before running all the way to Mitch's house. Standing on tiptoe, he rapped on the window pane he knew belonged to Mitch's bedroom. It took another ten minutes for his friend to respond, then minutes more to explain what they had to do. Mitch jumped into his clothes and climbed out the bedroom window to join Buddy. They ran the whole half-mile to the library.

The boys slipped into the basement via their original entry window and made their way upstairs. Somehow it felt easier breaching the sanctity of the library the second time. Their mission was to right a wrong.

Putting things right took time. Buddy first turned the right-hand drawer right-side-up. Next he attacked the pile of stuff he'd dumped out, neatly placing each item back in the best order he could remember. Mitch refilled the stapler. Next, he corrected the month, day, and year on the date-due stamp, and re-matched all the rubber-stamp labels. Squeezing the excess ink from the stamp pad proved messy. He ended up with telltale black ink spots on his fingers. But the worst was yet to come.

Mitch lifted Barney out of the bottom file drawer, but underestimated his pet's distress—and smarts. Barney leaped out of his hands onto the floor and escaped. Chasing a loose bullfrog through stack after stack took not only time, but acumen and swiftness as well. Mitch finally pounced on him and returned him to his glass jar.

The boys left the library as they had before, remembering to tape the cardboard over the empty window frame. By now it was four a.m. Buddy and Mitch had one last chore. They trotted the eight blocks to Grady's Pond, where Mitch solemnly returned Barney to his rightful home. The boys returned to their beds an hour before sunup with none of their parents the wiser.

During the next few weeks of his exile from the library, Buddy had plenty of time to think. Revenge had not brought the feeling of triumph that he'd expected. In fact, it had made him feel like crap.

These days, while sitting on the library steps, he's taking a different tack, asking his mother to bring him books to read. He surprised the dickens out of himself by enjoying them. And when he was finally allowed back inside, Mrs. Pritcher discovered a polite visitor and enthusiastic reader.

One afternoon a month later, as the boys were walking home from school together, Mitch abruptly stopped on the sidewalk and faced his friend. "Wait, Buddy! I have something to tell you." His round face flushed. "Hey, Buddy. I know I let you suck me into our…thing…because I wanted your brother's baseball cards. But I can't keep 'em. It's just not right. They're valuable. One is Hank Aaron! So here they are." Mitch pulled them gently out of his cargo pants pocket. "Take 'em back to your brother."

The freckles danced on Buddy's cheeks as he broke into a broad smile. Carefully tucking the cards into his backpack, he said, "Thanks. I felt real bad. I just didn't know how to ask for them back." The boys hugged.

Even Barney the bullfrog learned his own lesson. He never swam near the shallow shores of Grady's Pond again—at least not when any kids were in sight.

§

The Library Dwelf

by David W. Jones

If you went into the community library in the small town of Blue Diamond, Colorado, looking for a librarian, you would be excused for thinking this library completely lacked a librarian. Or it only had a *bad* example of that unique and wonderful species.

The children's librarian's desk would be vacant, with a small sign on it directing you to the information desk.

The information desk would have its empty chair neatly tucked up against it, with a sign directing you to the checkout counter.

The checkout counter would be *sans* humans. A pair of computer terminals sitting on the counter would give you baleful looks, wondering what you were doing there.

But in these pre-Internet days, you need a new roommate, and the library has copies of the local newspaper where you can check the "Looking for roommates" ads.

Unfortunately, they're kept locked up because the librarian (yes, this library has a bad example of a librarian) hates people messing them up. So you must ask the librarian to unlock them so you can look at them.

The security guard nods distantly at you as you walk back to the front door and ask about the librarian. He only took the position to stretch out his monthly Social Security check while he thinks about writing the Great American Novel. He only stirs from his chair when his bladder calls for a toilet visit. As he is well up in age now, that happens frequently. So sometimes he isn't there either.

But today, you're in luck.

"Out in the stacks," he replies. "She's a firm believer in keeping them clean, organized, and free of vermin."

As he speaks, a small, dirty, smelly homeless "person" bearing a big backpack scuttles in through the front door. The guard glances as it aims for the restroom. "Long as it doesn't get into the stacks," he says.

You stare. It doesn't look to you like an actual person, but it's not an "it" either.

As you stand there expectantly, looking pointedly at the police-style walkie-talkie mic clipped to the guard's uniform, he continues. "The librarian also particularly loathes all forms of literature that involve outlandish fictions. So you might go check the Fantasy and Science Fiction sections. About this time of day she'll be there, removing books she doesn't approve of."

The guard leans back in his chair and closes his eyes.

The homeless person looks out the restroom door at the guard, then scuttles off into the stacks.

"You might go follow that elf-dwarf-whatever," the guard says. "They always like the Fantasy stacks best."

Then the guard starts to snore.

After looking back and forth between the guard and the direction the homeless person went, you follow the signs to the Fantasy section. You find the librarian standing in the middle of the aisle between shelves, frantically thumbing the security alarm button on the lapel of her prim and proper blouse, and angrily addressing the homeless person. "I've told you many times you're not welcome here," she hisses. Librarians never shout. They only speak in hush. "You have no business here. I don't care what you think is real or not. *Fantasy is not real* and I'll throw out the whole lot as soon as the district librarian approves my request."

"But this is my home!" The voice sounds like a voice that grating rocks might have and, simultaneously, a clear, clean, flute-like, melodious voice. As if there were two separate larynxes? It sounds like each different voice is actually speaking some other language besides English.

You look at the small homeless being. It stands about a foot taller than the librarian's waist. Of indeterminate gender? No. There's a beard. Definitely male—dressed rather archaically in a floppy leather hat, breeches, an undertunic, an overtunic, worn boots. With an old-style leather pack strapped across his back.

His face is an odd mix of features. On closer inspection, any part of the face you might consider graceful is coarser and slightly distorted. And any part you might consider ugly or malformed is actually more symmetrical and well-formed.

Thick, dirty hair hangs below his shoulders.

His beard is darker than you might expect, but thin in patches and rather ordinary.

The ears that poke through the hair show themselves to be fine and pointed.

"I don't care if this is your home or not," the librarian says. "If you cleaned up and got a job, you wouldn't be homeless. Where is that security guard?"

"Just coming up behind you," the homeless person says, making an odd hand gesture and muttering something under his breath. The librarian turns and suddenly starts talking angrily to the empty air.

"Where have you been? You let this filthy vermin in here," she hisses. "Get rid of it."

You look at where she's looking, and see something that might be a faint image of the guard. The image looks past the librarian, then looks around. It's clear that the image sees neither the homeless person nor you.

You hear a thin, almost-might-be-the-sound-of-a-voice say, "Ma'am, what are you talking about?"

As the librarian turns round to the guard and starts verbally berating him, the homeless person looks over at you. "Oh, you're still here and you can see me?"

Listening to the librarian's increasingly less chaste idea of curse words, you nod.

"You must be a fantasy reader. Only fantasy readers can see me."

You nod again. "What's going on here?"

"Just a bit of magik. Let's get out of here while she's busy." The guard's image is looking more bewildered, and the librarian's voice is edging more and more out of "hush" territory as the homeless person turns down the aisle away from the argument. "Come on."

You follow him without more than a passing thought. Could fantasy be real? As you turn the corner, you think, *Would that be good—or bad?*

The homeless person takes a couple of twists and turns that don't quite seem to match up with the arrangement of shelves in the library. After a final turn, you follow him into an alcove. It seems to be in a corner, where some shelves meet against a wall, but all the book spines face *away* from the alcove. Like you're on the inside of the shelves. You glance out over some books, through the space between the top of the books and the shelf above. Everything out there looks normal: fluorescent lights, carpeting, people sitting at tables reading books.

When you look back, everything inside looks like it came out of the Middle Ages. A small fire provides flickering light near a bed formed from piles of old cloth. A window looks out over a forest lit by a full moon.

The air out there is clear, unlike the town's usual gray haze. The air in here smells of smoke. The smoke swirls around the space before floating out through the window.

The homeless person shrugs off his pack. "I don't feel like spending magik to make you forget me, so sit down. Have some beer."

You look at him. You look back the way you came. Your mouth hangs open. You look back at him. He's holding out a wooden tankard with a yeasty smell and a head of foam. "No better beer in all the world, even if I say so myself."

You meet his eyes. You remember those years growing up, when classmates made fun of you for reading *The Lord of the Rings*; talking about *The Worm Ourobouros*; inventing role-playing games; and attending the Black Pointe Renaissance Fair instead of football games and parties.

You decide something, sit across the fire from him, and accept the offered tankard. He raises his own, and you self-consciously tap yours against his.

"Thank you, sir!" you say.

"I'm no knight." He pauses, tips his tankard back, and drinks some down. You can hear him swallowing. Even gulping. "Just Oaktree Stonebreaker, as my accursed parents named me. You can call me Oak." He takes another gulp or two. "No one would make me a knight. Even if I weren't what I am, I'm not old enough for that. You have to be sixteen. I ran away well before that."

The beer is a bit flat, but the taste is rich and yeasty. As if it had never heard of homogenization. Fresh from malt, hops, pure water. You find yourself very thirsty, and down half the tankard without thinking.

You hope this isn't one of those strong beers. You remember the one time you went to a party in high school. Someone tricked you into drinking a strong beer, and you ended up throwing up, completely embarrassing yourself while everyone laughed at you.

Oak looks up at you, a glint in his eye. "Don't worry about that. This isn't one of your modern alcohol-loaded beers. This has just enough brewing to make the water it comes from drinkable."

You consider this a moment, then drink some more. "You can read my mind?"

Oak smiles. "Only through my elvish side."

"So you're elvish?"

"Half."

You study Oak's face and form again, matching things up with memories of what you've read. "And the other half is…dwarf?"

Oak nods warily.

"But elves and dwarves can't interbreed—"

Oak grunts. "Tell my bloody parents that."

You think about it. *Oak exists, therefore it must be possible, therefore…* "I might call you a Dwelf then."

"If you must."

"You said something about your *accursed* parents?"

"According to my father, my mother seduced him. According to her, he raped her. They were both drunk. I think some evil wizard cursed them. Either way, neither of their peoples accepted them. After I was born, they considered me too ugly to be claimed by either race, so they abused me until I finally ran away."

"How old were you when you ran away?"

"Twelve."

You mull over how you'd report child abuse in a fantasy world. "Does anyone else know about this?"

Oak grimaces. "I told the librarian about it once. When I first met her. I thought she might be more open-minded than she turned out to be. She proceeded to insist that dwarfs and elves don't exist. Couldn't accept the evidence of her own eyes." Oak sighs, a combination of rumble and flute. "That happens to me a lot."

He sags and gulps down some more beer.

You heft your tankard, finding it somehow full again. You take a big swallow and study Oak some more. Now that you think about it, you can see the places where the elf and dwarf parts come through. Some patches of skin, swarthy and rough, other patches pale and smooth. One eyebrow is thick and curly. The other eyebrow has the thin fineness of an elf. His eyes are dark and sunken under a strong brow, but there's elvish light in their depths.

"I think you are both, just unevenly mixed by whatever magik brought you into being," you say.

"The curse. Neither elf nor dwarf. My parents used to say that I'm so ugly I must be human." Oak chugs down some more beer. "But you humans don't accept me either. I'm filthy vermin. Ignored. Hated. Chased out whenever they can find me. Hear what I mean?"

The librarian's voice comes as if from a distance, still berating the illusion of the guard, but now much louder than a mere hush.

"But she's wrong," you say. "Not all humans are like that."

You drink more beer as Oak gives you a skeptical look. Then you meet his eyes.

"That was a slick illusion spell you worked on the librarian. Do you think the real guard has even budged from his chair?"

Oak smiles.

"And I bet you're just as good with dwarf magik as you are with the elvish."

Oak's smile widens. He scoops up some ash from the fire, closes his fist, mutters some words over it, then opens it to reveal a small rough diamond.

Your jaw drops in amazement. "And if something unfriendly came through that window from the forest, you'd be able to take it down equally well using either elvish or dwarven weapons."

"Damn right."

"Well, Oak, all my friends are fantasy readers. So they could see you. And they all invent role-playing games, too, so they'd think you were the ultimate in cool. They'd accept you," you say, and stop with a sudden touch of shyness.

Oak raises his thick eyebrow.

"And…my roommate just moved out, so I could use a new one. How'd you like to move into a real home?"

"I don't have a job," Oak says. "What about rent?"

You grin. "Oh, a diamond or two would be more than enough. I'm sure you could find other work with your stone-working skills. Do we have a deal?"

Oak sticks out his hand. "Put it there, roomie."

A few magik gestures by Oak return the library alcove to normal and the pack to his back. Then you two trace the path back into the library, walk unseen past the shouting librarian and the snoring guard, then go out the front door, heading for home.

§

A Needle in a Library Stack

by Shauna Jones

Julia Francine Saville slammed the door closed after entering her attorney's office. Steaming silently, she watched Russell Harrison half-jump in his chair. All his desk papers flew throughout the room.

Russell, the newest counselor in her late grandfather's San Francisco law office, stammered, "What the…" The tall auburn-haired man leaned down to pick up the fallen documents, scooping up an armful. "Hello, Julia. I take it you got the letter from Angela's lawyer." Russell pushed his hair off his forehead while putting a calming smile on his face.

"You didn't bother to tell me these past three months that I'll be homeless within a week of graduating from UC Berkeley, courtesy of my cousin." Julia balled her fingers, ready to punch his sympathetic face, then found herself fighting off the urge. "Graduation's in three days!"

"Mr. Harrison, do you need any help with the papers on the floor?"

Both turned to see the long-time secretary, Mabel Curtis, standing in the now-open door. As far as Julia knew, the statuesque woman had been around since before her grandfather started with the firm over half a century ago.

Russell smiled, "Thank you for asking, Miss Curtis." He gathered up the last few sheets from the floor. "I think we've got everything. We're good here."

Julia stared at the floor as the secretary left the room and quietly closed the door.

Russell cleared his throat. But before he could say anything, Julia put up her hand and said, "I'm sorry."

She crossed the room and sat down in a brown leather chair. As she felt her body meld into the chair, the past happiness and joy of being with her grandfather as a child stirred in her mind. The refusal to be silent deepened in her soul.

"Staying in the sorority house on campus is easier with my classes than traveling back and forth from the family Berkeley Hills cottage. Now that I'm graduating and leaving the sorority house, I plan to move back full-time to the house I grew up in and love. My grandparents have told me since I was ten years old that the house would belong to me after I received my college diploma. It was what they wanted for me. But according to this letter, my cousin Angela now owns the house."

"That letter from Angela is a lot of hot air," Russell replied. "Her attorney doesn't have the documents."

"The letter says I can't go onto the property until the court date for a judge to listen to our case. I have to move out."

"Not true," said Russell. "You can stay on the property until the hearing. If we can find your grandfather's original final will and property deed, then we can prove you are the only benefactor."

"Where are the documents that show that I am now the legal owner? I've been meeting with you for the last three months on this." Julia's anger turned to a quiet simmer. "All I know is Grandpa hid the will and property deed inside one of his books. I remember him saying that the book was in his law office. He died before telling me the title."

"Do you have any ideas which book?"

"I don't know which book! I remember that small bookcase filled with first-edition classics in his law office. It was leaning against the wall next to the window overlooking the Golden Gate

Bridge. It was a great place to read. Where is it now?"

"I don't know." Russell looked around the room. "I remember seeing it when I took over this office. I glanced over the titles on my way home last Friday afternoon. I thought I'd look at them more closely after the weekend."

"So what happened to the bookcase, and the books in it?"

"They were gone come Monday. I asked around and never got an answer."

Russell picked up the office phone and dialed. "Miss Curtis, could you please come in?" He paused. "Very good. Thank you."

The secretary came in with a notepad and pen. "What can I do for you?"

Julia looked at Russell. He nodded. She said, "We were wondering what happened to the small oak bookcase that was in this room. It held my grandfather's first-edition 19th-century British, French, and American children's classics and mysteries. Grandpa had the books mainly for kids who came with the adults to have something to do. I read most of them myself while I hung out at his office at various times over the years. Some of my happiest memories growing up were being with Grandpa Art and Grandma Letty."

"I remember the books," said Mabel. "Your grandfather loved reading them himself. It provided short moments of relaxation for him during a busy day."

"Do you know what happened to them?" Russell inquired.

"That's the strangest thing." Mabel took a deep breath. "Early on Monday, I got a memo from one of the firm's partners asking me to empty the bookcase and box and catalog the titles. I sent everything to the Rare Books Librarian at the UC Berkeley Library before 9 a.m."

"Do you still have the memo?" Russell asked. "How many books were there?"

"There were 120 books. The weird thing is the memo disappeared from my desk while I took the books down to be shipped to the university. I couldn't find it anywhere. It's the only time that has ever happened to me." She sighed. "But I still have the book catalog list in my files."

"Is it possible for us to see that list?" Julia asked. "It's really important."

"Of course. I'll get it right away." The secretary returned with two copies of the book catalog list. She gave one to Russell and the second one to Julia.

"How many boxes did you send to the university?" Russell asked.

Mabel answered, "Four boxes. Anything else?"

"Thanks. That's all." Russell smiled.

She returned to her desk, leaving the door open.

Julia got up from her chair and closed the door. "Someone else in this firm sent those books to my university library. Not me. We may never find out who or why."

"But they were rare books. Do you know the Rare Books Librarian at UC Berkeley?" Russell asked.

"Not personally. I know him by sight." Julia blew out air from her mouth. "Benjamin Thompson has only been around for a few years."

Russell looked up from the catalog list. "The books have probably been cataloged and placed on the library shelves."

"It will be like looking for a needle in a haystack," Russell and Julia said at the same time.

"So let's get started," Russell said, and picked up his phone. "Let's talk to him right now." He dialed the UC Berkeley Library.

"Good morning. May I speak with the Rare Books Librarian?"

Julia prayed that Mr. Thompson was still around. She sat leaning toward the call.

The attorney nodded toward her with a thumbs-up.

With a sigh of relief, Julia edged back into her chair.

"Good morning, Mr. Thompson. I'm calling on behalf of my client about four boxes of first-edition classics my law firm sent to the UC Berkeley Library by accident on Monday of this week. Have you received anything like this? We would like to get the boxes back as soon as possible."

Silence reigned as Russell listened to the man's answers.

"Thank you." Turning to Julia, he said, "The boxes are still in the back room waiting to be looked at."

Julia smiled for the first time since receiving her cousin's letter.

"My client will be there this afternoon. Her name is Julia Saville."

Nodding toward her lawyer, Julia mouthed, "Is three o'clock okay?"

"She'll be there at three o'clock. Thank you for your help. Have a good day. Goodbye."

"This is great! Thank you so much." Julia smiled at Russell.

"Thompson has an off-campus appointment this afternoon and will not be around. His assistant, Daphne, will help you."

"Fine. I'm off to hunt for that book."

"Speedy luck. Bring back the books and the documents as soon as you can," said Russell.

* * * *

Julia walked into the library a few minutes before her appointment. Her sorority sister, Susan Rose Montgomery, was waiting in one of the chairs near the entrance.

"Hi, Susan. I'm glad I called you, and so relieved that you could make it. You know the library staff better than I do."

"Happy to help," Susan said. "I already talked with the library assistant, Daphne Williams. She's in the library basement still looking for the boxes from the law office."

"Good, let's go help her. I have the copies of the book list for everyone." Julia pulled the sheets out of her purse and handed a copy to Susan. "The documents have to be somewhere in those boxes."

Susan smiled encouragement to Julia as they walked down the basement stairs. As they entered the room, Daphne slowly dropped a heavy box next to two others onto the table.

"We're here to help go through the books," said Julia. "Where's the fourth box?"

"Good question." Daphne stretched her hands and fingers from the heavy weight. "This morning there were four boxes. I know because I filed the paperwork after receiving them when they were delivered."

"Could anyone else have been down here with these boxes?" Julia asked.

"Not today. I've been down here most of the day organizing the donations. Besides, I've locked the door every time I've left the room." Daphne rolled her eyes. "That fourth box has to be somewhere in the library."

"Well, let's tackle these three boxes and see what we find." Julia opened the nearest box. "By the way, here's the list of the books we want to check."

In the second box, Susan opened up a copy of *The Wind in the Willows*. She sighed. "The illustrations are really beautiful. The colors still shine even though it's a first edition."

Susan thumbed through the book. On the inside of the back cover, she noticed a small tear that had the look of being glued back together. The glue had dried out and the paper had come apart again.

Carefully, she lifted the page apart from the back cover. A thin envelope that people used to send letters via airmail became visible. She pulled it completely out. "Look what I found!" She handed Julia the envelope.

Julia turned it over. "The letter is addressed to my grandfather from my uncle, Robert Morgan Saville." She pulled out three thin sheets of paper, laid them out, and stretched the pages on the wood table. "Thankfully, his handwriting has always been easy to read. I got a number of letters from him while growing up, especially after my dad died. And believe it or not, I still use the same airmail stationery."

After speed-reading the letter, Julia looked up at the two other women with tears slowly running down her face. "I had no idea of any of this."

Susan wrapped her arms around Julia. "Tell us what happened."

She took the letter from Julia's hands and gave it to Daphne.

Daphne paged through it. "Oh my God. No wonder these books were sent here and one of the boxes is still missing."

"Having me own the Berkeley Hills cottage is not popular with everyone in the family," Julia said, studying the pages again. "My grandfather's family has owned the cottage since the 1890s. It was always a vacation place for them. All the holidays were spent at the cottage with the family and cousins." She wiped the tears off her face with a tissue that Susan gave her. "According to this letter, both my grandfather and uncle were unhappy with the way my father handled his marriage to my mother. My mother always told me during her young and crazy phase that I was the greatest blessing that ever happened to her. I've always felt complete love by everyone in the family, even by a father who I only saw a few times a year, as he was constantly traveling."

Susan took her turn slowly reading. "Your uncle was furious that his brother, Theodore MacDonald, divorced your mother, Francine Marie Cresson, and left both of you destitute while he was on business trips that lasted three to four months. He left no money for your mother to pay the bills. By the time you were five years old, your grandparents and uncle decided to move the two of you into the Berkeley Hills cottage. The grandparents visited on the weekends. Your uncle arranged a job for your mother at a nearby bank."

"My mother did well, and eventually became the bank's vice president. She was always there for all my sports and other activities."

"Also," Susan added, "your uncle paid for court costs for your mother's divorce. He didn't want his brother to know that. He was adamant about you having the cottage. After your father died in the plane accident, he was your grandfather's only child left alive."

Daphne blew air through her mouth. "Uncle Robert bypassed his three children so you could be the only heir to the cottage."

Susan sighed. "What an amazing guy that uncle of yours is."

Julia nodded. Tears formed in her eyes.

"I've gone through the third box and didn't find the documents," stated Daphne. "That means we have to search through this basement for that missing box. The will and the property deed have to be somewhere."

A loud bang sounded behind them. The door to the room swung open. A tall, thin brunette with a short pixie haircut filled the doorway carrying a large box. She walked over to the table and placed it in front of them.

Shock ran down Julia's spine. "Angela, what are you doing here?"

"Good to see you too, Cousin. You may not be happy with me after what I have to tell you."

Angela moved the books around inside her box. "What you're looking for is in here." She gently rubbed her hand over a first edition of *The Secret Garden*, then handed the book to Julia. "This is where Grandpa Art hid the will and property deed."

"But why?" Julia stammered.

"I know that I've driven you crazy these past three months because I've been adamant about owning the cottage instead of you." Angela rolled her eyes. "And now I'm giving you the missing documents on a silver platter." She sighed. "The truth is my 'perfect' dad."

Julia shook her head. "What does Uncle Robert have to do with this?"

"How about everything?" Angela said. "He had known that I was jealous of you since we were kids. All everyone talked about was how you love the cottage, helping with the garden, taking care of everything in and around the property. You were the perfect caretaker for the cottage."

Angela swallowed hard. "I had told my father that I wanted to inherit the Berkeley property after your father's plane accident. I figured since Dad was the last surviving son, he would get all the family properties. I was entering college at the time. The property would help me after I got my degree. My plan was to rent it out when the family wasn't using it for their own vacation times. I cooked up the plan with my boyfriend. To my greatest anger, Dad told me 'No.' As Uncle Ted's daughter, the land was yours."

Angela paused for a moment to collect herself. "Dad found out what my boyfriend and I were doing, along with my mother's blessing through my two brothers. Just a few hours ago, Dad told her he would divorce her and disinherit me by next week if we went through with our plan. To say the least, my mother caved on the spot, leaving my boyfriend and me hanging in the wind."

"Did Julia's lawyer write the memo?" Susan asked.

"No, I wrote it," Angela answered, then took a deep breath. "My boyfriend just delivered it. The law partner had nothing to do with it."

Julia glared at her cousin. "You'd better hope Russell is more forgiving than I would be."

Angela stared at the floor. "I hope so." She sighed. "The will is inside the front cover of *The Secret Garden* and the property deed is in the back cover."

"That has always been my favorite childhood story," Julia mused. "That is how I got interested in gardening." She spotted her cousin's shame. "Thank you for bringing the documents and books back to me."

"I'm sorry this happened between us."

"What are you going to do now?" Susan asked.

"Well, the good news is, Dad won't charge my boyfriend or me for any illegal doings."

"I'm glad about that." Julia smiled. "So, what are your current plans?"

"I broke up with my boyfriend. I've bought a one-way ticket to London. Dad has arranged some job interviews."

"When do you fly to London?" Julia asked.

"Red-Eye tonight. I've always had a boyfriend since I was fourteen. I think it's time for me to fly solo." Angela shrugged her shoulders. "Now you can rest peacefully, as you are the proud owner of our family Berkeley Hills cottage."

Julia looked a bit sad after saying goodbye to her cousin. The basement door closed.

"Let's get the four boxes into your car, along with the documents." Susan said. "I'll drive with you into San Francisco. Afterward, we can find a great restaurant to celebrate your victory."

"I can't wait to return the books to their rightful place." Julia laughed with joy.

§

Sherlock Goldlock and the
Case of the Missing Library

by David W. Jones

The village of Upper Lower East Midgewick-by-the-Thames was just outside the greater London area, and felt rebuffed at not having been included. However, it was proud of its exceptional Community Library. Scholars from around the world sought it out due to its range of resource materials and its world-class, award-winning librarian.

So when the village found that someone had stolen their library, the word quickly went out for help.

The security guard nodded respectfully at the tall, muscular man clad in an overcoat and wearing a deerstalker cap. Under the cap, the man's hair hung heavily down his back, gleaming like metallic gold.

For it was metallic gold. The world-renowned *Fae*-cursed detective Sherlock Goldlock was dispatched to solve the mystery.

Where the library had been was an empty space.

"Sir, I swear it was here yesterday when I left," the guard said.

The detective studied the remnants of the library's foundation. "I see no footprints other than yours. Where was the librarian when you left?"

"She said she was going to make one last sweep of the library to make sure no vermin had sneaked in after closing time. She locked herself inside the library."

"So we are not only missing a library, we are missing a librarian."

"Yes sir. And, begging your pardon, if you don't mind me asking, is your hair *really* gold?"

The detective drew himself up to his full height and looked down on the guard. "Begging *your* pardon, if you don't mind me asking, is your head *really empty?*"

"Please excuse Mr. Goldlock," said an Italian greyhound seated beside Goldlock's feet. A talking dog? The guard stared as the dog continued. "He finds it challenging when dealing with people he regards as less smart than he is."

"Shut up, Gelert," Goldlock said angrily.

The small dog stood, stretched, opened his mouth, and tugged on Goldlock's long hair. "Getting time for a trim, eh? The Faery Queen isn't nearly as stupid as the way you treated her."

"Oh shut up," Goldlock's shoulders slumped. He looked down at the dog. "So…anything there where the library was?"

The dog stepped to the edge of the sidewalk. It listened, lowered its nose to the dirt, and sniffed.

"I smell magik there. Can't tell if it's dark-evil, or merely someone playing a prank."

"Pretty potent magik then! Is it…" Goldlock paused. "The queen?"

The dog looked up at him. "Don't be silly. Not someone as powerful as she is."

"You mean there are *other Fae* as crazy and mean as she—"

The dog glared at him. "Keep insulting her, and see how long it takes before she lifts her curse. I tell you, having eighty pounds of gold hanging from your head *when you are eighty* will be *no fun at all.*"

The dog pointed its head into the empty space. "I smell some intense magik that direction. I think it's in the middle. Also, something there really stinks. See anything? Human eyes are better than mine."

The guard looked. "No, the place is empty."

"Not you," the dog said, then nudged Goldlock.

Goldlock put his hand on the dog's head, and saw into the space via the dog's magik. He stared into the lot. In a distance that seemed far too great to fit inside the space of the missing library, he saw something. He squinted.

"It looks like a well. A low, circular stone wall, a couple of posts holding up a roof, maybe. A bucket sitting on the wall with a rope attached to it." Goldlock studied it some more. "And there seems to be a dark bird sitting beside the bucket. Larger than the bucket. Maybe a crow? Although it looks so far away, it could actually be much larger."

"Thought I smelled something," the dog said. "We don't know who's behind this, so we better be careful. We don't want more curses!"

Goldlock nodded. His neck and shoulder muscles bulged as he shook his hair out—the curse, and benefit, of having hair made of gold. Then he turned to the guard. The guard stared in confusion at the empty lot, then at the detective.

"Tell them I'm taking the case." Goldlock stared at the well in the empty lot. He saw the bird return his stare. "Come on, Gelert. The game is afoot!"

He and the dog stepped off the sidewalk together, and that step took them straight to the well. The bird hopped to the opposite side of the well. This close, it was no mere crow but a raven. A large raven. And it really, really stunk.

"Took you long enough," it said. "I thought you'd stand around there forever."

Gelert growled, stalking around the well. The raven hopped up onto the small roof above the well.

"Don't you try it, you stupid dog. You deserve what happened to you," the raven said, then looked at Goldlock. "Or you, you stupid changeling. Are you here to fight, or to solve the mystery of the missing library?"

Gelert growled. "I'm happy with the fight option."

Goldlock joined the dog. "No, we must save the library. And

the librarian."

At the reminder, Gelert stepped back. Goldlock studied the bird and glanced at the well. "It's in the well, isn't it?"

The bird snickered. "Of course."

"And to get it back, one of us must go down the well," Goldlock added.

"Why, you *are* almost as smart as you think you are," the bird said. "Of course, if either of you just jump down the well, you'll fall to the bottom and kill yourself. So you have to climb down the rope." The bird glanced at the dog, then stared straight at Goldlock. "And that requires hands."

The dog jumped and snarled, but the bird flew up out of reach and circled. "So what's it to be?"

Goldlock looked at the dog. "I'm the only one who can do it." The dog growled. "I'm sorry. What I need you to do is to stay here and make sure that bird behaves itself until I'm back."

The dog whined. Goldlock smiled. "I'll be okay, as long as I have a way back up from this well."

The bird settled back on the roof of the well.

The dog's whine turned into a low growl. "Don't you try anything, bird," the dog said, fixing its predatory gaze on the raven. "I've got your number."

The bird watched as Goldlock climbed into the well and went down the rope, hand over hand.

As Goldlock disappeared into the darkness, the bird sprang into the air laughing. "My, are you two idiots!"

As the dog leaped, the bird vanished, the roof fell into the well, and the well collapsed into nothing but a pile of earth. The pile scattered as the dog dug frantically, howling. But all it found was more earth. The well was gone.

At the bottom of the well, Goldlock looked up and noted the lack of any daylight. As he expected, the well was a trap. While the bottom and sides seemed dry, it smelled close and humid, earthy, with the stench of bird poop. That made sense. Whoever that bird was, it wasn't a nice bird at all. He hoped Gelert got it.

Going back up wouldn't help. He could climb the rope, but he was certain the opening of the well was closed now. And there was still a library and an innocent librarian down here to save.

He saw two doors on opposite sides of the well: an old Victorian one, thick and wooden; the other a modern glass door. In fact, it was the front door of the library. Modern lighting shining through the glass lit up the entire well.

He opened the library door and stepped through into modern air-conditioned comfort, with no stench of bird.

The librarian ran up to him, looking relieved.

"You're the famous detective! I've tried to get out, but every door out of the library takes me back in the front door. I even tried the door to the roof. And the phones don't work. The water, lights, and toilets still work, but I ate my lunch yesterday, haven't had dinner, and I'm starving!"

Goldlock looked around. He pushed discreetly at the inside of the library door and felt it move. He glanced back through the glass and noted the well still visible outside. He thought it likely that he could get out. The foul monster behind this couldn't be interested in a library, no matter how knowledge-filled it was, and a librarian, no matter how irreplaceable she was.

He gave her a quick summary of what he'd discovered so far: how the library had been sucked into the land of Faery by parties unknown for mysterious purposes. "That's why I'm on the case."

"Oh dear!"

"You'll be okay. I'll get to the bottom of this, don't you worry! I've never failed to solve a case, and it won't happen now," he said confidently.

"I'm sure you will. I've heard you're very smart!"

"Why yes, I am. I practically grew up in a library! I read everything I could get my hands on." He paused. It was easy to talk, but in the middle of a case the outcome could still be uncertain. What if the librarian really was the criminal's target? "I'm not about to let anyone steal a library! Or you."

"So what do we do?"

"I'm going back out that door," he said, gesturing towards the library door. "Across from this door is one that looks like it goes into an old Victorian building."

"I saw it through the glass. May I go with you?" she asked, trembling slightly.

"I don't think you want to. I think the criminals behind this whole case are there. Who knows what they might do to you if you came through their door?"

"Something awful, I'm sure! But I still want to go, now that you're here. You're very handsome and well-muscled, you know."

"Why thank you! You are quite pert and attractive, and, being a librarian, very smart yourself. Perhaps after I solve this case, you would like to join me for dinner tonight?"

"Oh, that sounds lovely," she said. "Now can we try going out the door?"

"We can try, but I don't think you're the one they want." He paused. "In fact, I think you'll wind up back here…"

"Let's try! I've got to get out of here. My parents must be horribly worried by now!"

Goldlock looked at her. "You have no special man waiting for you?"

"No, I live alone. The right man just hasn't come along yet, so I still want to go out with you, I mean, out the door."

"You're very brave."

"Before I was a librarian, I was a Girl Scout Guide. I can handle anything!"

"Okay. Let me lead. You follow as close behind me as possible."

"Yes, sir!"

He faced the door. She stepped up close. Pleasantly, perhaps even indecently close, especially for a Girl Scout. Then he pushed the door open. The well was still there, the Victorian door still across the well from the library.

They stepped through as one…and he felt the library door slither from his grasp and heard the librarian cry out as she stumbled back into the library. The door now closed again behind her.

He looked back, and saw that she had fallen to her knees inside the library, crying. Clearly, the library, and the librarian, weren't what the criminals wanted. That left only him. And his hair. But he must solve the case. He would solve the case, and put an end to this unfair abuse of a lonely, attractive librarian and her library!

He studied the Victorian door. It looked like one that would let you into someone's drawing room. He gripped the knob, turned it, quietly opened it partway. Yes, a drawing room! He threw it open and stepped through, shouting, "I have you now!"

Then the door snapped shut behind him, and he found himself standing in a large cage.

A familiar-looking bird looked at him from the desk on which it stood. Outside the cage and out of reach.

"No, *I* have *you* now. You're finally here. You're really slow."

"Who and what are you?"

"Who I am doesn't matter. I knew you once, when you were a baby, but you weren't big on names then, and you didn't know me. What I am is a Nachtkrapp, a powerful faery that even the queen fears and avoids."

"Then undo her curse on my hair," Goldlock demanded.

"Umm, well, no. Sorry," the Nachtkrapp replied. "I'm nowhere near as powerful as she is."

"I thought so. She avoids you because you stink!"

"Yes, I stink. Not everyone appreciates my beauty. But I'm more powerful than you are. Why are you here?"

"To find a missing library and librarian!"

"You have. In fact, I've already returned them to the human world. Too bad, so sad. With the door closed, no one else can follow you here now. So why are you here in this cage?"

"That's a good question," Goldlock sneered. "Are you foolish enough to tell me so I can put an end to your evil plot?"

The bird's cold gaze rested on Goldlock's hair. "Because the first crop is ready for harvest, and I have customers waiting. Human customers."

Another door into the drawing room opened, and two men in

dark suits stepped through, the second taller and bulkier and carrying a gym bag.

"How heavy would you say your hair is right now?" the bird asked. "About eighty pounds?"

The men turned greedy expressions toward Goldlock.

"Of course you're after my hair," he sneered, then shouted at the gangsters. "But it's faery gold! When you take it back with you, it will turn into ordinary human hair!"

If it were possible for a beak to smirk, Goldlock was sure the bird was smirking. "But yours isn't faery gold. Yours is gold from the human world. And it will still be gold after they cut if off and take it back."

The smaller mafia man nodded to the bigger one. The henchman walked over to the cage door and put the gym bag down. Reaching into it, he pulled out a sturdy set of garden shears. He also pulled a gun from under his jacket and handed it to his boss.

"Wouldn't want to tempt him, would we?" the henchman said. His boss smiled.

"Good thinking. We want him to stay perfectly healthy and live a long life, right here, while his hair regrows. And regrows. Again and again, forever and ever. Right, Nachtkrapp?"

"Right," said the bird. "I look forward to regular future business with you. I've spied on him in your world. His hair grows fast. Doesn't it, Goldlock?"

"Damn hair," Goldlock muttered. He threw off his coat and cap, then stepped to the barred cage door. Muscles rippled all over his shoulders, neck, chest, and abdomen. His thighs and calves were thick as tree trunks. Bearing such heavy hair around made him very well-muscled indeed. "You just open this door and see what happens, eh?"

The henchman looked uncertainly at the boss. The bird chirped a bit, and suddenly something hard, hot, and painful poked through the bars into Goldlock's belly. He doubled over, groaning. A similar poke hit his side, knocking him over. The bird nodded. The henchman opened the barred door and stepped through. He rolled Goldlock onto his belly with a kick, knelt and set one knee heavily on the middle of Goldlock's back. He slid a blade of the garden shears under one of Goldlock's gold dreads.

Suddenly, a greyhound leapt out into the room through the unbarred door, howling. With a snap of his jaws, Gelert ripped out the mafia boss's throat. Then he sprang onto the bird, snapping and biting. The bird shrieked as the dog ripped off one of its wings. Whatever magik it was trying to use availed it nothing as Gelert tore off its other wing.

Inside the cage, the henchman stared, frozen, as his boss's body spurted blood and collapsed. Goldlock stared at Gelert, as con-fused as the henchman for a moment.

When the henchman started to stand, Goldlock pulled his arms beneath himself and did a fast, hard push-up. He knocked the henchman over and jumped to his feet. The henchman scrambled to his feet against the bars, hand diving to his waist. Hah! He did have another gun!

Goldlock swung his head around once, slamming a whip of gold hair heavily into the side of the man's head. The man's neck audibly snapped and his body toppled sideways.

Goldlock looked up. The bird was still alive, but Gelert snarled. "Treat my boy like that, will you? You shouldn't have opened the door."

Gelert's jaws clamped shut on its neck with a harsh, final crunch. The bird shuddered.

"You've done it again, Gelert," Goldlock said. "They would have kept me here forever, an endless gold mine."

The greyhound dropped the twitching bird. "Call me 'Father'."

"Father?"

"Yes. I know you always wondered where you came from and how you landed in the human world." The greyhound looked down as the body of the bird stilled. "You were my son in Faery. Until this filthy Nachtkrapp snatched you and took you to the human world. When I found your crib empty and my faithful hound with blood on its mouth, I thought it had eaten you, so I drew my sword and stabbed him. As he died, he cried out his innocence—and his curse. On me. For the blood on its mouth was there because he had bitten the Nachtkrapp as it fled with you.

"My hound cursed me to be a hound until I found you and killed the Nachtkrapp. Time flows differently in Faery. By the time I crossed into the human realm and found you, you had grown into a human child. You were about eight human years at the time, already smart. And arrogant. You know, that's what earned you the queen's curse."

Goldlock hung his head.

"Son, you really need to do something about the way you look down on everyone else. Whichever world you live in."

Goldlock looked around. All doors into the room were gone. He saw no way out.

"Umm, so, how do we get out of here?"

"First, where do you want to go—Faery or human world?"

"You're really my father?"

Gelert nodded. "I'm sorry I couldn't keep you from being stolen, or cursed. I missed you desperately until I found you."

"What about my human father and mother? The ones who took in an orphan foundling and raised him as their own? And took you in when you showed up on their doorstep."

"I bless them for adopting you. I'm not here to take their place. They know me as the Italian greyhound that showed up on their doorstep about the time they thought you were responsible enough for a pet. Although they probably wonder how a dog with an average lifespan of fourteen to fifteen years is still alive at twenty-five."

"You could have told me earlier!"

"I couldn't, until the curse was lifted. Anyway, human or Faery? Choose."

Goldlock pondered a moment. "Not Faery. Not until I break the queen's curse."

"There is that," Gelert laughed. "Come out of that cage and let's shake hands."

Gelert sat and raised one paw. Goldlock stepped through the

cage and took it.

The dog looked up and loudly declared to the air, "I have found my son and slain the Nachtkrapp. The curse is ended."

The body of the bird dissolved into black dust that filled the room with darkness. That faded, and Goldlock found himself standing on the sidewalk in front of the library. People brushed past him, going to and fro into the library. It was a bright, sunny afternoon.

Then he heard a voice beside him. "Ahem."

He looked down at an Italian greyhound standing beside him. "Gelert?"

"The one and only."

"But I thought you weren't cursed anymore!"

"I'm not. Now I can choose which shape I take." For an instant, visible only to Goldlock, the dog flickered into a tall human-like Faery shape. Then it was a dog again. "I like being a hound with you. The whole human 'boy and his dog' tradition is wonderful fun!"

Goldlock gazed at him, ignoring the odd looks passing people gave them. "I've got to learn that shape-shifting thing, too."

"Later, son. Shall we go inside and see how our lonely librarian is doing? She's been through a bit of an adventure of her own, you know. She's probably a little alarmed by it all. And worried about you. You two *do* have a date tonight."

Dedicated to Gelert. Look him up.

§

Operation FULL-filled

By Dawn Knox

Victor Mason wasn't useless.

It was just unfortunate that nobody else appeared to see his value.

When Britain declared war on Germany in September 1939, Victor immediately tried to join up. He'd wanted to do his bit to end the hostilities quickly.

However, flat feet, knock-knees, and one shoulder higher than the other had prevented him. He'd tried all the Armed Services, but recruiting officers hadn't been able to see past his ungainly gait and lopsided appearance to spot his enthusiasm.

During the first few months after war had been declared, Victor carried on working as an office clerk in a clothing factory. For him, life hadn't changed a great deal, other than the factory began to produce uniforms for the Armed Services, rather than civilian clothes.

The press had dubbed those months the "Phony War" as if Britain wasn't really at war at all. Of course, life had changed—people now always carried gas masks when they went out. There were blackout regulations at night to prevent light from leaking out of houses and alerting Luftwaffe pilots that there was something worth bombing below. At first, there were shortages of food as people stockpiled supplies—until the government introduced rationing of meat, butter, and sugar. Children had been wrenched from their families and evacuated to live with strangers in rural areas, where it was supposed they'd be safe from bombing raids.

However, as the Phony War progressed, and the dreaded aerial attacks failed to materialize, many children returned to their homes in Britain's cities.

Now, at the beginning of 1941, Victor huddled in Fremford's underground bomb shelter, near central London, along with many of those children who'd come home and their mothers. The Phony War that had lulled people into a false sense of security had ended with shocking abruptness at the beginning of September the previous year, on what later was called "Black Saturday." The Germans had mounted an unbelievable aerial offensive against London, targeting the docks.

Wave after wave of Luftwaffe planes had swarmed across the south coast and continued towards the East End of London, where the docks and associated factories were located. It was also a densely populated area that housed many of the poorest families in London.

And as if that wasn't enough, the Luftwaffe kept up their terrible nighttime raids for months. Six months so far, to be exact. Victor knew because he'd kept a careful record.

The result was that at night, and often in the day, when the air raid siren began to wail, the population huddled in underground shelters, listening to the explosions above them, shuddering with each tremor and wondering if their home would still be standing when they climbed up toward the dust-filled, smoke-laden street.

Victor shifted his weight. He should have brought another cushion. It didn't take long for the cold to seep out of the concrete floor and creep into his body to chill his bones.

Opposite him, a mother with a baby asleep in her arms closed her eyes. Her head nodded and then rested on her chest, but even in her sleep, she kept tight hold of the baby. Sunken, dark-shadowed eyes told Victor the poor woman had been deprived of many nights' sleep.

Next to the mother, a young, red-haired girl sat upright, awake, yet not exactly alert. She stared straight ahead as if she couldn't see the others lying crammed together on the floor like jigsaw puzzle pieces. Mimicking her mother, she held a doll in her arms. Victor wondered if perhaps she was asleep with her eyes open. Was that possible? However, when he shifted his weight again, the girl's eyes flickered toward him, then immediately away as if she knew it was rude to stare. Victor smiled, but he was a second too late. She'd missed it.

Minutes later, he looked back, and the girl's head was against her mother's arm, the doll now lying discarded in her lap. Her eyes had closed and her red hair flopped forward.

She wasn't the only one around him who was asleep. The sound of rhythmic breathing echoed in the underground chamber; snuffles, snores, grunts, and bodies shifting, trying to find a comfortable position on the unforgiving concrete floor.

Victor suffered from insomnia. He was lucky he only needed a few hours' sleep each night. Taking his book out of his bag, he strained to read the words in the subdued lighting.

A little later, he checked his watch and realized, with surprise, an entire hour had passed. Time had lost meaning as he and the hero in his book had escaped from a deserted island, battled with pirates and explored exotic lands.

If only everyone in that shelter could have escaped for an hour with him. He was sure each person would have felt more refreshed by the morning.

And that was how the idea popped into his head. It had been as easy as that. The more he thought about it, the more his pulse raced.

He could do this.

And no one could tell him otherwise.

First thing in the morning, he'd find the shelter manager and his Air Raid Precaution wardens. Once he had permission, he'd enlist the help of everyone who was involved in the running of the underground shelter: the nurse in the sick bay and the ladies in the

Women's Voluntary Service, who served tea, sandwiches, and cakes for those who sought safety underground. Yes, Victor would ask everyone.

In the morning, people filed out of the shelter, clutching their thermos flasks and blankets as they climbed the steep stairs to the chilly February day. Victor, however, didn't leave as usual. Having gained permission for his idea—or "Operation Distraction"—as he'd begun to think of it, Victor rushed back into the now empty underground chamber. He started at the corner of the end wall, placing one foot in front of the other—heel to toe, counting as he went until he reached the other corner. That gave him a rough idea of the width of the wall. Then he reached up to the low ceiling. Yes, now he had an approximate idea of the height as well.

He would begin work as soon as he left the shelter. Thankfully, the bombing hadn't been severe in the area around Victor's house, but he knew a street that had been devastated the previous week. There would be plenty of wood available there. He wondered if people would approve of taking timber from bomb sites. What would people think when they saw him picking over what remained of people's homes? However, he was certain that, by the time he explained what he was going to do, he'd have their support. After all, what good were broken planks and splintered wood simply lying in the street?

Victor smiled as he spotted some good, sturdy pieces of timber and helped himself. He may have a crooked skeleton, but he knew how to wield a saw and a hammer.

That day, he put his tools to good use, and by the time the first people filtered into the chamber that evening, he'd made good progress.

"What's that against the wall, Mummy?" the little girl with the red hair asked as the weary woman and her baby entered the chamber and took up the space they'd occupied the previous night.

"Don't point, Mary, it's rude," the woman said, but her weary eyes roved over Victor's construction and, for the first time, they showed life and interest.

"What is it, though?" the girl persisted, her fists clenched as if to stop them involuntarily pointing.

"I don't know, love," her mother replied, sinking wearily to the floor. "Probably nothing."

Victor stood by his handiwork proudly. As soon as a few more arrived, he'd reveal "Operation Distraction."

As other people entered, they stared at the shelving that covered half the wall. It was time to explain. Victor stood back, so everyone had a good view of the empty shelves.

"Good evening, ladies, gentlemen and, of course, children. I've had an idea and I hope you're going to help me make a success of it—"

"Are we going to have a singsong?" someone called from the back.

Victor held up his hand for silence. "We have so many children in this shelter who have nothing to do and nothing to take their mind off..." He glanced meaningfully up at the concrete ceiling, hoping the adults would realize he was indicating the skies far above them and the inevitable swarm of Luftwaffe pilots and their bombs.

"I am proposing to set up a library. If you have any books that your children have grown out of, would you please bring them in?"

"I'd rather 'ave a singsong," someone shouted from the back, but his voice was drowned out by the others, who told him to shut up.

By the end of the week, not only did the shelving extend across the entire back wall of the chamber, but people were also bringing in books. And not only children's books, but adults' books, too. The shelves were three-quarters full, and several people had volunteered to help Victor log all the books and make library tickets.

"We need a name," Rose, one volunteer, said.

"Operation Distraction," Victor replied. "That's what I call it. 'Operation' makes it sound like a military maneuver."

"That's too much of a mouthful," Rose said.

"What about Fremford Underground Lending Library?" Val,

the other volunteer, asked. "We could shorten it to FULL."

"Operation FULL?" asked Rose.

"No," said Victor. "I've got a better idea. How about 'Operation FULL-filled'?"

That night Victor settled down after most of the others in the chamber were asleep. It had been a busy evening with a succession of people from his room, as well as other rooms in the shelter, hearing about the library and coming to borrow books. So many had been borrowed that there were now large gaps on the shelves, but the newcomers had promised to bring in books they no longer wanted the following night. The library was set to grow.

Opposite Victor sat the weary woman, her baby in a basket by her side. She'd already fallen asleep. Next to her, the little girl with red hair looked up from her book, smiled at him, waved shyly, and immediately looked back down. A wisp of red hair fell over her face, covering one eye. She tucked it behind her ear and carried on reading. Twenty minutes later, the book was in her lap—closed, and she too was asleep.

Victor sighed with contentment.

He wasn't useless at all. In fact, not only was he imaginative and resourceful, but he was practical, too.

Operation FULL-filled was a success, and that was due to him. He remembered the various recruiting sergeants who'd turned him down at the start of the war. Well, perhaps that had been a good thing. After all, if the military had accepted him, he wouldn't have been in the Fremford underground bomb shelter, nor setting up its new lending library.

Everything happened for a purpose, he thought.

Victor put his book back in his bag. He was too tired to read that night. He closed his eyes and joined in the collective sounds of sleep—safe—deep beneath the streets of Fremford.

§

Something Different

by Kelley Garcia

Dinnertime at the O'Malley house is usually stressful. The four of us seldom choose to be together at any other time, but Mildred O'Malley insists that if she can spend the time toiling over creating a meal, the rest of us can make ourselves present for it.

Father, having finished his fried chicken and mashed potatoes, was pushing the Brussels sprouts around on his plate They'd been left for last. He didn't appreciate vegetables.

Looking over at Mother, he asked, "Mildred, is there more chicken and gravy?"

"There is, but please don't let those Brussels sprouts go to waste, Norman. They're from our garden and they're so good."

Father rolled his eyes and stabbed one.

My little sister, Regina, was staring with disgust at her mashed potatoes. It was a mystery to all of us why Mother made mashed potatoes nearly every night when Regina hated them so much. I wondered if Mother thought the chicken gravy would be helpful in that regard. When she prepared our plates she would make a pocket in the mound of potatoes and ladle in the gravy, creating a pool in the middle. Regina made a show of getting up to fetch a spoon and then had very carefully dipped the gravy out and consumed it like soup. She'd been careful to not disturb the potatoes underneath.

Father had laughed about that and shook his head.

Mother just looked annoyed and said, "That's ridiculous, Regina."

As usual, I had better things to do than sit with my family. I'd finished all my food and was slowly emptying my glass of milk. I took care not to rush, else I'd be chastised for being ill-mannered. I wiped my mouth with my napkin and asked to be excused.

Mother nodded, but quickly followed up with, "Wait just a minute. You have to be at the library in one hour. You have just enough time to clear what you can from the table and clean yourself up."

Shocked as only a twelve-year-old-girl can be, I lost my ability to be well-mannered and demanded, "What do you mean the library? I'm going over to Molly's house. It's all set. Her mother said it was fine."

"Oh no you're not, young lady. I've paid for you to take a class at the library. It starts this evening at six o'clock and you will be there."

I could feel my cheeks getting hot, "A class?" I felt so angry I couldn't complete my next sentence. I started to sputter. "I don't… what do you…I can't believe you…"

Father interrupted me, "Stop right there, Clara. You'll get yourself in trouble if you continue with that tone." He glared at me, warnings flashing in his eyes.

I plopped back down in my chair. There was never any success when it came to pushing back against Mother. She dominated her home. We knew it was her way, or a hard way would follow for all of us. "What class is it this time?" I asked, defeated.

Since the beginning of summer break Mother had gotten into this thing where she thought we all needed to have stuff to do and, of course, she knew what would be best. She'd not had much luck with Father. He did put his foot down on some occasions, and her controlling all his free time was one of them. But poor Regina and I had been subjected to one sort of class or training adventure after another. Regina was in the midst of being tutored by a teenager who lived a few houses down from us. Neither Regina nor I liked Jackie Baker, but that's who Mother had hired to teach Regina how to twirl a baton. Yes, twirling.

The last class Mother had subjected me to was one carried out at the local Girls Club. It was two weekends of arts and crafts. I didn't know anyone there, and by the end, all I had to show for my efforts were a clay teacup that was severely deformed and several different pieces of jewelry made of painted macaroni that went straight into the trash as soon as I got home. And I hated spending two weekends battling mosquitoes while sweating in the scalding Texas heat at a camp where nearly every other child there was a year or more younger than me. It had been outrageous. Now what? What new torture had she come up with for her older daughter?

I didn't dare ask again. That would be rude. So I just stared and waited.

Mother sipped her iced tea, then took the folded napkin from her lap and dabbed at her lips before turning to face me. "It's a poise class."

Regina and I both said at the same time, "Poise?"

"What's that?" Regina directed her question to me. I shrugged and turned back to Mother.

"I know what the word poise means, but a class about it? What…?" I didn't know what to ask or why even bother to ask anything. I was filled with dread and deep unhappiness.

"Why me, God? Why?" I thought to myself. It was the question I always asked. It was the question that I could ask that helped me not scream and leap at her with my fingers in a claw-like position, ready to rip apart her horrible-looking beehive hairdo.

"You'll see when you get there," was Mother's smug reply. "Now go get ready. Regina can clear the table when she finally finishes her potatoes."

A great groan escaped my little sister. Father said, "Same to you, little girl. Mind your manners."

"Yes, sir," Regina muttered as she picked at a tiny lump of mashed potatoes that had a little covering of gravy.

I didn't do anything to clean myself up. I just went straight to my bedroom to fling myself onto my bed and scream into my pillow. It was better than crying. I'd learned that crying caused red and puffy eyes, and if either of my parents saw me like that they'd get annoyed and I'd be further badgered.

"What's wrong with you? Don't you know how good you have it? You should be grateful for what you have in life. You could have been…"

Blah, blah, blah. It was a no-win situation, always.

Father drove me to the library. I knew he was going to his favorite spot to see his friends after he dropped me off. We all believed he'd be at George Wesby's pub every minute of his free time if he could. He was just as unhappy at home as we all were, Mother included. I was old enough to realize she was miserable, and tormenting us was her only entertainment. I wished I could go to the pub with Father. He rolled his eyes at the idea when I mentioned it.

"Just go to the class and make the best of it, Clara."

I pushed back in the old Buick's passenger seat. My arms across my chest. Trying to stay calm. Then I noticed we weren't heading for the library. "Wait, where are you going?"

"To the library, of course. Oh." He looked over at me. "You didn't realize there's a new one? Well, there is. Construction is done. It opened a few weeks ago."

The old library had been in the annex of the huge Methodist church over on Broadway. Father had told me that it was only a temporary place since the main library had burned down. I didn't much like going to the church library. My family is Catholic, and being as we were in a small town, that was well-known. All the Catholic kids were thought of as different, and were not exactly welcomed by good Methodist families.

This news about a new building was interesting. My day instantly became a little brighter.

Father turned off of Main Street and left onto Liberty Avenue. There, to my surprise, was a gorgeous, large, white stone building with a water fountain in front of it, but on the other side of the street. "Oh, I remember seeing this being built. I had no idea it was the new library. It's so beautiful!" I couldn't keep the enthusiasm out of my voice.

"Well, now you know. Our city tax dollars at work." He didn't sound thrilled. He pulled up in front and said, "Mother will be here to pick you up when the class is over. Do us a favor. Have fun for once, will you?"

And with that I was deposited onto the sidewalk in front of the new building, watching the old black Buick belch smoke as Father put it back into gear and headed toward his reprieve.

My parents weren't the type to hover around Regina or me. Mother made the decisions about what we should do, but then had the full expectations we'd just do it. Father said it was their way to help us be more independent. I thought it was just their way to be selfish.

I took in the beauty of the new building. I couldn't believe it was in our little town. It seemed like it would be more fitting in a fine city. There were glass doors that led into a foyer decorated with a couple of statues. I didn't take much note of them. They were on either side of a glass display case that looked to hold history stuff. It felt like a real library, a special place. And, again, much too nice for our town.

Once inside, the first thing I noticed was the smell. Not only did it smell like new construction, but I could also smell the books. It sort of smelled like the church library but better, newer, fresher.

I saw a sign on a flip board that read, "Poise Class, 6 p.m. to 8 p.m." and it had an arrow pointing to the left. I looked in that direction and the first thing I saw was Sally Sue Parker. The most loathsome girl in my sixth-grade class. Also the most popular. She had on a colorful, pretty summer dress and white sandals. I looked down at my grimy shorts, faded top, and dirty Converse sneakers.

"Nope." I said out loud. "Not going to do it." And I turned in the opposite direction.

It was the greatest act of defiance in my young life. I wasn't sure what the consequences would be, but at that moment the one thing I knew for sure was that I was NOT going to that stupid poise class.

I looked around and decided that it was much more worthwhile to explore this new library. I thought of my favorite show. I would boldly go where no girl had gone before! I smiled. I was going to discover all there was to be found. Perhaps I could get lost among all the shelves and simply disappear. Teleport to another time or be lost in space. I could be like those children in *From the Mixed-Up Files of Mrs. Basil E. Frankweiler.* They ran away from home and lived in a museum, only coming out of hiding at night.

In a moment of clarity, I realized I'd have to figure out how to deal with Mother later, but decided that, for now, I'd simply explore, and I knew it would be worth it.

I headed for the stairs.

§

This Is Not Your Place

by Bob Newell

Dr. Yule Masters was writing a book. That was nothing special in and of itself, but Dr. Masters was an academic at a major New England university where publishing was the way to the top. Papers were great, but books were even better.

Writing a book, an academic treatise actually, is a lot of work, and in Dr. Masters's field, that included months or years of research tracking down often obscure references. Which was exactly what he was doing now.

After nearly eleven hours in an airplane, flying from Boston to a city on an island in the middle of the Pacific Ocean, a cab ride in traffic, and a ten-minute walk, Dr. Masters found himself in front of a small library at the edge of the city's tourist district. The library happened to hold a set of references that couldn't be found anywhere else. Via email, the library had informed him they didn't have sufficient staff to make copies, but he was welcome to come and visit in person, as indeed other academics had done on occasion before him.

The library sat on a large, grassy lot at the end of a waterway. Its architecture was striking. Dr. Masters found it hard to believe that it had been in existence for more than seventy years. He was a bit surprised to see various people lying on the lawn, many with battered suitcases or large plastic bags. Most were sleeping and paid

Dr. Masters no attention as he walked down the sidewalk to the main entrance.

He went to the service counter and introduced himself to the woman working there. "Delighted you're here," she said. "I'm Cynthia. Let me introduce you to our head librarian, Miss Jenny Wu."

Cynthia showed Dr. Masters into a staff room just behind the main service counter, and then departed. Miss Wu was a small woman of an indeterminate middle age with hair that was just beginning to gray. After mutual greetings, she told Dr. Masters that she had been the head of this particular library branch for about five years and had been a librarian for all of her working career. Then she got down to business.

"I needn't tell you about the precautions you need to take in handling such valuable materials," Ms. Wu stated, "but there are other things you must know."

"Of course," said Dr. Masters, as amiably as possible. He was anxious to get to work, as he could only stay a few days before he had to return to his teaching duties. "I'm very familiar with document preservation protocols. What else is it I need to know?"

"Well," Miss Wu said, "we are just a small branch of our state-wide library system. We only have four staff, and all but me are part-time. We're not open very many hours either. We do open at nine, but we close at four because...well, you'll see. And the budgets...yes, the budgets. We are always short of funds. Unfortunately, our state just doesn't put much value on intellectual pursuits."

"A common problem," Dr. Masters stated, although in fact he had never heard of a library in a major city that closed every day at the early hour of four in the afternoon.

"Look, Dr. Masters," Miss Wu said. "You're a noted academic with many years of experience in your field and a sterling reputation. We are privileged to have you visit us and want to extend you every courtesy. We know your time with us is limited, so if you need to work later than four o'clock, you're welcome to stay. The doors will lock behind you when you leave. But I must warn you not ever to be here after dark."

Surprised, Dr. Masters said, "But you know us academics. We often work late into the night, and since the materials can't leave the library…"

"I'm serious," Miss Wu said. Her tone was much firmer and more authoritative than Dr. Masters had thought possible from someone of such diminutive stature. "Do *not* stay after dark."

"Can you tell me why?"

Miss Wu gave an involuntary shudder. "Just heed my words, Doctor. Now, I need to get back to my duties and I'm sure you want to get started yourself. I'll have Bernard, one of our staff, show you where you can work and where the materials are located."

At that, a young man dressed in casual attire came over and introduced himself. "I'm Bernard," he said, offering a hand.

"Dr. Yule Masters," the scholar replied. "Pleased to meet you. And Miss Wu, thank you for your courtesy."

Bernard then led Dr. Masters to a locked bookcase containing the rare materials that the doctor wished to consult, and offered him a copy of the key to the case. "I'm afraid with our workload and my fifteen-hour-a-week schedule, I can't offer you any assistance, but I'm sure you'll manage. Now, let me show you your workspace."

"Unfortunately," continued Bernard, "we don't have a spare private office. In fact, we don't have any private offices, just that staff area in the back. But we've reserved this desk for you." Bernard pointed to a desk along one of the walls in the main room and handed Dr. Masters another key. "Be sure to lock everything up when you depart in the evening," he said "as we have…um…let's say, an unusual situation and we can't guarantee against theft. Well, then, I'll leave you to it."

"Thanks, Bernard," Dr. Masters said, perhaps a bit warily.

Bernard started to walk off, but then turned back and said, "Oh, did Miss Wu tell you about not staying here after dark?"

"Yes, she did, but she didn't tell me why."

Bernard's expression turned somber. "Just do as Miss Wu told you." He hurried off.

* * * *

Dr. Masters worked for two days, arriving at the library's nine o'clock opening time and working until after the four o'clock closing. However, he always made sure to leave by about six o'clock, allowing for a good margin until local sunset, which at this time of year was near six-thirty.

Another day passed and finally it was his last day of work. He would be able to work the full day, as his direct flight to the East Coast wasn't until just after eleven in the evening. He brought his single small suitcase along with him and resumed his efforts.

At quarter to four the staff appeared to wish him farewell.

"I'll be staying just a little longer," Dr. Masters told them. "Thank you for all your kindness and your warm welcome."

"I speak for all of us when I say that it was an honor to have you here," Miss Wu said. "We hope that one day you'll be back. Now, we'll let you carry on, but just remember..."

"...don't stay after dark," he said. "I know!"

The staff made their way out as Dr. Masters returned to the books he had open in front of him.

The time again passed quickly and soon he realized it was six o'clock, his usual quitting hour. But then he thought, my flight isn't until after eleven tonight. I can catch a cab at nine-thirty and be at the airport in plenty of time. I should take advantage of my last few hours here. What can really go wrong? It's just local superstition.

And so he stayed. Darkness was complete at seven o'clock. That's when it all began to happen.

* * * *

It started gradually and then accelerated. At first there were a few noises that sounded like they came from various points outside the building. They did little more than briefly interrupt Dr. Masters's focus. But then the sounds seemed to get a little closer. A few banging noises like a door opening and closing. No, not exactly a door.

A bit perturbed, Dr. Masters got up from his desk and went across the room to the entrance. It was closed and locked, just as he would have expected. He shrugged his shoulders and started back toward his desk.

The banging occurred again, this time much closer. Dr. Masters looked around. The door to the back storage area opened and through it came a figure. It was a man dressed in a soiled and yellowed ruffled shirt that must have once been white, formal trousers that had seen much better days, and a ragged dinner jacket. He was carrying a couple of bulging plastic bags.

Dr. Masters suddenly had trouble finding his voice. "Who… who are you?" he croaked weakly. "What are you doing here? How did you get in?" The doctor's last sentence sounded a bit more stern, as he recovered at least a little of his composure.

The figure looked up. "My name is Raymond. But who *you* are is really the question." He was weathered-looking and probably younger than he actually appeared.

"If you don't leave I'll call the police," Dr. Masters said.

"Oh you will, will you? Well, that's pretty funny. A bit sad, actually. You must not know very much, seeing as you're the first one we've caught here in a long, long while. Police, huh?" Raymond laughed.

A few more raggedy figures came through the door, both men and women, all of them with a uniform sort of disheveled appearance and different sorts of tattered and dirty clothing. Some carried plastic bags and some suitcases.

"Where are you all coming from?" Dr. Masters asked.

"There's a trap door in the back," Raymond said, "and no one will ever lock it or board it up, just like no one will ever call the police."

"I'm going back to my desk," Dr. Masters said. "This is all too much to believe. I'm imagining it. I've been working too long. I'm hallucinating. I've been working too hard on my treatise and I need a break."

"Hallucinating, are you?" Raymond said. "Well, I'll tell you what. We'll give you one chance."

By now, thirty or forty people had come through the door.

"Go back to your desk," Raymond went on. "Get your stuff, and leave. Right away. Well, after you settle up with us. Like I said, one chance. And you better do it before my friends find whatever you've got over there and decide it's finders keepers. We are all very poor and we own next to nothing of any value. So any personal property left behind after dark is up for grabs. It's only fair that wealthier people share with us those things that weren't important enough for them to remember to take along. That's part of our arrangement."

"Arrangement?" said Dr. Masters. "I don't understand."

But the rest of the people were starting to move toward the interior of the library, all of them shuffling slowly, carrying their respective belongings. Some of them were eyeing Dr. Masters's desk.

Alarmed, he said, "No! They wouldn't dare..."

He hurried back to his desk. One woman had already spotted his laptop computer and was reaching out to pick it up.

"Leave that alone!" Dr. Masters shouted. "Don't touch my computer!" He reached out, slapped the woman's hand away from the desk, and pushed her off to the side.

The woman let out a piercing scream and then a stream of invectives. Several others came over and surrounded her. Raymond quickly arrived. He shook his head in a wistful manner and said, "Now you've done it. You've blown your one chance. How dare you put your hands on our Tilly?"

Tilly, the woman in question, had stopped yelling and was now sobbing loudly. Raymond placed his hand on her shoulder. "It's okay, Tilly, it's okay. This bad man isn't going to hurt you. We'll take care of things."

Raymond turned to Dr. Masters, a very cross look on his face. "I don't know who you are," he said. "Maybe some sort of fancy professor or something. We've dealt with those before. But you... you went much too far. Listen carefully, for I'm pretty much the leader here. I decide what happens and what doesn't. I was going to let you go after you paid us, but now I don't think so."

"Paid you?" Dr. Masters said. "What do you mean?"

"This is not your place," Raymond replied. "After dark, it's *our* place. That's the arrangement, and you broke it. I was just going to make you pay a fine and a little rent, but now it's a lot worse."

"*Your* place?" Dr. Masters said. "This is a public library. How can it be *your* place?"

"See, this is how it works. We stay here overnight. The place is ours after dark. The staff here kind of takes pity on us. They know we have nowhere else to go, so they don't close up or lock that hatch door, and they certainly don't call the cops on us. We have a tough life and they help us out. In return, we don't make any trouble, or hassle, or beg from the library patrons. I make sure everyone stays orderly. It's a good arrangement. But part of that arrangement is that no one hassles us either, and that's why we have our hours, and the staff and patrons have theirs, and the hours are kept separated. And respected."

Raymond continued. "Now, once in a while we catch someone here, like you. Well, not as bad a person as you seem to be, but you get the idea. Like I said, they pay a fine and some rent money, and then they get sent on their way. The staff here warns everyone who might want to stay late, so there are no excuses and no pretending you don't know the rules. And they also make sure they close at four, so even in the winter everyone is out of here by dark, including the weekly cleaning staff. The rules apply to everyone with no exceptions."

"I don't understand..." Dr. Masters began, but Raymond interrupted.

"A smart fellow like you doesn't understand? Well, you will, that's for sure. Now, let's get ready for your trial."

"My...what?"

Several large men encircled Dr. Masters. Other members of the group started arranging chairs. They placed a table in the center of the open space with a chair behind it, where Raymond took a seat. Another chair was placed facing Raymond, a few feet away. The large men pushed Dr. Masters down into the chair, but remained standing around him, preventing him from getting up and trying to run away.

Everyone else sat in rows of chairs behind Dr. Masters, also facing Raymond.

Raymond banged a fist on his table several times. "The Court of the Unfortunate People is called to order!" he exclaimed. "The prisoner will rise."

The large men roughly pulled Dr. Masters to his feet.

"Prisoner, you are accused of violation of the Tenancy Agreement and Failure to Pay Rent by virtue of your staying past dark. You are also accused of Assault with Intent To Inflict Bodily Harm on our precious Tilly, as well as Causing Extreme Emotional Distress and Preventing Lawful Acquisition of Found Property. Prisoner, how do you plead?"

"Plead?" Dr. Masters said. "Is this some kind of joke? You're the ones guilty of..."

He was pushed back into his seat.

"The prisoner shall be silent!" Raymond said. "You are now facing additional charges of Contempt of Court, Disrespect for the Unfortunate People, and Failure to Properly Plead."

Raymond pounded his fist again. "Jury, what are your findings?"

"Wait...I thought this was a hearing," Dr. Masters began, but he was quickly cut off.

"Guilty!" everyone in the seated rows shouted. "Guilty, guilty, guilty!"

"The prisoner has been found guilty on all counts," Raymond said, "and due to his multiple offenses and their serious nature, the court will show no mercy. Jury, what sentence do you recommend?"

The crowd once more began to shout. "Living death! Living death! Living death!"

Dr. Masters again tried to stand, but the strong men held him down firmly. "What is this! Let me go! I'll leave! I'll leave at once! I'll never bother you again."

One of the men clouted him on the head and Dr. Masters fell silent while Raymond spoke again.

"Sentence is as follows. All of this person's property of any value is confiscated. That includes his computer, everything in his suitcase, and those nice clothes of his. Property to be divided at the dictates of Tilly, who is the most injured party here. Of course, all of us have been injured in some way. The Court of the Unfortunate People has spoken."

Raymond paused for a moment before going on. "The sentence of living death is ratified. Bailiffs, proceed."

The strong men tore off Dr. Masters's clothing and gave it and his laptop and luggage to Tilly, who screamed again, this time with glee as she extracted his wallet from his trousers and started to count the cash within it.

* * * *

On the following morning, Miss Wu was the first to arrive, as was almost always the case. She unlocked the front door and entered the library.

It didn't take her long to see that the reference books on the desk Dr. Masters had been using had not been returned to their proper place, as any scholar would have done out of habit and respect for the sacredness of priceless research materials.

"Oh my," she said to herself. "He didn't listen, did he? What a shame. Such a great academic and a nice, polite man, too. Yes, really a shame."

Miss Wu tidied up the desk, then returned all the precious volumes to their cabinet and locked them up, safely preserved for the next scholar who might one day come to visit. Hopefully, whomever it would be, whenever it would be, would be someone who would heed her warnings more carefully.

* * * *

Just after dark that evening, the banging noises resumed and the same crowd, led again by Raymond, made their way into the library through their hatch and through the supply room door.

But the very last one to enter, dressed in rags and carrying a nearly empty plastic bag, was a brand-new member of the group.

§

I've Never Done This Before

by Michael Little

"I've never done this before," she said.

"Me neither." I studied her dark eyes in the soft light that came through the hallway from the living room lamp. Bedroom eyes. Not the way she looked earlier, annoyed, when we both reached for the same book in the public library that morning. *Fifty Shades of Grey.* She won. She yanked it off the shelf and made a beeline for the desk to check it out.

"Not in the kitchen," she said. "I mean I've never done this in the kitchen before."

"Me neither," I said. "I've done *this* before, of course. Lots of times."

"How many times?" she asked.

"Who's counting?" I wasn't going there.

"I don't want you to think I'm easy," she said. "First date and all. Besides which I've never had a date with a guy I just met in the library stacks. Normally, you can't get me into the kitchen till the third date. Fourth even. Depends on the guy."

"Lucky me. Are you comfortable? Is the countertop too hard?"

"I'm fine," she said, "but let's switch."

"Switch places?"

"No, I mean switch ice cream. I want to taste your Cookie Dough. You can have my Cherry Garcia."

"She smiled sweetly. We swapped the pint cartons.

"Mmmmmmmmmm," she said. "Gotta love the Cookie Dough."

"Love your Cherry Garcia," I said.

Pinching my ear, she asked, "You don't mind the guys being here?"

"What guys?" I looked around.

"Ben and Jerry," she said.

"Oh."

She laughed. She always laughed at her own jokes.

"You like to laugh," I said.

"You haven't heard anything yet." While I thought about that, she moved her lips to my ear and nibbled on it. Her lips were cold from the ice cream. I didn't complain. I made a note about ears and filed it away. Then I took the note out and returned the favor, my lips on her ear.

"You can do that whenever you want," she said.

"You are easy," I said.

"You're learning all my secrets."

"Tell me more of them," I said. I brushed her lips with mine. Cookie Dough and Cherry Garcia go well together.

"No," she said. "You have to find out for yourself."

I took another spoonful of the ice cream, then turned my attention to the side of her neck, my lips in no hurry as they explored this new territory.

She moaned, almost inaudibly. "Damn, you're finding out all my secrets."

"I could stop," I said.

"Stop and I kill you." Her words threatening but warm, her hand on the back of my neck performing a massage maneuver that was new to me.

"I think Ben and Jerry are melting," I said, my exploration of her neck about mid-journey.

"I think I don't care," she said.

"We could save it for later. Seems like such a waste."

"Or we could do this," she said. She nudged me away from her neck, but not far. I watched as she reached into her carton and came out with Cookie Dough ice cream on the tip of her finger. It looked interesting next to the red fingernail. Then I watched her move the ice cream slowly to my neck, her mouth following closely, sure of its reward. Her tongue took over from there. My skin went from Antarctica to Maui in record time. Then she smiled and reached into the carton again. Then it was all Antarctica, Maui, Antarctica, Maui.

"Your turn," she said.

"Wait, you have a little Cookie Dough on your lips."

She stopped her Swedish massage on the back of my neck and pulled my mouth to hers, stopping an inch before they met. "Lick it off," she said.

"Yes, ma'am." I was in no condition to disobey orders. Besides which I was seriously jet lagged from the rapid travel between the South Pole and Hawai'i.

Then it was time to switch flavors. Cherry Garcia. Her neck. My lips and tongue. We were consuming and burning calories in a kind of wild, binge-eating workout. Do the reps. Do the reps. And four more. And three. And two. One more. I was beginning to fall in love with my trainer.

Was it hanky-panky? Maybe. I'm a guy, what do I know? I think this was what women call prelude. It's the part leading up to the main event. An old girlfriend took me to a talk once where a woman with a twinkle in her eye told us that hanky-panky, like Rome,, was divided into three parts. There was prelude: the touching and tenderness, then the actual hanky-panky, then something called afterglow. I'm not sure, but I think afterglow is the part where guys fall asleep. I do know that the prelude part is very important. It's important to a woman because it's like starting up a car on the coldest day of winter. You can't even start the engine until you've scraped the ice off the windshield. You know you're going to be in that driveway a while before you can get on the road. Guys, on the other hand, don't know the meaning of the word "winter." Guys live in Hawai'i, where it's always summer and there's no ice on the windshield, and the engine turns over as soon as you turn the key.

Anyway, the woman with the twinkle in her eye told us that prelude is essential, and that men might as well enjoy it. I remember going home from the talk and making a mental shopping list. Ice scraper was at the top of the list. I had some of the traditional stuff on the list, too, like flowers, chocolate, soft lights, and make-out music. I made a second list. It consisted of moves that had worked for me in the past. These were old friends. Whispering in the ear was one of them. Kisses on the cheek were another. I always liked that one. Kisses on the cheek were nonthreatening. You almost never got shot down for that one. It was a good first move.

I don't remember everything on my techniques list. Somewhere along the trail it disappeared. I hope it didn't land in the hands of an old girlfriend. I try not to think about it. One thing I'm sure of, the list did not include Ben and Jerry. If I were to make a new list, however, I think old Ben and Jerry would be right up at the top.

"Oh look," she said. "It's all gone. No more Ben. No more Jerry."

"We could go to the store for more," I said.

"We could do that."

"We could buy all the flavors." All the flavors. Endless trips from Antarctica to Maui.

"I think I've had enough ice cream for one evening," she said.

"Are you tired?"

"No, I didn't say that."

"Hungry?" I asked.

"For what?"

"We could see what else is in the fridge." It wasn't far. I reached over to the fridge door and swung it open. We studied the shelves.

"Oh my," she said.

"What?"

"Strawberries."

"You like?"

"Only if you have whipped cream," she said.

I looked in the fridge door. Peeking out behind a milk carton was the bright red top of the whipped cream container I had bought the week before. I reached in and slid it out.

"Look what I found." I held it up, like Indiana Jones with the Holy Grail.

"Oh my," she said. Spinning around, she reached for a book lying on the kitchen table and held it up for me to see. *Fifty Shades of Grey*. "Shall we read to each other?"

I grinned. "I thought you'd never ask."

Years from now, when I'm an old man sitting in our library's reading room, I will close my eyes and remember the night of Ben and Jerry, and the strawberries, and the whipped cream. And maybe, just maybe, there will be someone sitting next to me, perhaps remembering the same evening. Perhaps she will snuggle closer, then turn to me and whisper in my ear, "Oh my."

§

"Help Me, Tiger Princess"

by Rose Tigarden

Helen Santos, a widow of the Gulf War and mother of two daughters, is on her home computer, setting up a Yahoo personal ad. She thinks long and hard and finally selects a photo. Helen is lonely and looking for male companionship. With two daughters at home, she doesn't have time to frequent the gym or bars. So, in desperation, she adds a photo to her online personal ad. But not hers. The photo is of her seventeen-year-old daughter, Lillian.

Several weeks have passed and Helen is driving Nancy, her younger daughter, to Jefferson Elementary School only a few blocks from home. Nancy climbs out of the back seat and enters the elementary school grounds. Then Helen drives Lillian to Kaimuki High School. on Kapahulu Avenue.

From there, she drives back down Kapahulu to the Starbucks on Mooheau Avenue. Helen has been making dates to meet men at this convenient Starbucks, just down the street from the Safeway where she works. She recognizes the man she arranged to meet from his photo on his personal ad. But he's expecting to meet someone who looks like her teenage daughter. Another strikeout.

This Starbucks is busy in the morning. Helen has always tried to make small talk with the men waiting to order, and offers to share her table. But they always decline, saying they're meeting someone else. She wonders what makes these overweight men think someone who looks like her teenage daughter would be interested in them. She works hard to stay in shape with diet and exercise. She's a kindly, friendly, not unattractive, shapely, thirty-eight-year-old local woman, but men *her* age are all looking for younger women. It just isn't fair that none will give her a chance.

It was hard on the Santos females with the COVID pandemic and quarantine. Helen, a cashier at Safeway, was considered an essential worker. With the churches, schools, and libraries closed, she had nowhere to leave the girls. With a seven-year difference in their ages, COVID made it even harder, so both girls had to grow up faster. Sometimes she felt like they had their childhoods hijacked. On her days off, instead of just doing housework, she would spend as much time as possible running in the park with them and joining them at the beach swimming.

That particular afternoon a dark-colored SUV is following Lillian as she walks up Kaimuki Avenue after school to the bus stop in front of the Kapahulu Safeway. Since her mother doesn't get off work for several more hours, Lillian takes the bus down Kapahulu to the Waikiki library. The dark-colored SUV stays behind the bus as it heads in the *makai* (seaward) direction toward the library. It never attempts to pass the bus. Lillian gets off at Leahi Avenue and walks into the library, where she meets her little sister. The dark-colored SUV pulls into the library parking lot. The two Santos girls always study in the library after school until their mother gets home from work.

Weeks later, still hoping to meet someone at Starbucks, Helen finally lands a boyfriend, and after dating for a month, he spends most nights with her at her Campbell Avenue apartment. Ten-year-old Nancy does not like him. She thinks he's creepy. Lillian notes his dark-colored SUV parked in front and wonders whether it was the vehicle that followed her. But she dismisses it from her mind because he seems to make her mother happy.

* * * *

Maile Young, a Jefferson Elementary School teacher, is sitting in the teachers' lounge when Ms. Kaiolu, the librarian from the

Waikiki library, approaches her.

"Do you remember me?" asks the elderly Ms. Kaiolu. "Your mother and I went to school together many years ago. She brought you and your brothers into the library to get books to read. It's times like this I just don't know what to do. I don't know if the *keiki* (child or children) is imagining or exaggerating things."

"What's this all about?" Maile asks.

"One of your students asked me how to contact the Tiger Princess."

"Do you know the student's name, Ms. Kaiolu?"

"Yes. Nancy Santos. I asked her how she knew about the Tiger Princess. She told me she'd heard that the Tiger Princess protects all the *wahine* (women) of Honolulu and that she also saved the *tutu* (grandmothers) in our neighborhood from a serial rapist-murderer."

"Do you think Nancy might be in danger?" asks Maile.

"I just don't know," says Ms. Kaiolu. "The *keiki* watch so much television, I can't tell if the threat is real or if she's exaggerating. I thought since your sister-in-law, PeggySu Wong, is known as the Tiger Princess, that I'd ask you what to do. PeggySu has a reputation for helping people in trouble."

Maile thinks for a few moments, then tells the librarian, "Have Nancy write the Tiger Princess a letter asking for her help. She should say what kind of danger she thinks she's in and how the Tiger Princess might help her."

The next day Ms. Kaiolu hands Maile a handwritten letter in a child's script. She admits to helping Nancy write the letter. The librarian tells Maile, "You never know what the right thing to do is. You don't want to overreact. But then we don't want to be like the school where that girl Kalynn West was kidnapped and went missing all those years. I remember she was found by your brother, Officer Keanu Wong, with *keiki* of her own. "Do you know how they are doing?"

"Now she and her *keiki* are living with her mother," Maile says, remembering how, as children, they had all searched for Kalynn. "It so happens," Maile continues, "that an FBI profiler, a friend of

PeggySu, is putting together a program where Kalynn will make a video warning *keiki*, their parents, and teachers of the very real threat of *keiki* abductions. These videos will be aired on television, at schools, and at libraries."

"That's a good thing," Ms. Kaiolu replies. "Keanu has grown into a great police officer. I remember how smart and determined he was, even as a *keiki*. He told me that he was going to be Marshal Wong and ride in all the parades."

Both women chuckled at that.

Maile calls her mother, Gloria Wong, and says she needs to meet with PeggySu. "I have a letter from one of my students asking the Tiger Princess for help." Gloria checks with PeggySu and says "Come right over."

Maile is buzzed onto the estate from the street and parks as usual at the small bridge to the Buddha garden. Gloria is waiting at the front door. In the living room, she has a cart with tea and almond cakes set out, and pours as PeggySu joins them.

Maile hands PeggySu the handwritten letter. It reads: "Dear Tiger Princess, Please help me. I think a bad man has moved into our *hale* (home) and he will hurt us. *Mahalo nui* (thank you), Nancy."

"Nancy is the younger of two daughters," explains Maile. "Her mother is a widow of the Gulf War with a teenage daughter as well. It's hard sometimes to tell if the *keiki* are imagining or exaggerating, because they're so bombarded with images from television. I felt it best to have you check it out if you're not too busy."

PeggySu assures her that she did the right thing and says, "Unfortunately, they fit the profile of a sexual predator's preferred victims. I'll have my dad, Commander Lee, check it out and make sure the *keiki* are safe." Maile finishes her tea and leaves.

PeggySu emails her dad a copy of Nancy's letter and the pertinent information on the Santos family on Campbell Avenue.

Commander Lee, a former Navy SEAL, now runs his own company, Lee Investigations, Ltd. He pays a midnight visit to the Santos apartment and lets himself into the dark-colored SUV parked out front. He opens the glove compartment and records the name, Mario Grosso, on the vehicle's registration. On his way out he taps a taillight and the lens breaks silently.

Commander Lee runs the name, Mario Grosso, owner of the dark-colored SUV. He is on the sex offenders list for Kailua and Kaneohe. The commander alerts PeggySu that he will have words with Grosso that afternoon when he shows up at the Santos *hale*. He will persuade Grosso that the Santos *hale* is not a good place for him to be staying."

PeggySu calls Maile and tells her, "Mrs. Santos's new boyfriend is on the sex offenders list for the Windward side."

"Oh my. I'm so glad we took Nancy seriously," Maile says.

PeggySu tells Maile that her dad will have words with him when he shows up that afternoon.

Maile nervously chuckles, "I don't imagine your father has to repeat himself very often."

Peggy replies, "Lee Investigations has eyes on both the Santos daughters and they should be fine."

Maile drops by the Waikiki library and tells Ms. Kaiolu, "The *keiki* was right on. The new boyfriend is on the sex offenders list for the Windward shore."

"We all dodged a bullet on that one," says Ms. Kaiolu. "Please thank the Tiger Princess for her help."

The next day, when Nancy Santos arrives at school, her teacher, Maile, takes her aside and tells her that the Tiger Princess is on her case, but she still needs to be careful and watchful. Nancy is excited. She thinks that she will get to meet the Tiger Princess. This school day cannot go by fast enough.

Finally, school lets out. Nancy walks to Kapahulu and Ala Wai Blvd. and looks all around. Lillian meets her at the Waikiki library and they study before heading home for dinner. On the way home, the sexiest car Lillian has ever seen comes up Leahi Avenue. The black Lamborghini Countach LP400S cruises slowly as the Tiger Princess follows the two Santos girls home.

Nancy excitedly tells her sister, "That's the Tiger Princess. I wrote her asking for her help."

Her big sister says, "You've been watching too much television. There's no such thing as the Tiger Princess. It's just a myth."

Nancy insists. "Just you wait, you'll see that she is the Tiger Princess. We're safe now that she's watching over us."

Once the two Santos sisters reach their apartment and are about to go inside, Nancy turns and waves. PeggySu revs the Lamborghini engine and drives off. Neither girl has noticed the drone overhead.

An hour later, Mario Grosso arrives at the Santos apartment, parks across the street. and exits his SUV. Commander Lee, a formidable man with a shaven head, approaches and speaks to him in a hushed voice, almost whispering. "The Santos *hale* is not a very good place for you to be staying. I've declared it a pervert-free zone. You need to go inside, get your things, and leave permanently. Nod your head if you understand."

Mario nods, never looking directly at the commander. He scurries off across the street to collect his things and leave as he has been instructed.

When Helen Santos arrives home Mario is not there. She carries in takeout from the Panda Express, which is in the parking lot at Safeway. She asks the girls, "Do you know where Mario is?"

Lillian says, "Some big scary guy with a bald head said something to Mario. He came inside and got all his things and left." She turns to Nancy, "It's all your fault that Mario left."

Nancy says, "It is not! Mario left because he's in some kind of trouble with that big scary guy, which wasn't my fault."

Helen sets the Chinese food down on the kitchen table and says, "Come and eat before the food gets cold."

Nancy tells her mother, "That Mario is a bad man."

This hits Helen like a punch to her stomach. She runs into her bedroom crying.

Lillian almost screams at Nancy, "Mario is not a bad man, he loves us. Now you've made Mom cry."

Nancy whines, "Why am I blamed for everything that goes wrong around here?" She starts eating her Chinese food.

The next morning Helen drives her daughters to school. At the elementary school, Nancy gets out of the car and walks over to some man with a fuzzy little dog. Helen says to Lillian, "Remind your sister not to talk to strangers and be sure to walk her to her classroom."

Lillian gets out of the car and takes Nancy's arm. "How many times have you been told not to talk to strangers?"

Nancy protests. "He's a neighbor and I was just being friendly. What now? I can't even talk to our neighbors?"

Lillian looks over at her mother, who motions for her to walk Nancy to class.

They don't notice the drone hovering overhead. Commander Lee has captured all this on video, and he will have their "IT" guy run facial recognition on the neighbor. His old SEAL buddy, Smoke, a large muscular black man, launches another drone from the big white step van parked behind fire station #7 on Leahi Avenue. This drone follows Helen's car to Kaimuki High School. Now they have eyes on both of the Santos daughters.

That afternoon, as Lillian nears Jefferson Elementary School to pick up Nancy, she sees an older man and a big German shepherd playing frisbee with a younger woman on the grass. And twenty yards away, Nancy is speaking to the man with his fuzzy little dog. Still, no one seems to notice the drones overhead.

When Lillian reaches her little sister, she asked her, "What have you been told about talking to strangers?"

Nancy snarls at her big sister. "Just because we don't know the man, that doesn't make him a 'stranger-danger.' I'll talk to anyone I want."

Lillian takes her little sister's elbow and tries to steer her toward the library.

Nancy says, "Since Mom won't let us have a dog, I'm going to stay and play with this little dog on the grass."

"Nancy, come with me," insists Lillian.

That is when the man with the fuzzy little dog reaches for Nancy and grabs her arm to lead her away. In the blink of an eye, both the large German shepherd and the young woman, PeggySu, are on the man with the fuzzy little dog. The German shepherd, Butch, has the man pinned on the ground and the man's shoulder clamped in its jaws.

PeggySu tells him, "Stop struggling, and the dog will not hurt you."

Sundance, the German shepherd's owner, picks up the fuzzy little dog, who has now started barking and growling. Parents picking up their children from school, as well as pedestrians walking by, are all watching.

The Tiger Princess—PeggySu—winks at Nancy, then states loudly, "That is not your child, sir. Do not touch her, I've called the police. Just relax, lie there, and don't fight. Butch won't hurt you unless you resist."

Soon they can hear HPD as the police car drives the short distance, Code 3, lights and siren, from the Waikiki substation on Kuhio Beach.

PeggySu introduces herself and Sundance to the Honolulu Police Department officers who have arrived on the scene. They show the officers their Private Investigator identification.

PeggySu tells the officers, "We received a complaint and Lee Investigations has had the two Santos sisters under protective surveillance for a few days."

By this time both Maile and Ms. Kaiolu have arrived at the scene.

"Can the two sisters go into the library to wait for their mother?" PeggySu inquires.

"Sure," replied the senior HPD sergeant. He recognized PeggySu from her help in a rape-murder case a few years before, and calls the chief of police.

Chief Shing asked to speak with PeggySu Lee-Wong. She tells the chief, "The Tiger Princess received a letter from a student at Jefferson Elementary saying she was afraid of the bad man who had moved into their *hale*. Turned out, it was her mother's new boyfriend. My dad has taken care of it. He ordered the guy to leave permanently and the guy did. But the sad thing is, Chief, this same young student thought the man with the fuzzy little dog was their neighbor. She loved petting the dog and refused to listen to her big sister who warned her the man was a stranger and not safe. This afternoon that man tried to grab her, so I made a citizen's arrest." She hands the phone back to the sergeant.

The senior HPD sergeant handcuffs the man with the little fuzzy dog and takes him into custody for questioning downtown. As he loads him into the police cruiser, the sergeant reads him his rights.

Ms. Kaiolu tells Lillian to call her mother at work and ask her to come down to the Waikiki library.

"Is Nancy okay?" asks Helen.

"Mom, Nancy is fine, but some woman from her school and the police need to speak with you," replied Lillian.

"I'll come right down," says Helen. By the time she arrives at the library, the police have reviewed the Lee Investigations surveillance report and interviewed both Santos girls, as well as their teacher and the librarian.

Ms. Kaiolu shows Helen into her office and says, "Through the quick action of law enforcement, neither of your girls was harmed."

PeggySue pokes her head in. "Sorry, but I need to commandeer your office to speak with Mrs. Santos in private."

Once Ms. Kaiolu has left, PeggySu hands Helen her daughter's handwritten note. "The Innocents Fund had it checked out and they discovered this threat."

In tears, Helen says, "I'm just a poor working mother trying to make ends meet. I can't afford something like this."

"This is what the Innocents Fund is designed for. It won't cost you anything," says PeggySu. Then she gently continues. "Mrs. Santos, during the course of the investigation, we uncovered your personal ad on Yahoo. We always tell everyone never post any personal information online where just anybody can view it. You never know who is searching. The person claiming to be a teenager might really be a 400-pound sex offender. A sexual predator, the man with the little dog, spotted your personal ad. It fit right into his preferred victim profile—a lonely widow, a teenage daughter, and a younger one he could easily manipulate."

Helen turns pale and sweaty. "Oh my God, I don't know what I would do if one of my girls had been harmed."

PeggySu says, "I assure you they are now safe. But you need to take your personal ad down and try to find someone from your church. The churches have a Christian Singles website and socials where you can meet men known by the congregation and not a total stranger off the Internet."

They leave the office and Helen hugs her two daughters. Lillian gives her little sister a "stink face" and says, "See, I told you."

Meanwhile at HPD headquarters, the man with the fuzzy little dog has been photographed, fingerprinted, and a DNA specimen taken. He will be questioned for several sex crimes, but for now, they leave him waiting in the holding cells while they wait on the AFIS and NCIC data checks.

Chief Shing goes into Homicide and tells Detective Keanu Wong what PeggySu has been up to. "She made a citizen's arrest of a man with a fuzzy little dog." The chief's phone rings. He says into his cell, "Oh really, multiple matches." After hanging up, he tells Keanu, "Looks like PeggySu has captured a pedophile...Mark Pence, wanted for questioning in multiple cases, not only here in Honolulu but throughout the state and in Florida also."

Chief Shing explains. "Since the COVID pandemic and quarantine, there has been a huge uptick in domestic violence and child molestation cases. Mark Pence was in awfully good shape, considering coming face-to-face with the Tiger Princess. He complained that the German shepherd bit him. PeggySu didn't lay a hand on him."

Keanu says, "That would mean that he didn't really get his hands on the *keiki*." The Homicide detectives chuckle. They know what Keanu means. None of them wants to see what would happen if the Tiger Princess catches a pedophile red-handed.

After the chief of police has left Homicide, Keanu calls PeggySu. He tells her, "You all did a very good thing today. Mark Pence, the man with the fuzzy little dog, is wanted for questioning in multiple child molestation cases."

§

Turtles

by Rose Tigarden

Wendy and Peter Weber, a healthy elderly couple with silver hair who own the forty-eight-foot wooden ketch *Darling*, enter the Waikiki Yacht Club. They have been to Chinatown to shop for fresh fruits and vegetables before having lunch and walking home. When they arrive at their condo in Waikiki they find that the power is out and the elevators are not working. Rather than climbing thirty floors to their apartment, they decide to go to the Waikiki Yacht Club to sit out the power outage.

At the yacht club they see their old friend Bob from Lahaina sitting with a couple who just arrived from Seattle a few days ago on their forty-eight-foot sloop *Sea Symphony*. Heather and Harvey, the new couple, had asked him about the beautiful wooden ketch *Darling* docked at the yacht club. Bob told them, "*Darling* is owned by one of my oldest friends, Wendy Darling and her new husband, Peter Weber. I sailed around the world and raced three TransPacs with Wendy and her first husband, Captain Michael Kirkpatrick."

Bob follows the Webers down the dock to *Darling* and down below. Bob says, "I don't think that couple will make it as "turtles." I heard them arguing. I don't think they realize that everyone can hear them when they argue."

Wendy explains to Peter that live-aboards are referred to as turtles, carrying their homes on their backs. "If you add something new, something old has to go or the boat will sink. Cruising is not the solution for trouble in your marriage. If you aren't getting along in your big spacious home, getting into a cramped sailboat isn't going to fix it."

After dropping off the fresh fruits and vegetables in *Darling's* galley, Peter, Wendy, and Bob go back up to the yacht club. Wendy heads to the shelves of used books in the lending library. Bob and Peter join the new arrivals, Harvey and Heather, at a table by the bar. Wendy sits on the floor in the corner as she peruses the paperback books that reside in the yacht club's lending library. Unlike a regular library, yacht club libraries operate on an exchange basis. You take one and leave one. It's common for sailors to put their name, the boat's name, and the harbor where they took the book from on the inside of the front cover.

Wendy excitedly stands and holds up an old battered yellow paperback with a photograph of a bikini-clad babe on the cover. *The Tan and Sandy Silence*, #13 in the John D. MacDonald Travis McGee series. She walks over to the table and shows it to Peter. Opening it, she proudly points to the names on the inside of the front cover. Michael Kirkpatrick—Ring Anderson—English Harbour Yacht Club, Antigua. Wendy Darling—Schooner *Lord Jim*—Grenada Yacht Club.

Peter exclaims, "Wow! It traveled from Antigua to Grenada and now it's here."

Heather says, "I enjoyed rereading *A Tan and Sandy Silence* on our trip here from Seattle on our sailboat *Sea Symphony*."

Wendy smiles and remarks, "I read it a long time ago on a delivery from Grenada to here." She opens the cover and shows Heather the name. "I'm Wendy Darling...or I should say I was Wendy Darling once upon a time when I was much younger, in another life. I brought this book with us on the seventy-five-foot-schooner *Lord Jim*. And now, somehow, it has found its way back here to Waikiki after all these years. I read the first part of this book sitting on Grand Anse Beach in Grenada, the location where the bad guy buried Travis McGee up to his head in the white sand and left him for the tide to take care of. Charter guests would bring paperback books with them on charter and leave them."

"I remember the Travis McGee books. John D. MacDonald wrote something like twenty of them," Peter states.

Wendy smiles, "I must have read a dozen of them. Maybe I'll check out the beautiful old downtown library and see how many they have and reread as many as I can find."

Bob chuckles, "We would always pick up paperback books to read in-transit. Youngsters have no idea what it was like at sea before satellite navigation, cable TV, cell phones, and ebooks."

The salt-and-pepper-haired senior citizens, Heather and Harvey, arrived two weeks after Bob fled the devastating Lahaina fire with his sailboat *Blue Moon*. Their *Sea Symphony*, tied up behind Bob's, is a fiberglass Catalina yacht with all the modern cruising bells and whistles.

Peter chuckles. "Wendy, after John's and your adventures, I'm surprised your parents let the two of you read any books."

Wendy remarks, "They encouraged our reading the classics: Robert Louis Stevenson's *Treasure Island*; *Mutiny on the Bounty* by Nordhoff and Hall; Herman Melville's *Moby Dick*; and Richard Henry Dana's *Two Years before the Mast*. I always called it Five Years before the Mast—it must have been hell on board back then. While most kids read The Hardy Boys and Nancy Drew, we read Joshua Slocum's book *Sailing Alone Around the World*, published in 1899, the story of his single-handed voyage on *Spray*, his thirty-six-foot gaff-rigged oyster sloop. We also read C.S. Forester's Horatio Hornblower series, and books about surviving at sea in life rafts.

Bob remarks, "*Treasure Island* was originally titled *The Sea Cook, A Story for Boys*, the saga of buccaneers and buried gold. I imagine every little boy read it." He laughs out loud. "I'll always remember how Joshua Slocum put tacks on his deck to keep natives off the boat when he was anchored."

Peter questions Wendy. "So after reading *Two Years Before the Mast*, you and John took off in your sabot for Catalina to see the dead body. How old were you?"

Wendy doesn't say. "Yes, Captain Peoples spotted us as we sailed out of the harbor headed for Catalina. By the time he got to us with the Boston Whaler, we were taking on water and bailing. Before that fiasco, John and I attempted to fly to Paris in a hot-air balloon. We had fashioned it from three weather balloons attached to my mother's wicker laundry basket with fishnets."

Peter chuckles. "You got that from Jules Verne's *Around the World in Eighty Days*. And you told me about the time you and John attempted to join a cattle drive with your little red Radio Flyer wagon and your pony."

"Didn't everybody have adventures as children?"

Peter responds, "Not that they lived out…Most children only imagined them." Then he tells Heather and Harvey, who are listening intently, that John was Wendy's twin brother.

Wendy says, "John and I joined Captain Michael Kirkpatrick on the delivery of the 76-foot schooner *Lord Jim*. Of course, this was long before Michael and I became a couple. Michael was the paid captain and he was stuck with the owner, Mr. Collins, his wife, and a couple of their friends. They were all day sailors except one mate and his girlfriend. He was happy to have John and me, the blond curly-haired twins, and our experience with him on board for the long journey to San Francisco. That was without a doubt the delivery from hell.

"The owner of *Lord Jim* tried to repair the starboard marine toilet. He hit one of the thru-hull fittings with a pipe wrench and the toilet started leaking in the middle of the Caribbean. We had to heave-to so that Michael could go overboard and nail something over the thru-hull fitting. He and John were in the water for well over an hour with the boat rolling onto them as he tried to nail a copper plaque that said "Welcome to Bequia" to the wooden hull. He was mad as hell and swallowed gallons of sea water trying to make the repair at sea. I thought Michael might just keelhaul the owner."

Wendy took a breath and half-smiled. "That was just one of the screwups by the owner, his wife, and their friends. One day his wife announced that she was going to make a special birthday dinner for her husband and all of us. I pulled a couple of chickens that we had purchased while we were in Martinique out of the freezer and set them to thaw in the sink. A couple hours later I heard this blood-curdling scream from the galley. When I got there, the wife was pointing at the two whole chickens, which were on the floor. I picked them up, one in each hand, and she screamed again, pointing. They still had their heads and feet attached, and their innards were on the floor."

Everybody laughs.

"I told her the women of Martinique would have the shop-keeper beaten if they did not get the head, feet, gizzards, and all the innards. Mr. Collins came down into the galley and screamed at me, saying I should have warned her. Michael defended me. He told the wife, "Just because it was a French supermarket, and the chickens were wrapped in a cardboard container in plastic, didn't mean they wouldn't have head, feet, and innards. After all, it wasn't an American supermarket."

Wendy shakes her head and continues. "They would stand at the rail and pee into the wind. They never got it...the whole time they were on board *Lord Jim* they would pee into the wind. The thing was, Michael had been delayed by the owner, his wife, and their friends and was weeks behind schedule leaving Miami. They didn't understand the urgency. They were heading into hurricane season."

Peter asks, "Couldn't Michael just throw them off the boat?"

"He sort of did in the end," says Wendy. "The owner and his friends picked up a stray sailor who was stuck in Aruba. He brought drugs on board and wanted John and me to join them in taking over *Lord Jim* and throwing Michael off the boat since we knew celestial navigation."

Peter questions, "What did you do?"

"I told Michael, and when we cleared Customs in Colon he took me with him. I reported the planned mutiny to U.S. Customs and that the stray sailor had brought drugs on board. U.S.

Customs came on board and searched the vessel with a drug-sniffing dog who hit on the stray sailor's gear. John went up the mast and found his stash. Someone from U.S. Customs explained to the owner and his wife how close they came to being arrested and having their boat seized in Panama. The group decided to fly back home instead of making the remainder of the voyage."

Harvey asks, "What happened then? How did Michael get *Lord Jim* to San Francisco?"

Wendy replies, "We all sent word out that we were looking for experienced crew to help deliver *Lord Jim* from Panama City to San Francisco. We picked up a few crew hands from other cruising boats for the transit through the canal, and waited for crew reinforcements. Every time we transited the canal, it reminded me of a Los Angeles freeway with large bright lights along the sides."

Heather asks, "How many times have you gone through the Panama Canal?"

Wendy counts on her fingers before answering. "Six."

Harvey asks, "Weren't you worried about the Pacific hurricane season?"

Wendy shrugs one shoulder. "Sitting in Panama City we were safe in the horse latitudes where hurricanes really don't venture. We sailed up to Puntarenas in Costa Rica to wait out the remainder of the Pacific hurricane season and catch some awesome waves in Nosara. We discussed the pros and cons of making one long tack to weather and restocking in Hawai'i before heading to San Francisco. Or else tacking up the west coast of Mexico and California. In the end, Michael decided to make a run for Hawai'i and take our chances in the cooler, deep Pacific Ocean, rather than tacking up the coast of Mexico in hurricane season. It was a very wise choice. Our delivery crew met us in Puntarenas and we sailed for Hawai'i with an experienced crew of seven on *Lord Jim*. The trip from Costa Rica was uneventful and Captain Kirkpatrick navigated us straight into Hilo Harbor.

"After clearing Customs and restocking, we sailed for Honolulu. *Lord Jim* sat here at the Waikiki Yacht Club. I took Michael and his girlfriend to several free hula shows. Michael said that his father had died in World War II. While here in Honolulu, Michael took a tour of Pearl Harbor and the National Memorial Cemetery of the Pacific at Punchbowl. While in Waikiki, we hauled *Lord Jim* out of the water and did a proper repair on the marine toilet. We also scraped, sanded, and painted *Lord Jim's* bottom."

Wendy's voice rose as she continued her saga. "Then Mr. Collins, the owner of *Lord Jim*, and his wife showed up in Waikiki with more of their friends. They attempted to throw us off the boat! They said they could sail *Lord Jim* to San Francisco and didn't need or want us on board.

"Michael immediately notified the International Seamen's Union, and an official representative came to the Waikiki Yacht Club. By that time Mr. Collins had called the Honolulu Police Department. The union representative informed the HPD that Captain Kirkpatrick had a contract to deliver *Lord Jim* to San Francisco and the insurance policy was issued in his name. He enlightened the HPD sergeant on maritime law, which was very clear in the regulations regarding the crew of maritime vessels. Then the U.S Coast Guard showed up. HPD was more than happy to leave this problem up to them and their expertise.

"Captain Kirkpatrick suggested that they move *Lord Jim* to the Coast Guard docks while this little problem was sorted out. Mr. Collins was not happy. Under maritime law he was required to repatriate Michael to Scotland and his girlfriend to England. Since both John and I joined *Lord Jim* in the Caribbean and transited the Panama Canal before sailing it into Honolulu, the seamen's union was requesting that Mr. Collins be required to fly us home to Los Angeles, the U.S. city stated on our passports. The U.S. Coast Guard required new proof of insurance before releasing *Lord Jim* and allowing her back in Waikiki at the yacht club. But the Waikiki Yacht Club refused to allow *Lord Jim* to dock there. Mr. Collins didn't belong to any yacht club with reciprocal privileges. *Lord Jim* had been a guest of the Waikiki Yacht Club under Captain Kirkpatrick's yacht club membership.

"John and I hung out with some surfers who had a trimaran in the Ala Wai Yacht Basin and went with them to Maui, surfing for a couple of weeks."

Wendy pauses for a moment, her voice flagging a bit. "We didn't see Captain Kirkpatrick again for a long while. Not until we ran into him in Puerto Vallarta while John and I were there with you, Bob, on the 76-foot schooner *Lady Luck*."

Bob reminisces. "That was so weird, running into Michael Kirkpatrick—a Sean Connery-looking Scot—there when he was delivering that big catamaran, *Randy Tarr*."

"Bob," says Wendy, "You know that John and I hated leaving you all in the lurch like that, but after what had happened on *Lord Jim* we really needed to leave. And again, Michael came to our rescue, offering a crew swap, two of his for John and me. He always remarked how sailors are just flotsam, adrift on the ocean."

Wendy's voice softens. "I really loved our time on the 80-foot ketch *Morning Star* in Bermuda. I don't think of it as the time we lost Joshua Slocum III and the replica of his great-grandfather's gaff-rigged oyster sloop, *Spray*, in the hurricane.

Wendy turns to Heather and Harvey and explains. "Teddy was a treasure hunter, marine salvager, pioneer of underwater archaeology and deep ocean research, plus a whole lot more. I choose to remember our time with Teddy Tucker, not just on the National Geographic dive shoot of the 1596 wreck of the Spanish merchant ship *San Pedro*, but tagging fish for Bermuda Fish & Game as well. Teddy was in the habit of dropping little sharks on unsuspecting sunbathing females. He took great pleasure in watching them jump up squealing and losing their bikini top. He would also slit open any large shark that he caught just to see what it had been eating. His friend, the author Peter Benchley, used that in his book *Jaws,* and later in the movie.

"Peter Benchley was on Bermuda after they had wrapped up the filming of *Jaws* from his novel. He would regale us with tales from the shoot in Australia. Stories about the midget they had hired to make the great white shark look larger. How the midget hid out in the boat after the great white shark tore the shark cage apart.

"Peter autographed hardcover copies of both *Jaws* and *The Deep* for us. We left the books at the Royal Bermuda Yacht Club when we sailed away. I've kept watching for them to show up someplace. I've made it a habit to check out all the yacht club libraries for interesting books. Books make the best sailing companions. I picked up the Travis McGee book *Turquoise Lament*, the only Pacific story, while I was at the Bequia Yacht Club in the Caribbean and brought it along on *Windward Passage* for that delivery to Hawai'i."

Harvey comments, "Bob told us that you, Michael, and John sailed around the world."

Heather says to Wendy, "That must have been so romantic!"

Wendy shakes her head. "We were working most of the time. What is romantic anyway? How much money do the advertisers say we need to spend on chocolates, flowers, perfume, sexy lingerie, dinner and champagne for Valentines Day to qualify as romantic? Did we find standing four-hour watches in-transit for days and days romantic?"

Bob asks her, "Didn't you find Michael singing to you in French, Spanish, and Italian a giant turn-on?"

Wendy replies, "Romantic is subjective, like the difference between sensual and sexual." She reaches over and touches Peter's face.

She looks out over the Ala Wai Canal at Diamond Head and recalls, "The owner of *Morning Star* sent us to the Caribbean island Martinique to pick up his wife's niece and her husband for their honeymoon. We took them up to Saint Pierre and anchored in the shadow of the inactive volcano. I think it's the most beautiful place in the world. After the 1902 eruption, when the people returned home, they just swept the volcanic ash out of the way and piled it up on the leeward side of their homes and buildings, and orchids grew. The newlyweds were sure they'd had the most fantastic, romantic honeymoon ever and they had the pictures to prove it. A honeymoon in Martinique, on a big beautiful private sailing yacht, with fine meals and French wines."

Harvey asks Peter if he knew the Darling family. Peter says, "I went to school with Wendy and John Darling."

Bob sighs heavily, reflecting on the Maui tragedy. "I had just picked up a new book at the Lahaina library. We lost so much that day. The books can be replaced. The cost of life, property, and history...not so much. I don't think I'll ever go back. They called me a hero just because I hung around to pull people out of the water—that is what seamen do. At first I was angry because the Lahaina day boat to Lanai didn't hang around, but instead headed straight to Ma'alaea Harbor, Lanai. Michael always said that the captain is responsible for the vessel and all those on board. I couldn't understand how you didn't blame someone for John and Michael's deaths."

Wendy says, "They died rescuing people."

Heather says to Wendy, "You should write a book about your adventures with Captain Michael Kirkpatrick."

Harvey nods. "That would be a book I would have to read."

The early TV news is just starting. A banner states today's new body count from the Lahaina fire. The news broadcaster leads off with a story of a new power outage. "A rooster was blown into a transformer on Ena Road, causing a temporary localized power outage in Waikiki."

Harvey asks, "Does that sort of thing happen often?"

Peter answers, "Power outages are not uncommon. The Maui wildfire of August eighth was a 'perfect storm' scenario. With the drought and strong winds, it could happen again."

Wendy remarks to Bob, "You did all you could there in Lahaina. No one was lost in the stacks at the library."

Treasured Library Memories

Many of our contributing authors have fond, character-shaping, or unusual memories of public libraries in their past. They welcome this opportunity to share these treasured tidbits with you.

Moons and Junes and Ferris Wheels
Remembered by Brett Botbyl

The Louis Bay 2nd Library and Community Center. That's the name of my hometown library in the NY suburb of Hawthorne, New Jersey. Yuck. Why humans feel compelled to name structures after other humans never quite made sense to me. The original library was perfect and manageable for a young me. The iconic Hawthorne Public Library carried a whopping $7,000 mortgage and opened on Memorial Day of 1931. Brick, mortar, and hard work came together to construct that old box of books, meant to serve generations of knowledge seekers. The "modern" addition was tacked onto the original building in 1979. I was sixteen at the time. Ah, those were the days. I could reminisce for pages about my expeditions in those stacks. But I'd rather remember an earlier time, before the addition and the modern steel water fountain. Before the massive, palatial bathrooms opened for business, smelling like a brand-new toaster oven, offering an endless supply of never-quite-big-enough one-ply toilet sheets. We gave them the nickname "finger whoopies" for obvious reasons.

My family moved to Hawthorne halfway through the fourth grade. Well, most of my family. One day my mom packed up my brother and me and drove us away from the only home I ever knew. Divorce is difficult on children, but so is separation. And we were pretty separated. My new school was fine, except for Donald Gianella's constant teasing, nicknames, and mocking sing-song jingles. My brother was four years older than me and quickly found new friends and piles of fresh mischief to unearth. As a now-single parent, my mom had to work long hours. Brett was left alone to explore the strange new world in search of imaginative kid-friendly adventures.

The town library became a quiet, harmless oasis. I went there with my homework and planned out every theme and genre in the place. One afternoon, while browsing the Biography section looking for something Ben Frankliny, I came across an area I hadn't seen before. Three pairs of back-to-back study carrels were lined up along a large book wall. Upon closer inspection, I discovered that these were not ordinary reading nooks but rather fully powered listening stations complete with turntables and headphones. The mystery was alluring. Record players in the library? I looked back toward the front desk to see if Mrs. Lobe was on the prowl for library hooligans. But something called me to the carrel. That very seat before me. The first one in the carrel-cade, with its tempting headphones dangling from a hook with a "come hither" and "hear the secrets of the universe" taunt. A siren's song whispered just loud enough for any nonhooligan to hear. I approached the carrel.

The seat slid out with ease. One of those old library chairs, made of solid wood, with the butt-cheek indentation so you can get comfy while studying. But with my very own turntable, I wasn't planning an extended stay with any old hardcover. Nay, this was an audio Shangri-La, and I was about to become the mysterious High Lama of Library Listening. I settled into the butt groove, set my book bag down on the floor next to me, and prepared for some grown-up acoustics.

And then it dawned on me that I had nothing to play. There had to be records somewhere, right? This couldn't be some cruel *Twilight Zone* mirage, could it? A trick of the mind in a wicked oasis of the stacks? Ah, there is something. Sitting on the side of the turntable was an album with a thick plastic cover. I craned my neck to check one last time for librarian oversight. Nothing. Whew. The coast was clear. I fumbled for the record sleeve and turned it over to read the cover. *My Fair Lady*? I read further to discover that this was the original cast recording of the London musical starring Rex Harrison and Julie Andrews. *The Sound of Music* lady?! Okay, sure. After all, this was my only record option. I quickly placed the vinyl platter on the turntable, donned the headphones, and placed the needle at the beginning.

Orchestral music filled my ears with an overture that seemed to change moods and directions like magic. Then there was Rex Harrison, aka Doctor Dolittle, singing a rant about Englishmen not knowing how to speak. Then Julie Andrews wrapped her vocals around universal themes like chocolate, comfortable chairs, rain in Spain, and dancing all night. More. I wanted more!

Thus began my new hobby for the better part of my mid-childhood. Library for homework, research, and air-conditioning. Every Bookland excursion concluded at my carrel. I eventually named it Lewis. The literary reference should be obvious. What C.S. Lewis shared with me, once I located the record collection, was a vast aural soundscape, enriching the imagination of a Broadway-bound theater kid.

Lewis introduced me to Richard Burton over in *Camelot*, and Jesus as both a hippie in *Godspell* and a rock balladeer in *Jesus Christ Superstar*. I cheered with the entire U.S. Congress in *1776* as they debated independence in the sweltering heat of a Philadelphia summer. I sat in the studio mere feet away from John Gielgud as *Hamlet* while he suffered outrageous fortune from every sling and arrow. Laurence Olivier took my breath away with his *Macbeth*. Then Lily Tomlin made me giggle uncontrollably with *This Is a Recording*. But what was Lewis's most precious gift? The one album that seemed to celebrate my mom, Lois, and the strength she mustered every day of her single-mother existence. Joni Mitchell and her "Clouds."

My hometown library taught me the way of the book and all the magic books unlock. The vinyl records of my library spun life into all my fantasies. My dreams took flight in a beautiful praxis. For that, I honor that place. Moons and Junes and Ferris wheels.

* * * *

A Long and Winding Process
Remembered by Gail M Baugniet

For a couple of decades beginning in the late 1990s, family genealogy research occupied my free time. The first step entailed speaking with close relatives to build a framework of family lines back to second great-grandparents. Multiple letters and emails were exchanged with extended family members. Cemetery tours replaced normal leisure activity. Library microfiche viewers became invaluable sources of census information, birth records, marriage certificates, and death announcements.

Helpful librarians within Wisconsin were exceedingly patient with me when demonstrating the use of microfiche viewers. In Kewaunee, Manitowoc, and Kenosha counties, they knew some of the family names I was researching and shared information about life in areas where my ancestors had resided. With so much goodwill extended toward me, genealogy research became a pleasant source of entertainment. Each new ancestor "discovered" was cause for celebration.

Eager to learn more about the family of an ancestor who, at age three, had sailed from Cork, Ireland, to Woodstock, Canada, and eventually settled in a small Wisconsin town, I entered one county library to request a specific reference book that might reveal interesting information.

Other researchers had warned me the librarian in charge of genealogy materials harbored a fierce possessiveness toward the collection and required certain information before granting requests. With appropriate paperwork in hand, I asked for the specific reference book. The librarian advised me that, for the book to be of any use, I needed a birth certificate of the person being researched. I confirmed having a copy. Undeterred, she stated I should also have a copy of a marriage certificate. This was included in my paperwork. Finally, she wanted to know if I had census records for the family. I smiled and nodded.

With that, the librarian asked, "Then why do you need the reference book?"

After mumbling something about looking for personal details not included in public records, I was grudgingly given a request form to complete, along with a stern warning that the process could take weeks.

Over time, I gathered a substantial amount of information about my ancestors. Publication of my genealogical novel, *Shards of Memory, Oral History in a Heartbeat*, followed. But I never did receive that reference book.

* * * *

My Favorite Library Times
Remembered by Shauna Jones

I am a child of an eclectic-reading mother, who stacked bookcases with mysteries, novels, histories, and encyclopedias, along with piles of library books that caught her interest throughout my childhood home. From my earliest memories, books and libraries have always been a special part of my life. Even though we lived in a large city, my mother chose to take us to a small library several miles from our house. We went to this library twice a month until I graduated from junior high school. My favorite times were the children's reading programs in spring, summer, and winter that met on Saturday mornings. My brother, my sister, and I went to every event Miss Conway, the librarian, arranged. She also established a very large children's library, along with an excellent research section. My mother knew that the more books were checked out the more money the library would receive. Between the four of us, we checked out about thirty books at a time. The librarian helped us find books for school papers as well as stories that would entertain us. Also, Miss Conway shared friendship, peace, and a love of books with all of us.

* * * *

Heroism and Romance
Remembered by Michael Little

In my earliest library memories I am a second grader in Lampasas, Texas (5,000 inhabitants, not including the horned toads and rattlesnakes). My family will not own a TV set for another three years, so on a Saturday I can either walk a few blocks to the local movie house to watch Westerns, or I can read on the floor in the small children's section of the town library (they had chairs but I was more comfortable on the floor).

For my other Saturday reading I walk the three blocks to the local Piggly Wiggly grocery store (supermarkets were not yet invented). As soon as you walk in the door there it is, a long double rack of comic books waiting to be read. I sit there and read a comic book from cover to cover, and nobody objects. I could spend the ten cents for the comic, if I had it, but the management doesn't mind anyway. I read two types of comics: 1) Superman and Batman; and 2) Archie comics. So, from an early age, I want to learn all there is to learn about superheroes and teenagers.

Years later, when I begin to write my own stories, I will draw on the power of those early comic book stories. My characters will be people we can root for, and who are up to the challenges of life. It helps to give your hero a comic sidekick. Batman had Robin. Archie had Jughead. They will also be romantically attracted to others. Ah yes, teenage romance. There's the dark-haired Veronica and the blonde Betty, as well as rivals like Reggie. I was a little too young to date back then, but there was always the inescapable crush just waiting down the road. Blondes and brunettes would be finding their way into my own stories, especially blonde rodeo queens.

It was a long journey from those small kid reading-on-the-floor days to becoming Archie or Jughead myself. Besides learning about girls I even learned to read sitting in a chair. Now that's sophisticated!

* * * *

In the League of Nations Library
Remembered by Rosemary Mild

In my sophomore year at Smith College, I was accepted into the Junior Year Abroad Program to join the Smith Group in Geneva, Switzerland.

For the school year 1955-56, thirty-two of us attended the University of Geneva and the Graduate Institute of International Studies. All our classes were in French. Our group leader was Mr. Alan Overstreet, a Smith Professor of Government. Yes, "Mister." Smith College's tradition was to avoid students having to deal with the pompous "Professor" and "Doctor." Mr. Overstreet fitted his own course into our schedules, American Foreign Policy. We had no tests, just one term paper, requiring us to answer this question: "Was the United States justified in entering the Korean War?"

I spent glorious hours doing my research at the League of Nations Library in Geneva. The three-story building was made of yellow-orange stone with eight square structural columns and tall, narrow windows. I chose a spacious reading room for my research. I could hardly concentrate. Azure blue Lake Geneva, and in the distance, the snow-covered Swiss Alps! What a great privilege.

I proudly turned in my paper a day before the deadline.

One week later, our papers were handed back with our grades. I stared in shock at mine: a big fat red C, accompanied by Mr. Overstreet's comment. "Rosemary, amid all your research, you forgot to answer the question: Was the United States justified in entering the Korean War? That was the entire assignment."

* * * *

The Sacred Spark
Remembered by J. T. Page Jr.

My absolute favorite year in grade school (or, for that matter, high school, college, graduate, and postgraduate studies) was sixth grade. It was at St. Basil's Elementary School on the south side of Chicago where I grew up. Great memories and a happy childhood.

There were about fifty total sixth-grade students at St. Basil's that year, but the maximum classroom size was something like forty. As a result, and one of the things that made it such a unique experience was that my schoolroom was split between ten students in sixth grade and thirty students in fifth grade. (The rumor, never officially confirmed, was that my group were the students who could likely handle the rigors of sixth grade the easiest for both them and their teacher.) We had a wonderful Dominican nun, who taught both grades…but did so separately, usually fifth grade in the morning and sixth in the afternoon.

This left a lot of open time (and glorious freedom) for my sixth grade classmates and myself. The nuns were not oblivious to this and a practical decision was made. Our group (each eleven years old, relatively responsible, and well-behaved) would be put in charge of St. Basil's small, unmanned school library, which conveniently sat outside our second-floor classroom. Our group of ten would pretty much spend half our time sitting in the mini-library (while the fifth graders were being taught) and we would each take turns acting as the librarian to receive or check out books. The rest of the time we would be back in the classroom being taught. (The fifth graders had to tolerate our higher-level classroom lessons, but were happy to tune all that out, since they were able to routinely focus on and finish their homework before school ended each day.)

Having said all that, this special time in the school library is what lit the fire of my love for books. Many find classic novels like *Treasure Island* by Robert Louis Stevenson or *Robinson Crusoe* by Daniel Defoe as the genesis of their reading for pleasure. But the "spark" for me was something much different and quite obscure. One day I noticed a book on a corner library shelf and it was the cover that caught my eye. There was a spaceship and two men in spacesuits. Sweet! I picked it up and started reading. Wow! Oh wow! I literally could not put it down. Never had I felt this way before. I had to check it out and could not wait to get home to continue reading. This new discovery of reading for pleasure was marvelous and continues to this day.

That special book, by the way, was *Space Captives of the Golden Men* by Mary E. Patchett.

For some reason, I thought about all this some years ago and set out to find a copy of the book that started it all for me. It was not easy (or inexpensive) to find a copy…but I managed to do so. I honestly have not re-read it yet, perhaps out of fear of disappointment…but I keep it close in the event I ever have to rekindle that memorable childhood spark which, to me, remains sacred.

* * * *

Grandpa, My Inspiration
Remembered by Larry Mild

Grandpa, Charles Morris Glueck (1873-1955), stood tall for his generation, tall from the perspective of a doting preteen, and taller yet from my adult recollection of the man who made such an intellectual impression on my life. Though he grew up in Hungary and spoke most of the languages of Europe, I never knew him to speak with any kind of accent or abuse of the English language. I attribute this to the literature and newspapers he read, as well as his willingness to join any discussion. He instilled in me a love of literature and the arts and a will to study.

He painted houses for a living and oils on canvas for an avocation. He loved to copy miniatures of famous paintings on a larger scale with increased detail, always giving credit to the painter, and adding his own name in the opposite corner.

Invading my favorite reading haunt, our veranda rocker, he'd invariably discover me reading the forbidden comic book. Like so many of my young peers, I'd been seduced into reading mere pictures. Catching me red-handed, he'd trash the comic book and lead me off to the nearest library. He didn't say "Go pick one off the shelf." Instead, he whet my appetite with his description of a favorite character or a tantalizing plot. I'd reel myself in without realizing I'd been caught. Dickens, Dumas, and Stevenson became friends for a lifetime.

* * * *

A Library Offering

Remembered by Bob Newell

It must have been in 1965, at the Irvington Public Library in Irvington, New Jersey. That library was situated in a large space that
had once been a car repair shop. The library hired student interns
from Irvington High School, which I was attending, and one of
the interns was a good friend whom we'll just call Flo. She and I
visited on the phone a couple evenings a week and talked before
class most mornings, but she was just a friend. In fact, she was
quite attractive, and had lots of dates. I was a nerdy and clueless
sixteen-year-old and never would have dreamed of asking Flo out.
Yet I did frequent the library often and so ran into Flo there from
time to time.

One day after school I stopped in at the library. I was always
looking for sci-fi so here I was bending down, looking at books
on a lower shelf, when Flo came up to me. She had this big smile.
That was nothing new, but she started insistently rubbing her hip
on my shoulder, and then she said, "Guess who just turned sweet
sixteen and has never been, and would you like to be the first?"

So...remember that I said I was clueless? Well, sure I was. I
didn't know what she was talking about and the moment passed.
Looking back some sixty years later, it was probably just as well that
I was naive and completely missed the point.

Or was it?............I'll never know.

* * * *

Falling into Books

Remembered by David W. Jones

Buried in a high school yearbook is a picture of me. Scrawny, horn-rimmed glasses. I think I was a sophomore. Settled on a couch in the library, doing what I did best back then: Read.

If I recall correctly, the caption said something about me being completely unaware of the picture-taking. It's true. Fall into a book and the world goes away! I don't even remember seeing the picture in my yearbook! But someone somewhere scanned the yearbooks in, and there I was.

Libraries are the perfect places to fall into books. Our high school library had a huge variety of books. One was a book produced by the U.S. National Guard as a civil defense tool, about how to deal with nuclear attacks. (A popular topic among weird teens like me.)

It included a bomb effects calculator. Set the bomb yield and burst height, and it would show you how big and deep the crater would be, how far each of the different damages extended.

At the time, we lived within 10-20 miles of four places targeted by at least one 10-megaton warhead each. Today, we maintain the tradition by living 14 miles from Pearl Harbor, 16 from Schofield Barracks, 17 from Kaneohe Marine Corp Base.

What did I learn from that? I don't fear surviving nuclear war. We won't live past the first exchange. Maybe this is why I'm such a warm fuzzy person?

Thank you to all libraries and librarians everywhere!

* * * *

§

Aloha, Storytellers!

Hawai'i Fiction Writers welcomes all storytellers seeking community and craft. Our diverse group of passionate writers spans genres and generations. Together we celebrate the literary spirit of our islands and beyond.

Gather with us to meet fellow creatives, share your work-in-progress, and get thoughtful feedback in an encouraging, good-humored atmosphere. Our readings, workshops, contests, and publications showcase the talent flourishing in our island neighborhoods and global 'ohana.

Through the written word, we support and inspire each other's voice and vision. We laugh, learn, and grow as writers. Hawai'i Fiction Writers embraces the chance to meet, connect, and craft stories together. Let us be part of your literary journey!

Join us and let's talk a little story, shall we?

Visit us at: https://www.hawaiifictionwriters.com

Earlier Anthology (2020) by
Members of Hawaiʻi Fiction Writers

Michael Little
President and founder of Hawai'i Fiction Writers

In 2015, **Michael Little** co-founded Hawai'i Fiction Writers with Carol Catanzariti and Leslee Ellenson. In 2018, The Hawai'i Literary Arts Council awarded Michael the Loretta D. Petrie Award for outstanding service to the literary community of Hawai'i. He is the author of two comic novels set in Reno and small-town Texas: *Queen of the Rodeo* (2001) and *Chasing Cowboys* (2009). Another novel, *Escape from the Dream House*, is aging quite nicely at the bottom of a drawer.

His short stories have appeared in Bamboo Ridge's collections. In 2012, he co-edited an anthology of Hawai'i writers titled *Sunset Inn: Tales from the North Shore*, which includes two of his quirkiest stories, "Grace-Anne Discovers Mai Tais" and "Inga of the North," a heartwarming Christmas tale set in Santa's sweatshop days before Christmas and featuring Santa's estimable adopted daughter, who serves warm cookies and attracts the eye of an out-of-work actor who is sent north by his L.A. agent and finds himself sitting in an elf-size chair and popping Barbie heads onto the Barbie dolls. (The author confesses to a strange love of run-on sentences.)

In 2020 Hawai'i Fiction Writers published *Kissing Frogs and Other Quirky Fairy Tales*, edited with Gail Baugniet and Carol Catanzariti. Michael's stories in that collection are "Kissing Frogs" and "The Case of the Runaway Blonde."

Gail M Baugniet

Gail M Baugniet is the author of the Pepper Bibeau mystery series, available on Amazon. Early careers in law enforcement and the insurance industry fueled her interest in writing mysteries. She is a member of the national writers group Sisters in Crime, Inc.; and Hawaiʻi Fiction Writers. As president of Sisters in Crime/Hawaiʻi, she co-published two anthologies featuring short story mysteries by local authors. Gail's book of linked poetry, *Another New Beginning: 70 Poems for 70 Days*, was gifted to 70 family members and friends in celebration of her 70th birthday. A genealogical novel, *Shards of Memory—Oral History in a Heartbeat*, derives from her decades of family research. She also published *For Every Action There Are Consequences*.

After twelve years of security dispatching for Ala Moana Shopping Center in Honolulu, she turned to writing full-time, including novels, poetry, and short stories published in several anthologies.

Visit her blog site at: **https//gailbaughniet.blogspot.com.**

John E. Simonds

John E. Simonds, a retired Honolulu daily newspaper editor, has lived with his family in Hawai'i for more than 45 years and previously was a reporter for newspapers from Washington, D.C., and other cities. A Bowdoin College graduate and former East Coast and Midwest resident, he has been writing poems since the 1970s, including three previous collections: *Waves from a Time-Zoned Brain* (AuthorHouse 2009); *Footnotes to the Sun* (iUniverse 2015); *In a Roundabout Way* (Dorrance 2021); and *Walking the Sunset Home* (Atmosphere Press 2023). John has been involved in the Hawai'i Literary Arts Council, Friends of the East-West Center, and distance-jogging (now walking) events with the Mid-Pacific Road Runners Club. He and his wife, Kitty, have children and grandchildren in Wisconsin, Texas, and California, with many nieces, nephews, and in-laws in Hawai'i.

Dawn Knox

Dawn Knox lives in Essex, UK, about thirty miles from London. So, you may ask, what is she doing on a website featuring the Hawai'i Fiction Writers?

Well, it was one of the good things that resulted from the COVID-19 pandemic. As many of us went into lockdown, technology became increasingly important in keeping us connected. And not only maintaining contact with family and friends, but in making new friends in far-off places.

Dawn had been in contact with David and Shauna Jones for many years, and at the beginning of lockdown, one of her books was chosen as the pick of the month for their book club. Since the members were meeting on video link, Dawn was invited, too. When she was asked if she wanted to join their book club, she jumped at the chance, and since then, has met her friends in Hawai'i nearly every month via video link.

On the book club video meetings she met Michael Little, who invited her to contribute a story to the anthology *Kissing Frogs and Other Quirky Fairy Tales*. To her utter delight, it was accepted.

And now, Dawn keeps in touch regularly with David, Shauna, Michael, and Gail Baugniet by email.

Dawn often describes herself as an Accidental Author. She has a Bachelor of Science degree, which led to a career in pathology, so her head was firmly in the world of science, not literature. When she was younger, it certainly never crossed her mind she might one day write books. So, although she'd love to claim everything has been planned meticulously, the truth is, almost everything about her writing career has been a happy accident.

Neither did it ever occur to her that she'd write a play. She'd deliberately avoided learning much about the First and Second World Wars because she found the suffering too upsetting, then unintentionally became involved with a World War One commemoration group. She went on to write two World War One plays that have been performed in England, France, and Germany. And those scripts led to the book she hadn't intended to write that she now says has her heart and soul in its pages—*The Great War— 100 Stories of 100 Words Honouring Those Who Lived and Died 100 Years Ago.*

Three zany, fun-filled books came about completely by accident. She'd actually intended to write a few short stories, but the characters took over and their adventures grew into *The Basilwade Chronicles, The Macaroon Chronicles* and *The Crispin Chronicles.*

She'd never, ever have considered writing a book with anyone else… until her friend Colin Payn asked her to write a near-future, climate fiction book with him, and *The Future Brokers* was published!

There have, of course, been books she did intend to write—she's not a complete disaster zone! She has a series of romantic historical novels set in the 18th-century penal colony of Sydney in New South Wales, as well as historical novels set during the First and Second World Wars in England and France.

But recently, she's been at it again and accidentally joined a writing group in Hawai'i… Seriously, she's thrilled to be part of it. If only she could accidentally find her way out to Hawai'i…

But perhaps one day…

David W. Jones

Kapolei, Hawai'i author **David W. Jones** started writing and selling poetry his first year in high school. His stories have been published in two anthologies: "Champagne Twist" in *Dark Paradise: Mysteries in the Land of Aloha;* and "The Disrespectful Prince and the Frog" in *Kissing Frogs and Other Quirky Fairy Tales.*

A former professional musician and radio DJ, he sometimes blogs at **dancingtreefrog.com**.

Shauna Jones

Shauna Jones. With a degree in history and professional journalism experience, Shauna's work has appeared in the *Hawaiian Church Chronicle*, several newsletters, and in two anthologies: "The Breakup Queen" in *Sunset Inn: Tales from the North Shore;* and "The Stranger" in *Dark Paradise: Mysteries in the Land of Aloha.* She was the Hawai'i State representative for the International Women Writers Guild and the Aloha RWA chapter secretary. She co-led a weekly writing group from 2000-2014, and enjoys writing romantic suspense and historical romances.

Brett Botbyl

For over 35 years, **Brett Botbyl** has been a weaver of worlds. Fueled by a lifelong love of theater, he founded a production company at the young age of twenty, launching a prolific career that saw him push boundaries and redefine immersive storytelling.

Brett's visionary direction blurred the lines between cinema and live performance, transporting audiences to fantastical realms and historical eras. Under his hand, viewers traversed an ancient British hillside, a bustling 17th-century French village, an eerie Carpathian cemetery, and a sultry 1933 Marrakech nightclub. While the settings varied wildly, Brett's productions were consistently infused with passionate realism and undeniable excitement.

Now, after a pandemic-induced hiatus, Brett has turned his focus to the written word, channeling his passion for storytelling into vivid published fiction packed with adventure.

His books include: *The Ghost Hill Gang, A Horror Fiction Serial; The Minstrel's Mile, An Original Fantasy Adventure; and St. Alban's Cove, A Paranormal Cold War Thriller.*

For more, visit: **www.otherwyrld.com**

D.V. Whytes
(Don and Vicki)

Don was born and raised in the Washington, D.C., area. He received his BA degree in History at Evangel University, Springfield, Missouri, and his Master's in Counseling, at the University of Cincinnati. Don's vocation began in teaching history and evolved to counseling. For the past thirty-five years, he has been a general building contractor.

Vicki was raised in Austin, Minnesota, and received her national ARRT license as a radiologic technologist in Rock Island, Ill. She received her BA in Health Administration from Pacific Western University. She specialized in trauma and then moved into management.

Retired, Don and Vicki reside in Waikiki, enjoying the view of the Pacific Ocean from their home. Both are avid travelers with a passion for Africa.

Their books include a detective series: *Death in Full Swing; The Case of Bitter Melon and Peppermint;* and *Die, Die, Pumpkin Spy*. The Greystone Murder Mysteries: *Prism Poison* and *Cookie Crumbs, Green Eyes, and Murder*. Two Inspirationals: *Love Beyond Measure* and *Onions in My Ice Cream*.

Rose Tigarden

Rose Tigarden writes contemporary fiction novels based in her beloved Hawaiian Islands, published in large print for easy reading. Her novels include a romantic adventure on Maui called *Life's a Beach on Maui,* 2nd ed. and *Prophesy* and *Legend,* the first two books in the seven-book murder mystery series called Hawaiian Tiger Princess Chronicles.

Rose works with Page Publishing out of New York. She is a member of the Red Hat Society and Sisters in Crime. Rose writes strong female characters drawn from her many years of surfing, sailing, and flying. She has lived on sailboats in Hawai'i, Southern California, Mexico, and the Caribbean. She has over 30,000 blue water miles under her hull, crossing both the North Pacific and Atlantic Oceans, transiting the Panama Canal, and working on charter boats in the Caribbean. Rose has lived in Australia, Maui, Honolulu, Southern California, and in a nudist colony in Florida. During her time living in Marina del Rey, she worked as a sailmaker, a development assistant at a production company, and a commercial extra. She is herself a strong female character, often described as a free spirit. Rose now lives in Honolulu full-time.

Joseph T. Page Jr.

Joseph T. Page Jr. has a doctoral degree in business management from Nova Southeastern University. He served over twenty years as a U.S. Army officer, commanded military units on three continents, and is a decorated combat veteran. He also worked as a Department of Defense contractor for almost two dozen years in Europe. He and his wife, Gretchen, are retired and live in Hawai'i. They have five daughters and nine grandchildren. In addition to writing, he is an amateur magician and a major Sherlock Holmes enthusiast. Joe is the Gasogene for The Shaka Sherlockians of Hawai'i scion society.

His books include: *The Kingdom Queen: A Medieval Novella* and *Holmes and Me: Reflections on the World's Greatest Consulting Detective*.

The author can be contacted at: **shakasherlockian@gmail.com**

Bob Newell

Bob Newell is an MIT alum and a retired engineer who returned to fiction writing after an extensive hiatus. Now living in a Waikiki high-rise with a spectacular view, Bob was a long-time scholastic chess tournament director, scholastic debate judge, and literary society leader, but currently allows far too much of his life to be taken up by his role as Board President at the Waikiki Banyan.

Bob has published two novels and numerous short stories. He is perennially trying to finish editing his novel *From This Day, From This Night*, a *Pride and Prejudice* variant set in the last days of the Hawaiian Kingdom, as well as his French-language novel, *Le dernier couple*. He spends whatever time is left solving cryptic crosswords and playing 16th-century lute transcriptions on the classical guitar.

His books include: *Courting Jane; The Voyage of Admiral Grey;* and *Mr. Darcy plays Draughts and Other Stories.*

Kelley Garcia

Kelley Garcia is a passionate writer who, from an early age, found joy in journaling and crafting short stories. This passion for writing led to studying creative writing and journalism at the University of Kentucky. Despite transferring universities multiple times, Kelley's determination to pursue her writing aspirations never wavered. She wrote for three different college newspapers, gaining valuable experience.

In 1999, Kelley became a Project Management Professional for IBM located in New York. She continued to utilize her skills by writing technical manuals and creating cutting-edge methods of communicating that facilitated her team's successes. Her last projects were within the IBM Watson division and now her fourth novel, *Something About A.I.*, weaves a tantalizing tale around Artificial Intelligence.

Kelley and her dog, Zack, now live in Houston, Texas.

Larry and Rosemary Mild

Larry grew up in New Haven, Connecticut, and served in the U.S. Navy during the Korean War. After earning a BS in Information Systems Management from American University, he became a field engineer riding Navy ships for RCA. He spent most of his career at Honeywell/Alliant Techsystems, designing electronic equipment for the U.S. Government. Larry feels fortunate to have wed two terrific ladies. Losing Hannah to leukemia in 1986, he married Rosemary sometime later. They are members of Mystery Writers of America, Sisters in Crime (Larry's a Mister), and Hawai'i Fiction Writers. They write back to back in their Honolulu condo overlooking the Pacific Ocean.

Rosemary, a Smith College graduate and former *Harper's* assistant editor, also writes personal essays, published in the *Washington Post, Baltimore Sun, Chess Life,* and elsewhere. At Waverly Press in Baltimore, she was managing editor of *Chemical Times & Trends* and copyedited scientific and medical books and journals. For fun and fitness, she goes to Jazzercise, satisfying her suppressed desire to be a Rockette. She was divorced when she met Larry on a blind date. He told her, "When I retire, I'm going to write a novel and I want you to help me." She knew he was Mr. Right, so she chirped, "Okay!" Twenty books later, Larry still conjures up their plots while Rosemary adds the pizzazz. And they haven't killed each other yet!

Visit them at: **www.magicile.com**

Books Coauthored by Larry and Rosemary Mild

The Dan and Rivka Sherman Mysteries

- *Death Goes Postal*
- *Death Takes A Mistress*
- *Death Steals A Holy Book*
- *Death Rules the Night*

The Paco and Molly Mysteries

- *Locks and Cream Cheese*
- *Hot Grudge Sunday*
- *Boston Scream Pie*
- *The Moaning Lisa* (in progress)

Adventure/Thrillers

- *Cry Ohana, Adventure and Suspence in Hawai'i*
- *Honolulu Heat, Between the Mountains and the Great Sea*
- *On the Rails, The Adventures of Boxcar Bertie*
- *Kent and Katcha—Espionage, Spycraft, Romance*
- *Kauai Spy and Other Lies* (in progress)

Short Story Collections

- *Murder, Fantasy, and Weird Tales*
- *The Misadventures of Slim O. Wittz*
- *Copper and Goldie, 13 Tails of Mystery and Suspense in Hawai'i*
- *Charlie and the Magic Jug and Other Stories*

Science-Fiction Novella

- *Unto the Third Generation, A Novella of the Future*

Also by Rosemary

- *Miriam's World—and Mine*
- *Love! Laugh! Panic! Life with My Mother*
- *In My Next Life I'll Get It Right*

Also by Larry

- *No Place To Be But Here, My Life and Times*

All their books, print and ebooks, are available on Amazon.com.